May managed to unlock the driver's side door. She jumped in and unlocked the other side. Ignition. Where was the ignition? Palm let out a high-pitched squeal. Brooks reached over, grabbed her hand, and directed it firmly toward the ignition. The key slid into the slot, and the car roared to life.

"Drive!" Palm yelled.

Shift? Shift. Come on, May. Grab the shift. May threw the car into reverse, backing it out of the parking space. *Move it to D. Hit the gas. Go.*

The Golden Firebird peeled out into the balmy Baltimore night.

Also by Maureen Johnson

13 LITTLE BLUE ENVELOPES

THE BERMUDEZ TRIANLGE

the key
to the
golden
firebird

a novel

maureen johnson

HarperTrophy®
An Imprint of HarperCollins*Publishers*

The Key to the Golden Firebird
Copyright © 2004 by Maureen Johnson
All rights reserved. No part of this book may be used or reproduced
in any manner whatsoever without written permission except in the
case of brief quotations embodied in critical articles and reviews.
Printed in the United States of America. For information address
HarperCollins Children's Books, a division of HarperCollins
Publishers, 1350 Avenue of the Americas, New York, NY 10019.

 Produced by Alloy Entertainment
151 West 26th Street, New York, NY 10001

Library of Congress Cataloging-in-Publication Data

Johnson, Maureen.
The key to the Golden Firebird / Maureen Johnson.—1st ed.
p.   cm.
Summary: As three teenaged sisters struggle to cope with their
father's sudden death, they find they must reexamine friendships,
lifelong dreams, and their relationships with each other and their
father.
ISBN-10: 0-06-054140-7 (pbk.)
ISBN-13: 978-0-06-054140-8 (pbk.)
[1. Grief—Fiction. 2. Sisters—Fiction. 3. Fathers and daughters—
Fiction. 4. Automobile driving—Fiction. 5. Alcoholism—Fiction. 6.
Softball—Fiction. 7. Philadelphia (Pa.)—Fiction.] I. Title.
PZ7.J634145Ke 2004
[Fic]—dc22
                                                    2003021444

Typography by Christopher Grassi
❖
First Harper Trophy edition, 2005

Visit us on the World Wide Web!
www.harperteen.com

For my dad, Raymond R. Johnson, who gave me the following piece of advice when I started high school: "Take it from me, if you're going to sneak out of class through the window and climb down a drainpipe to the ground, wear shoes that don't slip." This is a foolproof suggestion, which only goes to show how smart dads can sometimes be.

Firebird, golden
(largous automobilus yellowish)

1. A car manufactured by Pontiac. In this particular case, a car painted a color called Signet Gold and built in Lordstown, Ohio, in 1967. Almost sixteen feet long, with extremely poor gas mileage and no modern amenities. Has a cream-colored interior and a black convertible top and belches noxious clouds of instant-cancer fumes whenever started. Attracts an unreasonable amount of attention from car buffs [for its collectability] and others [because it's brightly colored, noisy, and as big as a battleship].

2. A mythical creature prominently featured in Russian folktales. Possesses magical powers. Wherever the Firebird goes, princes, princesses, kings, and mad wizards are sure to follow.

3. Presumably, any golden bird that's on fire.

before

"*Ch*ome on," Palmer said, her words dulled from numb-tongue syndrome caused by the Icee she was slurping. "You haff to admit it *wash* funny."

May, who was sweating profusely and peering longingly through the bottom of the screened window at a swimming pool, turned and stared at her little sister.

"No, I don't," she said.

"It wash . . . ambhishious."

"Ambitious?" May repeated. "Looks like you got a new vocabulary word."

"It *wash*."

"They didn't play 'Wind Beneath My Wings' for *you*," May said. "Just be quiet for a minute, okay? I'm trying to listen."

She turned back to the window.

"I shtill can't believf the Oriole pickhed you up," Palmer went on, grinning at the thought. The Icee had turned her teeth a faint blue, which looked even creepier against her braces. It was as if the disguise was being dropped and thirteen-year-old Palmer was revealing herself to be a monster with blue metal teeth.

May wasn't smiling, because the memory wasn't funny to her. She was here for a reason. She was getting revenge— revenge that had been a long time coming. Peter Camp was going down.

Pete was the son of her father's best friend and had been eleven months old when May was born. There were pictures of him lurking above her as she was swaddled in baby blankets, unable to move. He looked surprisingly the same—brown curly hair, body covered in head-to-toe freckles, a slightly goofy, yet predatory expression as he reached for her stuffed duck.

Right from the beginning, May had been the unwilling straight man in Pete's ever-evolving comedy routine. There was the lick-and-replace sandwich gag from kindergarten. The yo-yo spit trick at the bus stop in third grade. The terrifying "lawn sprinkler" (don't ask) from fifth grade. The dribble holes in her milk, the lab worms in her lunch, the bike-by Supersoaker attacks . . . There was nothing too low, too stupid, too disgusting for him to try. Then Pete had moved on to Grant High, and they'd been separated. The next year May had ended up going to a different high school—to Girls' Academy, in downtown Philadelphia. Aside from the occasional whoopie cushion at holiday gatherings, she believed the menace had ended.

Until last weekend, when the Golds and the Camps had taken their annual trip to Camden Yards.

The Camden Yards trip was one of the major events of the year. Even May, who didn't like baseball, was able to work up some enthusiasm for it—if only because her father and sisters were practically humming with excitement. Also, May's dad always saw to it that she was entertained in one way or another. He'd let her choose some of the music in the car. (Along with the obligatory Bruce Springsteen. Her dad had to blast "Out in the Street" and "Thunder Road" as he tore down I-95 in the Firebird. *Had to.* As if the earth would explode if he didn't—or worse yet, it might rain and the game would be a washout.) He'd glance at her through the rearview mirror and make his "big tooth" face, pulling his lips back in a horselike grimace that always made her laugh. As a reward for sitting through the game, her dad would slip her some cash (he had developed a very slick move, which even Palmer couldn't detect) so that she could buy herself an extra snack from the concessions. So May had come to peace with the event.

On this last trip she had been biding her time during the seventh-inning stretch, staring absently into the depths of her cup of lemonade. The next thing she knew, a pair of huge and fuzzy black wings embraced her. Suddenly she was being lifted out of her seat by someone in a black bird costume and was on her way down to the field. Once there, she was immediately set upon by five members of the Baltimore Orioles, all of whom shook her hand. One gave her a signed ball. The crowd began to cheer her. Then, just when things couldn't get any weirder, she looked up and saw her own face—big as a building—stretched across the Jumbotron.

Underneath it was the caption *May Gold, formerly blind fan.*

She didn't even have time to react before she was escorted back to her seat.

It had taken over an hour to get an explanation because that was how long it had taken for Peter Camp to stop laughing. He revealed at last that he had told one of the public relations staff that May had been born blind, had just been cured by surgery, and was fulfilling her lifelong dream of seeing a live baseball game. It was an incredibly weird story—so weird that they'd actually believed him.

The audacity of the stunt had kept Pete from getting into any trouble; in fact, the Gold-Camp contingent now ranked Pete among mankind's greatest thinkers. May's father had immediately claimed the baseball and held it carefully with both hands for the remainder of the game, as though it were his very own egg that he was protecting until it hatched.

The rest of the night was ruined for May. She flinched whenever anyone came too close—even the waiters at the restaurant they went to for dinner. Her psyche was shot. Pete had finally gone too far.

The Camden Yards stunt had brought May to the pool house at the local swim club that afternoon after school. She and Palmer admitted themselves using keys borrowed from their older sister, Brooks, who was a lifeguard there. This was the day before the Memorial Day opening of the pool, so it was filled and ready but deserted.

Their accomplice was Diana Haverty, a fellow lifeguard and one of Brooks's friends from softball, who was known to be the current object of Pete's desire. Diana had obligingly asked Pete to meet her there for a private swim. Diana was going to dare Pete to disrobe. He would be ambushed by May and Palmer. From there, it was a simple grab-the-clothes-and-run operation, taking as many pictures as possible with May's Polaroid camera in the process. It was a beautifully simple plan.

Except that Diana wasn't there yet. She was fifteen minutes late. This worried May a great deal—even more than the fact that it was over eighty degrees outside and it was even hotter inside the crowded office, which was also the storage area for several vats of pool chemicals. They'd been waiting there for over an hour, crouched on the concrete floor. The hot chlorine vapors invaded all of May's pores. The smell burned her nose, stung her eyes, and infected her taste buds. She wondered if it was possible to die from inhaling chlorine fumes. It would be a stupid way to die.

Palmer drained her cup loudly and launched it across the room at the trash can. Just then May heard the front gate creaking open. There were footsteps in the breezeway. Someone was walking toward the pool. May silenced Palmer by raising her hand, but Palmer had heard it too and was frozen in place. May got a little lower and kept watching out the window.

"Please be Diana," she mumbled under her breath. "Please."

But it wasn't Diana. Pete emerged from the breezeway, looking somewhat baffled. He stopped and looked around, then started patrolling the far side of the pool in his slightly slouchy walk, his crown of finger-length curls bobbing with every step.

"We're dead," May said. "Let's get out of here."

"No, we're not," Palmer replied as she crept across the floor and joined May under the window. "Quick! Take off your shirt."

May's head whipped around in Palm's direction. Her green eyes, so similar to May's, were flashing maniacally. Her fingers were already clawing at one of May's short pink sleeves, trying to tug it down her arm.

"I am not taking off my shirt," May whispered.

"Just the right side," Palmer said. "That's all we'll need."

"What are you talking about?"

"Just do it!"

It was moments like this that May felt that nature had been much too unfair. Palmer, like their older sister, Brooks, had gotten all the enviable physical traits the family gene pool had to offer—the golden blond locks, the endless legs, the slender, boyish hips. It didn't stop there. From their father, an excellent baseball player, Palmer and Brooks had gotten exceptional athletic ability. They were all muscle and blessed with grace and speed.

May had hair that wasn't quite blond and wasn't quite red (she called the shade "anemic strawberry"). From her father, she'd gotten the high arch of her brow that made her look like she always thinking, *Huh?* From some unknown, less-evolved relative, she'd gotten shorter legs, pale, sun-sensitive skin, and a lack of coordination. The consolation prize was that she was supposed to have gotten intelligence, but intelligence doesn't matter when your thirteen-year-old sister can just sit on top of you and take your shirt by force if she decides she needs it for something.

"It's not enough," Palmer said, looking at the shoulder May had just freed from her shirt. "The strap is in the way. The bra has to go."

"Oh my God." May rolled her eyes. "I've wandered into a teen sex comedy."

"Would you shut up and take off your bra?"

"Okay, now you just sound like a scary boyfriend," May said, reaching under her T-shirt to unhook her bra. "Explain. Why am I doing this?"

"Bait."

"Bait? My shoulder is bait?"

"Show more if you want," Palmer said, flashing the blue

teeth again. She really did look like some kind of otherworldly predator when she did that—one that wanted May's bra for some insidious purpose and that now thought of May as "bait."

May yanked off the bra and covered the rest of herself as best she could by clutching her shirt against her chest.

"Is that better?" she asked.

"That's good." Palm nodded. "Now stick your arm out the window so it looks like you're naked. Then wave him into the water."

"*That's* your idea? He'll never fall for that."

"Don't doubt the power of a little suggested sex."

May looked over in disbelief. "Who are you?" she said. "What have you done with Palm?"

"Either you get him to strip and wave him into the pool or we go out there, hold him down, and get the pants. What do you want to do?"

Faced with this dire choice, May sighed. She took a moment to try to invest as much come-hither mojo into her bare arm and shoulder as she could. She imagined Nicole Kidman—how would *she* beckon someone with her bare arm? Slowly, she thought, with a little wrist action. Gracefully. Slight rotation in the shoulder. That's what she would try.

She put out her limb and waved. Her move didn't seem very seductive. It was a bit more ground-crew-guiding-in-the-plane in flavor.

"Diana?" Pete called to the arm.

May looked down at Palmer in panic. Palmer had to shove her fist into her mouth.

"What do I do?" May whispered.

Palmer replied by taking May's bra from the ground and shoving it into her sister's hand.

"Wave it," she said. "Like a flag."

May flapped the bra around. Pete stared at it but did nothing.

"Come on, Camper!" Palmer suddenly shouted in a remarkably good imitation of Diana's high, twangy voice. "Get in the pool!"

"Get in?" he called back.

"Wave the bra again!" Palmer hissed. May shook it around once more. It got stuck in a nearby bush and she had to pull it free.

"See? I'm getting undressed," Palmer yelled, her face turning red from the effort of holding in her laughter. "Come on! Take it off!"

Palmer pulled May down next to her. They waited, just under the window, unable to breathe. May expected Pete to come to the window at any minute. Something awful was definitely about to happen. This was going to end badly.

A very long minute passed.

Splash.

Palmer and May peeked out of the bottom of the window. Pete was in the pool, and his clothes were on a chair.

"I don't believe it," May whispered.

"See?" Palmer said. "Showtime! Come on!"

May pushed her arm back into her shirt, shoved the bra into the pocket of her long khaki shorts, and fumbled for her bag. Palmer was already slipping out the door. May followed her into the breezeway and concealed herself behind the soda machine.

Palm crept to the edge of the breezeway and crouched down to evaluate the situation. She nodded her readiness to May, and May nervously nodded back. Even though Palmer seemed as ready to go as a trained commando, May was not. But she was here, and it was happening.

Palmer counted down from three on her fingers and bolted for the pool. May heard Pete yelling, and Palm barreled back, grinning crazily, with a pile of clothes in her arms.

"Now!" she yelled as she passed.

May readied herself and raised her camera to her eye. Pete was about to come charging right at her, in his *natural state*. Yes, May knew what to expect. Yes, she knew what to look for and where to look for it. Still, she decided to just shoot straight ahead and not focus too much on what she was actually seeing.

And around the corner he came. All of him. May started snapping away.

On seeing May and the camera, Pete had the good sense to immediately turn and run back around the corner to the pool. Faced with the choice of running after him (and possibly being overtaken by a wet, naked nemesis) or running to the car and getting away, May opted for the latter. She turned and ran toward the lot. Brooks had already pulled up in the minivan, and Palm had the door open. May scrambled in, her hands full of still-gray Polaroids. Brooks peeled out of the lot and down the street.

The three Gold sisters were convulsing from laughter in the minivan as they drove away. The images on the Polaroids were blossoming. Many were blurry, a few were interesting studies

of the ceiling or the wall, but there were a few promising ones
in the bunch. These were examined closely and critically by
Palm.

"She-male," she said, holding up a streaky image.

"Cut the guy some slack," May said graciously. "He was just
in a very cold pool."

"I don't see any slack to cut," Palm said with a shrug.

"Come off it. These pictures are too blurry to tell. He was
moving too fast."

"I saw it."

"You didn't see a thing." May shook her head. "He was in
the pool when you saw him. But he ran right at me. I saw it.
And it was what you'd expect. Regular."

As she squealed to a stop at a red light, Brooks turned a
questioning gaze on May.

"And you're comparing him against . . . what?" Brooks
asked, one eyebrow raised.

"I'm . . ." Now Palm had fixed May with a stare as well.
Unless May had been withholding important information, they
knew she didn't have a clue what she was talking about.
"Guesstimating."

Palm snorted and fanned the photos out on the backseat.

"Here's one of his butt that's pretty good," she said, plucking
out a picture taken during Pete's hasty retreat. It caught him
midrun and was elegant, nearly classical in composition. Pete had
the naked flair of an ancient Greek, but his butt was highlighted
by the red glow from the Coke machine. Palmer named it *Naked
Running Rudolph Butt*, which triggered the laugh attack all over
again.

"Okay," May said, catching her breath. "We have five minutes to get home."

"Not a problem," Brooks said.

As Brooks cranked up the music and went into hyperspeed, Palmer and May examined the spoils of war: one pair of jeans (with wallet—that would need to be returned right away), one gray T-shirt, one red-and-white short-sleeved cotton button-down, one pair of boxers imprinted with pictures of chickens (very strange), one pair of gray socks with a thin red stripe. Palm hadn't had enough time to get his shoes, but they could live with that.

Brooks turned down the entrance to their road. The Golds lived in an old suburban development outside of Philadelphia. Back when it was new, it had probably been the neatest, most uniform community in the world, with its six different models of houses randomly and endlessly repeated down meandering tree-lined streets. But in the half century since it had been built, everything had been overgrown, and all of the houses had deteriorated or been altered or rebuilt. Their little corner in particular was the forbidden forest of mismatched additions and sagging garage porticos. They passed the Camps' on the way to their own house and gave a triumphant wave.

As May was in the middle of putting on Pete's shirt, Brooks suddenly turned off the music. May looked up from her buttoning.

"Why did you . . . ?"

May never finished her question because she soon saw what had caused the disturbance. In front of them was a parked police car with a silently pulsing siren light. It was next to an ambulance and a fire truck.

"What's that?" May said.

At first, May would remember, she thought that something had happened to their elderly neighbor, Mrs. Ross. But as they drove closer, they saw that the ambulance was in their driveway and that the fire truck and squad car were in front of their house. But there was no fire.

Though Brooks accelerated toward the house, to May it felt like the minivan was moving slowly. Now she could see the activity in their garage. Her father's Firebird was neatly parked in its spot, richly reflecting the late afternoon sun from its deep gold exterior. Three or four people in blue uniforms were calmly standing around the car. Some of their neighbors were on their front lawns, watching all of this.

Brooks brought the minivan to a jerky stop and killed the engine. Palm and Brooks ran out. May moved more deliberately, gathering her photos, picking up her purse and locking the doors. Then, when she was ready, she turned and walked toward the garage.

There was a large orange kit in the garage entrance. It sat open, revealing white sterile packages and plastic tubes from unseen devices. There was a stretcher set up by the tool bench. As May and her sisters approached, one of the EMTs pulled a sheet over it. One of their neighbors, Bonnie Stark, was in the driveway. She ran toward the girls, ushering them back. Bonnie had been crying.

"Girls," Bonnie was saying, "something happened. . . ."

May never remembered what it was that Bonnie told them; she only recalled that when Bonnie finished speaking, Brooks ran into the house. May looked down and with complete presence of mind counted every single one of the geraniums in the flower box by her feet. There were thirty-six. There was a whistling noise in her ears as she sat down in the driveway. Palm clung to her. Palm was crying—screaming, actually. May absently stroked her hair. It was slightly oily. Her poor little sister. She was so long and skinny, and she was clinging onto May like some violently terrified baby animal grabbing onto its mother's fur. Howling.

May started counting the tiles on the roof of the garage.

The next thing she remembered was walking into the kitchen. This must have only been a few minutes later. Pete's dad, Richard Camp, was there, on the phone. He was tall and thin like Pete and he was slumping a bit when May walked in, so he looked a bit like a drooping plant. He straightened up when he saw her and rapidly finished up his phone call with a curt, "Okay," and, "I'll call you back." She didn't really question why he was in their kitchen, on their phone; instead she wondered whether or not to tell him that Pete was stuck at the pool and that he had no clothes.

He hung up and walked over to her and tried to put his hand on her shoulder.

"May," he said, "I'm so . . ."

She moved away.

"Can you tell me, please," May said, reaching back and holding on to the kitchen counter, "can you tell me what's happening?"

"Your father . . . ," he began. He was speaking in an unnaturally precise manner, and he gripped the top of one of their heavy kitchen chairs until his knuckles were white. "He had a heart attack, May."

"When?"

It was the only thing she could think to ask.

"About forty-five minutes ago."

Forty-five minutes. You could save someone in forty-five minutes. That sounded reasonable. You hit them with the electric paddles or you gave them some medicine. Aspirin. She'd heard that aspirin could save you if you took it while you had a heart attack.

"Where is he?" May asked, surprised to hear the low insistence in her own voice. "Where did this happen? Here?"

"In the garage. In the car. He parked it, and then it must have happened."

"Have they stopped trying to . . ." May didn't know the words. "Those people, are they going to keep trying? You know. To help him?"

Mr. Camp didn't say anything for a moment.

"It was too late when they got here," he finally managed. "Do you understand?"

"Too late?"

"He was already gone, May."

No. He wasn't gone, not literally. He was out in the garage.

"He's dead, May."

May swallowed a few times in an attempt to get the whistling, air-suction noise in her ears to stop. It didn't work.

"Can I go see him?" she asked.

Mr. Camp sighed and ran his hand through his hair. It was straight, unlike Pete's, and turning a steely gray. Her dad had no gray hair.

"I wouldn't. Stay here with me, okay?"

"Where's my mom?"

"She's coming home now."

"Does she know?"

"She knows something is wrong."

"I'll call her." May walked toward the phone.

"She's on her way. She's not at work anymore."

"Cell . . ."

"Why don't you wait?" he asked. "I think that would be better. Safer. She's driving. Is that okay?"

May stopped halfway to the phone and thought about this.

"Safer. Okay. She's driving."

"Right." He nodded.

There was a lull. Neither of them moved.

"May," he finally said, "I'm so sorry."

"I have to go look for Palm," she replied. "I'll come back."

Halfway to the door, May realized that her bra was still dangling out of her front pocket. She yanked it free and threw it on the stairs as she passed. Stepping out the front door, she was shocked at how achingly sunny it was. Somehow she felt like it should have suddenly gotten dark. The paramedics were still there. They gave her sideways glances as she wandered to the quiet street, looked to the left and right, and wandered back toward the house. Another neighbor approached. So many neighbors. They were coming out of the woodwork.

The buzzing in her ears was getting louder.

"Have you seen my sister?" May asked anyone nearby. "Palmer?"

"She's over at the Starks', honey," one of the neighbors replied.

That's right, May thought. Bonnie had taken Palm to her house.

The neighbor was reaching out to her, trying to embrace her.

"Oh, right." May nodded, backing away. "Thanks."

She walked around the house, straight to the back of the yard, to the narrow, secluded space behind a bush that separated her sisters' pitchback and the shed. It was a damp, spidery spot, but it couldn't be seen from the kitchen window. She sank down into the grass and leaned up against a pile of cinder blocks that someone had stacked there six or seven years ago and never bothered to move. She started to laugh. It was completely automatic and spastic and so forceful that she actually gagged once or twice. She wasn't sure how long she sat there. It could have been five minutes or two hours. She didn't hear anyone approaching.

"May?"

May looked up to find Pete, now dry and dressed, standing next to her. He must have followed along to their house with his mother; she would have gotten the message as well. And of course Pete would know to look for her here. This had been a long-standing hiding spot in all kinds of games when they were kids. As for the incident at the pool . . . that had been sometime in the distant past or in another dimension.

Pete watched her. No jokes this time. Somehow having Pete standing next to her with a serious look on his face made the whole thing a little more real. And the real was horrible. The real made her panic. The pressure of his stare caused her laughter to evolve into a different, more logical emotion. She wanted to run, but she knew that she couldn't. Her legs, her arms—she didn't really know how they worked at the moment.

"Hey, Pete," she said as the last of the laughter died out of her voice, "I have your wallet."

next may

Babysitting

1. Since there's a baby in it, you'd think babysitting only meant babies. Then again, it also has a sitting. It's one of those things you can't get too literal about.

2. Something I first offered to do when I was four or five years old. I told my parents that they should go out because I could take care of Pawmer and Bwooks. They laughed and said that was really cute of me. I think they took it seriously on some level, though, because I feel like I've been doing it ever since. So it's also one of those things you have to be careful about volunteering for.

1

May Gold's actual name was Mayzie. As far as she knew, this was not a real name. It was a made-up, moon-man-language name based on Willie Mays, one of the most famous baseball players of all time.

All of the Gold girls were named after baseball players, a testament to their father's obsessive love of the game. Brooks was named after Brooks Robinson, twenty-two-year veteran of the Baltimore Orioles. Palmer was named after Jim Palmer, who was considered to be the best pitcher in Orioles history. May's sisters' names had relevance in their lives. They played softball. (Palmer was, in fact, a pitcher.) Also, Brooks and Palmer were kind of cool-sounding names. May could imagine a Brooks or a Palmer working in a law firm or becoming a famous artist. Mayzie was someone who had a washing machine on her front porch and turned up on some trashy talk show for the "My Mom Married My Brother!" episode.

So when the driving examiner, a woman with a helmet of tight, steel-gray curls, a state police jacket, and aviator glasses, came across striding across the lot, calling for "Mayzie Gold!" May nodded stiffly and felt the first tingling of nervous perspiration. She hated hearing that name announced in public.

"Get in, please," the woman said. It wasn't a friendly request.

May opened the driver's side door of the green minivan and

took her position behind the wheel. This was just a test, she told herself. An easy little test. And if there was one thing May was good at, it was tests. Okay, so she hadn't exactly prepared for this test so well. Who needed more than three or four sessions behind the wheel, anyway? She tried to relax, tried to release the tension-building death grip she had on the steering wheel, tried to send messages of peace along her arm muscles, tried to tell her eye not to spasm.

The woman got into the car. Now that she was so close, May got the full effect of the glasses and the hair and the jacket, and she saw the ashy gray color of the woman's skin and her purple-blue lips. She had a slight wheeze.

"Windshield wipers," the woman snapped.

May reached for the wiper switch. She had it in hand. Wipers. Definitely the wipers. But flicked the wrong way this switch turned on . . . the *high beams.*

Brain, May begged internally. *Brain. Do not send me bad information. DO NOT TURN ON THE HIGH BEAMS.*

Flick. Wipers squealed their way along the dry windshield. Flick. Wipers off.

The woman nodded.

"Hazards," she said.

Hazards. Yes. The panic button—the one you hit when something was going wrong with the car. She knew that one. May clicked the button with confidence, and the car responded with the comforting ticktocking noise of the flashing lights.

"All right, Miss Gold . . ." She snapped May's learner's permit onto her clipboard. "Hazards off and let's go. Straight ahead."

May turned off the hazards and toed the gas pedal.

"I'd like to finish this test today, Miss Gold. A little faster, please."

May put her foot on the pedal lightly, cranking the car up to about the speed of a casual bicycle ride. The examiner sighed and made a note. May's eyes flashed over to the clipboard. In the process she rolled five feet past the first stop sign. May hit the brakes hard, coming to an abrupt stop.

Well, that was wrong, she thought, easing the car back into motion. *Better keep going.*

May continued on to the serpentine, the pattern of orange traffic cones set up as a winding path. Unfortunately, the serpentine didn't look like any kind of path to May—it looked like a random mass of cones tossed into the road to block her. She dropped the car's speed even more and started trying to pick her way through the mess without hitting anything.

"Speed up," the examiner said.

May ignored this.

"You missed one of the cones," the examiner added as May struggled through the forest of orange.

Only one? May said to herself. *Better than I thought.*

From there, she faced the stall for the three-point turn. This was the dreaded part of the exam where she was supposed to pull the car into a tiny box, then had to figure out how to get out of it by backing the car up and only turning it three times. She pulled in carefully.

"All the way into the stall," the examiner snapped.

"I *am* in," May offered meekly.

"You're barely halfway in."

May blinked and looked around her. The low walls of the pen seemed to be coming in at her. It was like the examiner was saying, "Don't just tap that metal divider May—*ram* it. I want to see spare parts and twisted metal *everywhere*."

"Pull in!" the examiner repeated.

May pulled another half a foot forward.

"Miss Gold," the woman said with a sigh, "if you don't pull in, you can't complete this part of the exam."

"I'll hit the barrier."

"The barrier is over six feet away."

Six feet? No. It was right in front of her, just over the hood of the car. Any closer and they would be less one minivan. May felt the panic juices start to speed through her system.

Though she would have liked to, she couldn't just leave the car here in the middle of the course. Leave it and run. Off to someplace where cars were not a required feature of life. Maybe Holland, where her mother's parents lived. From what she'd heard, the Dutch had so many trains and trams and boats that no driving was required. She could see the canals and the tulips and try those fries with the weird mayonnaise sauce that her mom said were so good. . . .

"*Miss Gold.*"

"I can't," May said, looking down at her lap. "I'm sorry."

"Back out and turn around."

May managed to recall only one thing from her studies of the art of driving: when facing a collision that is impossible to avoid, relax—the impact is less damaging that way. She let her elbows drop, and her breathing became shallow. She slowly turned the car around and managed to wind her way back to the parking lot in front of the exam building. She stopped the car in the vicinity of the curb and killed the engine. The key stuck in the ignition. She had to wiggle it out.

May was calm through the quiet scribbling on the clipboard. She saw *x*'s being made at what had to be the wrong end of a chart. A slip of thin paper was handed to her, which she grasped in a slightly shaking fist and could not bring herself to read.

"I'm sorry, Miss Gold," the examiner said, not sounding sorry at all. "You'll have to come back."

"Thanks." May nodded. It seemed kind of stupid to thank someone for failing her, but it was an automatic response. The woman wheezed once more and exited, and May slid over to the passenger's seat and stared at herself in the side-view mirror. Apparently she was closer than she appeared. Another mystery of driving that she would never understand.

A minute later her mother's face appeared in the car window. She evaluated May with a quick glance, got into the driver's seat, and quietly started the car. She took her sunglasses from their resting place in the gentle blond spikes and put them over her eyes.

"It's no big deal. I failed the first time too," her mom offered when they were safely up the road.

"Okay."

"You just need a little more practice. Maybe you can take it again in a week or two. . . ."

"Can we talk about this some other time?" May said.

"Sorry."

May stared into the pile of rubble that had pooled in the

console. Coffee rings with change and grit stuck on them. Wrappers from candies and meal-replacement bars. Crumpled receipts from the hospital parking lot. A french fry container dotted with clear congealed grease stains. So gross. For a nurse, her mom could tolerate a pretty disgusting car. Even if May could have gotten through the test, she probably would have failed for poor automotive hygiene.

"Our car is nasty," May said, closing her eyes.

"I know."

Her mom switched on the radio, and they soft-rocked out for a few minutes. Neither of them really liked that kind of music, but it seemed soothing, numbing. One of the other things about May's mom was that she had once been a hard-core punk girl. The spikes in her hair had been harder, stiff with gel, formed into sharp points. Gone forever (but not forgotten—her father had taken a picture to use as blackmail) were the ripped fishnet stockings, the shock-white face makeup, the black eyeliner that stretched all the way out to the hairline, and the combat boots. Now she was a gentle, soccer-mom kind of punk. But the soft rock was still unacceptable.

"I'm working tonight," her mom finally said. "I asked Brooks if she could take you to work if—"

"If I failed. Which I did."

"I'm sorry I haven't had more time to teach you."

"It's not your fault," May replied. "We're just on opposite schedules."

"Could you make sure Palmer eats some dinner before you go?"

May wanted to say, "She's fourteen. She can feed herself."

But that would be ridiculous. Palmer would survive solely on Doritos and doughnut holes if she could get away with it. May's father, the security systems salesman, had been the great negotiator of the family, coaxing each bite of roast beef or tuna fish into Palmer with offers of softball catches and water ice. But Palmer was too old for that now, and her mom didn't have the time or energy to think about how things should be—she only knew how they were. She knew that Palmer needed to have an actual dinner put in front of her and needed to be watched to make sure she ate it. And that kind of job always fell to May. In fact, May didn't have to say anything at all to her mother's request because her mother knew her answer would always be yes. There was no room to say no anymore.

"I don't want to pressure you, May." Her mom sighed as she turned down the shady entrance of their street. "I'm sorry. You know how much I count on you. Brooks should be more responsible, but we both know she isn't. I need your help. And when you can drive . . ."

"It's no pressure," May lied. "It'll be fine. I just need a little more practice."

"Right. You'll have no problems the next time."

She gave May's ponytail a light tug. May forced a smile.

Inside, Palmer was sprawled all over the sofa, her long limbs draped in every direction. She tipped her head up on their arrival, took one look at May's face, and lowered herself back down and focused on the television again.

"You failed," she said. "Great. Now I still have to ride with Brooks."

May trudged upstairs, threw herself onto her bed, crawled under the quilt, and fell asleep.

It was late in the afternoon by the time that May woke up. Her room was dark and cold. She rolled out from the warm spot under her quilt, slid into her slippers and pulled on a sweatshirt, and made her bleary-eyed way downstairs. The television was blasting from the living room, and her sore head began to pound slightly.

A glance at the clock told her that her mother had already left for the hospital and that she had less than an hour to get ready for work. She headed to the kitchen to get some dinner together. Along the way, she picked up a cup and a coffee mug from the hall table. There were even more dishes scattered around the kitchen. May gathered them up and loaded the dishwasher. She wiped down the counter. She had to scrub hard to get rid of all the sticky juice and soda and coffee rings. The washcloth had a sour, fishy smell.

Dinner prospects were grim. The edible contents of the refrigerator consisted of one bottle of Brooks's spooky blue post-practice Gatorade (strictly off-limits to anyone else), year-old pickles, some tuna fish salad (age unknown), half a piece of fried chicken, and some brown iceberg lettuce. The pantry wasn't much better. There were some boxes of cereal that contained only dry, dusty evidence of their former contents. Some soups that had been around so long, they had become heirlooms. Crisco. Rejected packets of plain instant oatmeal.

May finally settled on a box of macaroni and cheese. She found some freezer-burned ground beef and decided to warm it and cook the two together. This "casserole" was one of the few foods that Palmer was sure to eat. Not the most nutritious meal, but probably better than a handful of chips. At least it was the good kind of macaroni and cheese—the kind that came with the pouch of cheese goo.

After starting the hot water for the macaroni, May sat at the table and pulled over the stack of textbooks she had piled in the corner. She had just enough time to finish up the set of trig problems for class on Monday. Grabbing a mechanical pencil from the fruit bowl, she set to work.

The phone rang immediately.

She stared at the cordless that sat just two feet in front of her, then smothered it with the quilted toaster cover.

"Get that?" May yelled in to Palmer.

No reply. It rang again.

"Palmer! Get that!" May repeated.

"You get it."

"I don't want to talk to anyone!"

"That's *your* mental problem," Palmer replied.

Why did the toaster cover have so many burn marks on it? That couldn't be good.

"What if it's Mom?" May called back.

"What if it is?"

One last ring and the caller was shuttled off to voice mail land.

"Thanks!" May added.

"No problem."

May heard the television volume increase. The kitchen wall began to vibrate. She got up and marched into the living room.

Palmer was huddled close to the television, basking in its glow. She wore her sweats, her fleece jacket, and nasty fuzzy slippers. Additionally, she had draped the old crocheted living room blanket over her head like a hood and was wearing May's chenille gloves. If she'd had a marshmallow on a stick pressed up against the screen, May wouldn't have been completely surprised.

"You know that you're not outdoors, right?" May asked.

A cold stare.

"Could you turn that down a little?"

Palmer turned the volume up another notch.

"Where's Brooks?"

Palmer shrugged.

"She's supposed to be taking me to work in an hour," May said. "Do you know what time her team meeting is over?"

"There's no meeting today."

"Then where did she go?"

"How am I supposed to know?"

"Did she tell you?"

"No. She just left with Dave when you and Mom were asleep."

"Dave?" May repeated. "Oh, great."

Dave had recently come into Brooks's life. He had wide brown eyes, high cheekbones, thick eyebrows, and a fringe of long hair all around his face. He was always smiling a slow, mysterious smile, and he had to lean against something whenever he wasn't sitting down. May begrudgingly admitted to herself that he was handsome—in a lethargic, werewolfy sort of way. She couldn't tell if the two of them were dating, since

Brooks never discussed it. And Dave certainly wasn't shedding any light on the subject. May had exchanged exactly two sentences with him in the three or four months he had been coming by. One was, "I'll go get her." The other was, "She's coming down."

If they were dating, Dave stood in stark contrast to Brooks's last (and only) boyfriend, Brian. Brian was the brother of someone on Brooks's softball team—a pleasant, extremely dull guy, who Palmer had blessed with the nickname "Nipplehead." (There was nothing specifically nipplelike about his head, but the name just seemed to fit. Even their mom, who liked Brian, said, "You know, he really is a Nipplehead.") He'd disappeared sometime during the events of the previous summer, and no one had asked about him since. Dave seemed nothing like Brian. When Brooks went out with Dave, she came back late and usually drunk. This was a new thing for Brooks. May was still getting used to the sound of hearing her come in and stumble around, doing everything too loudly and dropping stuff in the bathroom.

But only one part of this interested May at the moment: Brooks definitely wouldn't be back in time to take her to work.

"Put my gloves back where you found them when you're done." May sighed. "Those are my good ones, from Christmas."

Palmer plunged her gloved hand into the remains of a bag of barbecued potato chips that lay by her side.

"Don't eat those," May said. "I'm making you dinner."

Palmer shoved the chips into her mouth and turned back to the television.

Sighing again, May went back to the kitchen and headed straight to the refrigerator. She pulled out Brooks's bottle of Gatorade, poured herself a small glass, and dumped the rest down the drain. The empty bottle she placed in the middle of the counter. She looked out the kitchen window at the pounding spring shower that had come out of nowhere. This would prohibit her from getting to work on her bike—the trusty Brown Hornet, her dad's twenty-five-year-old brown three speed, complete with "guy bar."

She could call her mom on her cell and tell her what Brooks had done, but there was no point. Her mom would be halfway to downtown Philadelphia by now, weaving her way through Saturday night traffic to get to the hospital. She would sigh and swear in Dutch and say something about having to talk to Brooks, but she wouldn't. Lecturing Brooks was as useful as lecturing a cat.

So May sipped the Gatorade and looked out at the rain.

"Thanks a lot, Brooks," she said to herself.

Brooks had no idea where she was going. She had just gotten in the car when Dave pulled up.

At the moment there were five of them in his Volkswagen, even though it really only held two people comfortably since the front seats were always pushed back to the maximum. Brooks sat in the back with her face pressed up against the window. The rest of her was pressed deeply into Jamie. Jamie was giving off a powerful orangey-jasmine odor, almost candy sweet. Someone else reeked of patchouli incense, cigarette smoke, and fast food. Brooks considered trying to crack open the window a bit for some unfragranced air, but she would be guaranteed a wet head if she did so. The rain was practically coming down sideways.

"Come on!" Jamie yelled over the music pounding from the stereo. "It's pouring. So let's forget it. I want to go to that tattoo place instead, the one off of South, on Fifth."

Dave looked at Jamie in the rearview mirror with a bemused expression.

"For what?" he asked. "So you can stand there in front of the place for an hour again?"

"I'm going to get it this time," Jamie said. "And Brooks wants to go. Right?"

"Sure," Brooks said, barely listening.

Dave smiled at Brooks in the rearview mirror. It was his let's-humor-her smile. Brooks returned the grin.

"We'll go afterward," he said. "Relax."

Small exchanges like this one told Brooks that she was in Dave's inner circle now—the one whose only consistent members were Jamie and Fred. Jamie was an extremely tiny and pale girl with catlike features and black hair cut into a sharp bob. She always wore tight, clubby clothes and three or four necklaces. She waxed her black eyebrows into high, dramatic arches and wore stark red lipstick that never seemed to wear off. She was so strikingly feminine that Brooks occasionally felt like a lumbering guy sitting next to her. Fred always rode in the front seat since he was about six-foot five. He had white-blond hair cut into a little boy's page cut and a tattoo of Snoopy on his forearm.

Along with Jamie and Fred, Dave always had a bunch of guys around him. Different ones every time. Henchmen.

Tonight's random henchman was sitting on the other side of Jamie. He was a weedy guy in a hooded sweatshirt who was interchangeably called "Damage" or "Bob," but Brooks thought she heard that his actual name was Rick. Damage/Bob/Rick didn't speak. He spent the entire ride trying to remove a thread from the back of the driver's seat upholstery.

Fred passed a plastic soda bottle full of orange liquid into the backseat.

"Who wants it?" he asked.

"I'll take it," Brooks said, grabbing the bottle. "Jamie's wasted."

She uncapped the bottle and took a long swig. She shook her head from the force of the strange elixir—it was like gasoline with a little orange added for flavor.

"What is it?" Brooks said, trying to place the sweetness and the hard, burning sensation that came with it. "Rum?"

"King of Pain," Fred said. "It's got 151."

"One fifty-one . . ."

"A hundred-and-fifty-one-proof rum. It makes *really* good fires. You like it?"

"It hurts." She groaned as the burning in her throat stopped. "But I like it." This stuff was *fast*. Faster than anything she'd had before, even grain. She was laughing, and her head was thrumming within seconds.

"Hey, Dave," Fred said. "Can I light it?"

"Not in the car," Dave replied.

"I'll hold it out the window."

"Dude . . . ," Dave sighed. "Relax."

"This one time," Fred went on, "I flamed it, right? I was down the shore and I flamed some 151 on the beach. And I was looking at it. And I totally burned off my eyebrows. Check it out."

He pushed back his hair and tilted his big forehead in Brooks's direction. She saw that his blond eyebrows were very sparse. The skin underneath was all scar tissue, thicker and whiter than the rest of his face.

"That was hilarious," Dave said. Even Damaged Bobrick stopped thread picking for a moment to smile.

Jamie was whispering into Brooks's ear.

"I'm going to get it," she said.

Brooks nodded her approval, even though she couldn't care less if Jamie got a tattoo. She looked out the window at the flag-lined road they were driving down. They were downtown, on the Benjamin Franklin Parkway. In front of them, high above the road and looking like some Greek antiquity, was the Philadelphia Museum of Art.

"The art museum?" Brooks asked. "Is that where we're going?"

Dave smiled into the rearview mirror again. He turned off the parkway onto a smaller road that wound its way up to the art museum. They drove around its base to a small service entrance for emergency vehicles and maintenance crews, cordoned off by a single chain drawn across two poles. Dave stopped the car, and Fred got out and moved the chain so that he could drive through. The path was narrow, just wide enough for the car. The bushes rubbed at its sides as Dave slunk along, lights off.

"Should we be here?" Brooks smiled nervously.

She could see high windows through the greenery—bits of sculptures, walls of shadowy squares that had to be paintings. To

Brooks's amazement, Dave pulled the Volkswagen right up onto the grand plaza in front of the colonnaded central building and the grand fountain. The building's two wings spread out on either side of them, embracing the entire area. The fountains and buildings were lit up with golden spotlights. In front of them was a huge, steep set of stairs that led down to the boulevard. It was intensely bright, but it was so high up that it was also amazingly private.

"Rocky!" Fred screamed.

"Rocky!" everyone else but Brooks yelled back.

There was a scrambling all around Brooks. Doors flew open, and Fred, Jamie, and Bobrick tumbled out onto the brick plaza. They didn't seem to care at all that there was a deluge going on. Fred and Damaged Bobrick were now screaming out the *Rocky* theme and running haphazardly toward the huge steps. Jamie delicately followed them in her little boots.

Brooks noticed that Dave was lingering behind. Something told her to do the same.

"You going?" she said casually.

"No," Dave said. "Come on up."

She slid out of the back and joined him in the front seat, getting fairly drenched in the process. She brought the King of Pain with her.

"Ever see *Rocky*?" he asked.

"No."

"Well, he's this boxer, and he lives in Philly. There's a really huge scene where he runs up these steps. . . ."

Dave pointed to the huge slope of steps directly in front of them, which everyone else was now stumbling down.

"And that song plays."

Everyone else had passed out of sight by this point, but Brooks could still hear them screaming out the song. It grew fainter as they got lower. She took a long swig of the punch.

"We used to come here a lot last year," he said. "They do this every time."

"You don't do it?" She smiled.

"No." He shook his head. "I've never seen the movie."

Brooks laughed. Dave grinned back at her. He had a small scar above his upper lip that stretched when he smiled. Maybe they all had scars on their faces. She would check Jamie's face later.

"So," Dave said, "they don't make you practice softball on Saturdays?"

"During the day they do."

"How many afternoons a week?"

"All of them."

"Harsh."

"It takes up a lot of time," Brooks said, passing him the punch. Her hand brushed against his jacket. It was a heavy, soft corduroy, lined with a knobby wool that peeked out at the collar and the cuffs.

"You've been playing for a long time, right?"

"Since I was four."

"Aren't you sick of it?"

"Sometimes," Brooks said. She leaned against the dashboard and looked down at the view. The dark was dropping lightly, she noticed, like a falling blanket. It caught on the spires of the Liberty Towers first, and they lit up. The yellow clock on top of

City Hall was illuminated. The punch had gummed up all the vessels in Brooks's brain that juiced her nervous reactions. Of course she should be here, in this most illegal of spots.

"I used to dive," Dave said, taking a sip. "That took a lot of time too. I liked it, but—"

"Exactly," Brooks cut in. "I like it, but—"

"So quit," Dave said.

He said it like it was simple, like softball was just something she could give up.

"I can't." She laughed.

"Why?"

"Because . . . ," Brooks said, and then found that she had no concrete reason to give. She knew it had something to do with her dad and never having really known a life outside of softball. Her father had put a bat in her hand the minute she was strong enough to hold it up, and that was that. Afternoons and week-ends were for playing. She didn't even know what people who didn't play sports did with their time. But she had to admit, she'd seen less and less of a point in playing in the last year.

"Because why?" Dave said. "You don't sound like you want to do it."

"Sometimes I don't. Lots of times I don't."

"So don't do it."

Maybe it *was* that simple. Maybe the problem was that she'd just never thought about quitting as an actual option.

She heard Dave shift in his seat. Something was happening. Tonight was different from the other nights they'd gone out. She felt like he'd wanted to come here for a reason.

"Yeah," she said, "I guess I *could* quit. . . ."

When Brooks turned her head to face him, Dave kissed her.

A minute or two later Bobrick and Fred reappeared, winded and sopping wet, at the top of the steps. They ran over and threw themselves against the hood of the car. Dave waved them away with one hand, and they disappeared into the scenery, like all good henchmen should.

Pete had the radio blasting when May threw open the door to his old Cutlass Ciera. He'd been letting his hair grow, so now it was similar to the way it had been when they were kids—loose and crazy, sometimes forming perfect corkscrews, sometimes just flying out in mad, electrified strands. He was bobbing his head slightly and playing with the zipper on his blue hooded sweatshirt. As May went to sit down, he quickly reached over and grabbed a bunch of papers, plastic bags, unmarked CDs, and wrappers that covered the passenger seat and tossed them into the back of the car.

"I can't control the volume!" he screamed as a greeting. He killed the power so that the radio switched off. "Sorry," he said. "It's a new thing. The volume only goes up to eleven."

The last word was said in some kind of British accent.

"Eleven?"

"It's from . . . nothing. It's a quote. So what happened?"

"Brooks pulled a Brooks," May explained, throwing herself into the seat and shaking off some of the rain. "She knew I needed a ride, but she went somewhere."

"Oh. Well, good thing I was home. Let's go."

He turned the key. Nothing happened.

"Huh," he said, rattling the key in the ignition.

"What?"

Pete flicked the key several times and stomped his foot on the gas. Still nothing.

"It's been doing this," he said, knitting his brows together in concentration. "It usually starts. Eventually."

"In how long?"

"Ten or fifteen minutes. As long as I keep trying. The longest it ever took was like half an hour. Unless it's the transmission."

"The transmission?"

"Well, I had to have mine taken out last week," he said, flicking the key in disgust and shifting through the gears a few times. "They put in a dual battery instead. It was cheaper than getting a new engine, you know? But it's been weird ever since."

May faced straight out and counted the uncollected newspapers on the Starks' front porch. She told herself to be calm as Pete tapped strategically on the dashboard, trying to make the car come back to life.

"Just give me a second," he said, reaching under his seat. May heard a popping noise. "Be right back."

Pete jumped out of the car and disappeared behind the raised hood for a moment. She could hear him banging on something furiously. He came back a moment later, his great mass of hair sending water flying in all directions.

"Yeah, it's the transmission," he said, wiping his hands on his pants. "I don't think I should have let them take it out."

"Does that mean it isn't going to start now?"

"Probably."

May sank her head into her hands. Her desperate gesture must have touched the car because suddenly the engine purred. May refused to look up until it was actually moving for fear of making it stop again.

"Take out the transmission?"

May opened her eyes to see Pete grinning down at her. He was alternately glancing between May and the road, obviously pleased with himself.

"Take out the transmission?" he repeated. "Replace it with a battery?"

Age seventeen, tormenting May with little car pranks. Age seven, tormenting May by sneaking up on her and sticking Cheese Puffs up her nose and then pulling them out and eating them. It was all pretty much the same thing.

"What?" May shot back. "That means nothing to me."

"A *dual battery*?"

"Car isn't my best subject."

"The transmission makes the car go vroooom," he said. "It makes the wheels go round. If anyone offers to take it out of your car for you, say no."

"I'll remember that if I ever drive. But that's probably not going to happen."

"What do you mean?"

"I failed my exam this morning," May said.

"Oh," he said. "Sorry."

"It's fine. I just want to get to work."

"What happened?"

"What did I do wrong?" she said. "You want the list?"

"But you never fail things. You're test girl."

"Well, now I'm failure girl." She sighed.

"Who taught you?" he asked. "Your mom?"

"She tried, but she doesn't have a lot of time."

"What about Brooks?"

"Reliable Brooks? The one who's taking me to work tonight? The one who goes over speed bumps at eighty miles an hour?"

He nodded, understanding this. Pete knew a lot of things about them, including some things May would have preferred to keep private. Like the fact that they were broke, for instance, and that going to a driving school was not really an option.

Soon after May's father's death, an unpleasant fact had had to be faced: Life is not like the movies—you don't just get money when someone dies. Sometimes you lose money. There are strange expenses and taxes. Mike Gold had taken only minimal steps in the way of insurance, so without his income, they were in trouble.

In the summer and the fall, May had sat with her mother and helped work out their budget. They'd canceled her father's subscriptions to his sports magazines, turned off the cell phones, and limited the cable service. Her mother had switched to working nights and bumped up her hours. She'd also accepted a few small family loans—enough to pay for May's tuition and a bit of the mortgage. Still, things were not looking very good.

Pete's dad was an accountant. He did their taxes, and he knew the score. Pete's mom often sent over strange assortments of extralarge items she picked up at the wholesale club—jumbo bottles of dishwasher detergent, twelve-packs of soap, jugs of shampoo with pump dispensers. She'd say, "It was such a good deal, I couldn't pass it up!" or, "It was two for one, so I just figured I'd give this one to you!" to try to keep the whole thing from being awkward. It still always was.

They pulled into the shopping center where May worked, which was between a collection of housing developments and the access road from I-95. Pete drove up to the brown building in the far corner of the parking lot, the one that had been born as a Pizza Hut but had lived through several incarnations since then.

"Do you need a ride home tonight?" he asked.

May looked out at the rain. She had no other option, aside from walking through the downpour in the dark.

"I don't want to mess up your plans . . . ," she said.

"I just have to go over to school later and finish hanging some lights for the show. We're doing *Joseph and the Amazing Technicolor Dreamcoat.*"

"It sounds like an infomercial."

"It's a musical," Pete clarified. "They're always musicals. So, what time are you done?"

"Eleven."

"Eleven," he repeated, again in the strange accent. "So, I'll come back then."

With that settled, May stepped out into the rain and ran to the door, and the Cutlass rolled out of the parking lot and vanished beyond the gray horizon.

Presto Espresso wanted desperately to look like it was part of some huge chain of coffee bars. It had the wooden tables, the wall murals, and the recycled cups. It had drinks with catchy names, always prefaced with the words *our signature,* as if Presto Espresso made coffee in some special, famous way. It had generic jazz music pumped into the air from hidden speakers. What it didn't have was customers. Working there was a long exercise in killing time—stacking cups and grinding coffee and standing around. Specifically, it was an exercise in killing time with Nell Dodd, the assistant manager.

"My dorm was right near this massive cell phone tower," Nell was saying as she arranged a pile of cups in bowling-pin fashion at the far end of the counter. "And it's a well-known fact that cell phone signals give you brain cancer. So I talked to the residence life staff, but they completely refused to move me."

"Uh-huh," May said.

Nell had started college in September and left after two weeks. She'd been living at home and working at Presto for the last nine months while contemplating her "new direction." May had started working at Presto in December, and she'd heard this story at least fifteen times since then.

"Everything about the place sucked," Nell went on. "Like my roommate. My roommate was this total crypto-fascist sorority-girl wannabe. I mean, pretty much all she wanted from college was to pledge Sigma Whatever Whatever, which is just about the saddest thing I have ever heard. I showed her a book once and she kind of shrank away, like Dracula from garlic or something."

"Uh-huh."

"And my classes were just kind of stupid, you know? All kinds of stuff I didn't need. For my core science class I was tak-ing their highest level of Biology 101, which was for majors, and I wasn't a major. But it was *nothing*. I did *all of that* in high school because we had a completely amazing biology program. My high school was *so* much harder, you know? Because I went to an alternative school, right?"

May was taking seven periods of biology a week, along with an introductory chemistry class to prepare her for the two more years of chemistry she still had to face. She somehow doubted that Nell had ever done the same amount of work, but she said nothing.

"So I'm kind of taking some time to think it all over," Nell continued. "I want to reapply to some really good schools, like Bennington and Smith. You know Bennington and Smith?"

"What? Oh. Uh-huh."

"Bennington is like amazingly cool, but it's really expensive. Sylvia Plath went to Smith, and she totally exposed it for everything it was, but I think it's really cool now. Did you read *The Bell Jar*?"

Actually, May considered, this wasn't the worst of the stories she'd had to endure. Nell had once entertained May with a two-hour saga on how she'd been vegan for two years during high school, but then someone had slipped her some cheese-mushroom ravioli and the whole thing had fallen apart, ending with her decision to revert back to ovo-lacto. There had been another grueling evening in which May had learned all about Nell's eight piercings: the two on her face, the three on her ears, the one on her belly button, and two small rings that she actually called "knocker knockers." Now *that* had been a really bad night.

Nell snapped her fingers in front of May's face.

"What?" May jolted.

"A guy. A guy is here."

May followed Nell's gaze. She was staring out the front windows at Pete. He was getting out of his big gray sedan.

"What?" May said. "Him?"

"You see another guy?"

"That's Pete," May said. She realized as she looked at the clock that Pete was fifteen minutes early.

"Pete?" Nell asked.

"Yeah. That's Pete."

"Right. Got that part. And who is Pete?"

"Oh," May said, "he's kind of like our neighbor. A family friend. Kind of like one of our old friends."

"Boyfriend?" Nell said.

"What? Mine? No." May hastily dusted off her apron. "No."

"Check out that hair. He's got a full-on 'fro. You like him?"

"He's Pete," May said.

"Oh." Nell nodded. "It's like that. Okay."

"Like what?"

Pete came in before Nell could answer and before May could remove the baseball cap with the cartoon of the dancing bean on it. That was probably for the best anyway—Nell would have noticed if she'd taken it off.

As the assistant manager, Nell was able to use her rank to push the uniform to the limit, adding a studded black belt to her ragged cargo pants and wearing a torn black mesh shirt over her white T-shirt. She decorated her fiendishly healthy complexion with a few small bits of metal, including the stud in her nose and the ring through her lower lip. She didn't have to wear the hat, the name tag, or the apron. May did. Nell liked to point this out—as a joke, or so she pretended. Nell had an annoying sense of humor like that.

"You're early," May said. The abruptness of her remark caused Pete to stop in his tracks. Nell snorted. Her nose always whistled a bit when she did that as the air passed by the nose stud.

"If you're busy"—Pete motioned toward his car—"I can go. . . ."

"Are you kidding?" Nell threw herself down on the counter. "A customer! We are at your service!"

Pete stared down at the back of Nell's head, then looked at the pile of cups that she had arranged for her game of bowling for Kona.

"You guys are bored," he deduced.

"Is it that obvious?" Nell asked, looking up from her prone position. "Please stay. We are but two young virgins trapped in this remote outpost, with no men to talk to."

May winced. Okay, maybe Nell could joke around with a word like *virgin*—a description that probably didn't fit her—but May couldn't. She kept a wide berth around that term.

"We have nothing to do," Nell went on. "You know those people whose job it is to paint the Golden Gate Bridge? They start at one end, and it takes them a few years to paint all the way to the other side, and when they finish, they just go back and start over? That's kind of like what we do. No one comes here because this place totally blows. Right, Ape?"

"Ape?" Pete repeated.

"My nickname," May said, without enthusiasm.

"Yeah, when May first started, I had to make her name tag,

and I forgot which month her name was. I thought it was April." Nell reached over and grabbed at the strap of May's apron and flashed Pete the tag for proof. "So I call her Ape."

May silenced Pete with a stern look before he could make any reply. Nell was staring at Pete's chest.

"I like your shirt," she said.

Pete was wearing a T-shirt that read, mysteriously enough, Best Wishes to Your Family.

"Well," May said, quickly untying her apron, "we're pretty much done here, right?"

"Sure," Nell said. "Why don't you two go?"

"Okay, then," she said, before Nell could say anything else. "See you later."

May felt Nell's gaze following them as they left the store.

"So that's where I work," she said, sliding back into Pete's car.

"She's interesting," he said.

"She's a special person," May said, giving Pete a light punch on the shoulder. "Just like you, Camper."

"Not special. Challenged."

"So," she said, "what do you have planned as an encore? Are you going to fake a ten-car pileup or something?"

"Eleven," he said, once again in the weird mockney-Cockney accent.

Pete spent most of the ride back smacking and yelling at the radio dial, trying to convince it to work correctly. This didn't accomplish much. He gave up and switched it off when they pulled up to May's house.

"Listen," he said. "I can teach you, if you want."

"What?"

"Driving?"

"Teach me *driving*?"

"It was my mom's idea," he said. "I went home for dinner after I dropped you off, and she suggested it."

"Your mom wants you to teach me?"

"*I* do," he clarified quickly. "It was her idea, but I think it could be fun. You know. Spreading my knowledge."

More charity from the Camps. She should have realized this would happen. They sent Pete to do everything—cut the grass, deliver the bulk purchases, clean the rain gutters, shovel the snow.

"I don't want to take up all your time."

"It's not a problem," he said. "Besides, someone has to teach you, right?"

May couldn't argue the point, even though it made her sound somewhat pathetic. "I guess I'm on the to-do list," she said.

It took her a minute to figure out why Pete was staring at her so strangely.

"You know what I mean," she added.

"So? What do you think?"

What she thought had nothing to do with it. There was only one answer to give.

"Okay," May said. "Thanks."

Palmer was in the exact same position in front of the television that she'd been in when May left, even though four and a half hours had gone by.

"Brooks come home?" May asked, peeling off her damp jacket.

"No."

"She call?"

"No."

And that was it from Palmer.

May went upstairs to her tiny room. Her wallpaper was covered in pictures of white horses with pink ribbons in their manes. Most of her furniture was unfinished light pine, which tended to splinter a bit along the edges of the drawers. One snagged her favorite sleeping shirt, one of her dad's old University of Maryland shirts, as she pulled it from the drawer. She carefully picked the splinter out of the worn fabric, pulled the shirt over her head, and crawled under the quilt.

She turned off her bedside lamp and stared up at the shadow of her blinds, rippling across the ceiling. Someone drove by in a car with way too much bass, and the room thumped and rattled until it passed by.

"I suck," she said out loud. "How could I fail?"

The phone rang. Probably her mother's midway-through-shift call to check on them. May clawed around next to her bed for the phone and answered it. The person on the other end breathed heavily into the phone. She allowed this to go on for a minute or so.

"What's up, Camper?" she finally asked.

"Do you like scary movies?" the voice whispered.

"Do you like getting hot coffee poured in your lap? Because that's what's going to happen the next time I see you if you don't stop it."

Pete cleared his throat.

"I forgot to ask you when you wanted to start," he said. "Monday?"

"Okay." May yawned. "Monday."

"Six?"

"Fine." After a moment she remembered to add, "Thanks."

"No problem."

"Good night, Camper."

Shaking her head at the great unfairness of it all, May hung up and dropped the phone beside her bed.

2

Even though Palmer was only a freshman, she was already the pitcher on Grant High's varsity softball team. This would normally be a rare and remarkable accomplishment, but really, no one expected less from the little sister of Brooks "Solid" Gold— shortstop, Grant's record holder for most hits in a season and in a career, two-time All State selection, with the team-best batting average of .692.

Palmer intended to do even better than her sister. Along with the formal daily practice at school, she did a separate workout at home. Her father had helped her design this routine. It was based on his college workout, and he'd modified it carefully for her. She followed it religiously. On Mondays, Wednesdays, and Fridays she worked on her pitching. On Tuesdays, Thursdays, and Saturdays she stretched and ran a few loops around the neighborhood.

Since it was Monday, Palmer slipped on her fleece jacket (which she wore all year round, except in the most excruciating heat, to keep her body warm and prevent injuries), grabbed her small bucket of softballs, and went out into the backyard. First she set her face in her standard pitching grimace—she narrowed her eyes, sucked in her round cheeks, and tipped her head to the side. (It was actually her imitation of Dirty Harry. She thought it made her look a little older and more imposing.)

Then she started to throw.

Twenty wrist-snap pitches close to the pitch back. A series of fastballs, ten inside and ten outside. A few rise balls, a dozen drop balls and screwballs. Last, she worked the changeups, the balls that actually slow down as they travel. These were the hardest, but they were also some of her best. She wrapped the whole thing up with a dozen very fast, very accurate throws, aimed directly at the center of the net.

With the formal practice over, she allowed herself to throw whatever she liked as her brain tried to process the news, which she had gotten along with everyone else, dished out cold at an impromptu team meeting after practice. Brooks had quit the team that morning. In fact, Brooks was completely AWOL. She hadn't even been around to help Palmer get home. She'd had to bum a ride home with one of her teammates.

When she heard the minivan pull into the driveway, she stopped her practice and went inside. Brooks was in the kitchen, staring into the fridge.

"What's going on?" Palmer said bluntly.

"Yeah," Brooks said, "I was going to tell you."

"*Going* to tell me?"

"May made you dinner," Brooks said, pointing inside the fridge. "She says it's meat loaf, but it looks like one of those old Duraflame logs from the garage."

"You were *going* to tell me?"

Brooks let go of the fridge door.

"Look, I've just had enough, all right?" she said. "I've been playing for what, twelve, thirteen years?"

"You could get a scholarship," Palmer said, her lips clenched. "Or try out for WPSL or the Olympic team . . ."

"Palm," Brooks said with a laugh, "I don't want to go pro. And there's no way I'd even make it."

"Yes, you would. You could. Easy."

"It doesn't matter. I don't want to."

"Why didn't you even tell me?" The strain in Palm's voice was clear now.

"I just decided," Brooks said as she played with the fridge magnets.

"So? You should have told me before you quit."

"You're right," Brooks said. "I should have. I was going to."

May ran into the kitchen. Without bothering to greet either of them, she moved Brooks out of the way, opened up the fridge, and grabbed at the meat loaf. She cringed when she saw it—it looked kind of wet, and it was dotted with soft, sick-looking peas. She sliced off a chunk, dropped it on a plate, and tossed it into the microwave. Normally she went right upstairs to remove her school uniform. Today she just pulled off her maroon blazer and threw it on a chair.

"You're in a hurry," Brooks said.

"I have a driving lesson."

"With who?"

"Pete's teaching me," May said, dropping her bag onto a chair.

Brooks gave her a sharp sideways glance.

"Pete Camp?"

May pulled out a book and instantly started reading.

"What are you doing?" Brooks asked.

"Homework," May said, not looking up. "It's work. You do it at home. You take it back to school the next day."

"Ohhh." Brooks nodded, looking over May's shoulder. "*Romeo and Juliet*. How appropriate."

"What are you talking about?"

"Getting in the mood?"

"I'm getting in the mood to wing this book at you," May said, snapping to the next page.

"Touchy, touchy."

Palmer watched this exchange, then sat down next to May and folded her arms over her chest.

"Did she tell you?" she asked.

"Tell me what?" May asked, reaching around to grab the meat loaf from the beeping microwave.

"She quit the team."

"What?" May's mouth dropped open. "You quit softball?"

Brooks didn't reply. Instead she bunched all of the magnets together and then started dividing them into groups—picture frame magnets, fruit magnets, baseball magnets. . . .

"Can you do that?" May asked. "I mean, can you quit in the middle of the season?"

"You can quit anytime," Brooks said.

"But that's not good, right?" May persisted. "If you wanted to play again?"

"No, probably not. But I don't want to."

"Not even in college? I thought you wanted an athletic scholarship."

"Well, I don't anymore."

"A *scholarship*, Brooks. You're going to need it. Think about it."

"I *have* thought about it."

"You couldn't have, or you wouldn't be doing this. How else

are you going to get a scholarship? You're not going to get an academic one, and we can't pay full tuition."

"I'll work."

"And make ten or fifteen or twenty thousand dollars?" May said. "Doing what?"

"Why is this your business?"

"It's all of our business. There's only one pool of money for tuition. We have to figure out how to divide it."

"Like that's up to you," Brooks said. "Besides, you're the only one whose school costs money. Why don't you just go to our school?"

"We don't pay my tuition," May said quickly. "Grandma and Grandpa Gold pay it."

"So? Couldn't we use that money for something? It's what, six thousand dollars? Seven thousand?"

"It's different."

"How?"

"I don't throw it away," May said, her voice rising. "I actually work. If I get a scholarship, it will all be worth it. It'll be worth *more*."

Palmer started chomping furiously at her nails.

"I'm telling Mom," she said.

"Go ahead," Brooks replied, meeting Palmer's gaze.

There was a knock at the front door. May made a move to get up and answer it, but Palmer beat her to it. She had to get up or she would start screaming.

Pete was waiting there when she opened the door, dressed in a loose pair of jeans and a blue T-shirt that said 100% Hawaiian Pure.

"Hey," he said. "Is May here?"

He looked just over her head, in the direction of the kitchen. Palmer waited a minute before answering, trying to figure out a way to get him to come in and join the conversation. Maybe *he* could talk some sense into Brooks. Before she could think of anything, May came up behind them.

"I'm ready," she said, stepping around both Palmer and Pete and out the door.

"You can come in," Palmer said to Pete, even though it seemed like the wrong time to finally say this.

"That's all right," he said. He looked over his shoulder at May. "We're just going to go, I think."

"Uh-huh," May said, folding her arms over her chest. "Definitely."

She walked across the lawn toward Pete's car.

"See you later," Pete said, smiling at Palmer.

"Later."

Palmer watched Pete follow May. When she turned around, she saw Brooks coming up behind her and heading for the stairs.

"I'll tell Mom myself," she said.

Palmer shut the door.

"Whatever," she said. But Brooks was already gone.

Pete's car was saunalike. Waves of heated air came blasting from the vents.

"Sorry," he said. He threw his arm over her seat and craned his neck around to back out of the driveway. "My radiator is leaking."

"What?"

"My radiator. I have to keep the heat on so the car doesn't overheat."

"You have to turn on the heat to keep the heat down?" May asked. "That makes no sense."

"It pulls the heat out of the engine and pushes it inside the car. That's how heaters work."

"Is this a joke? Like the one from the other night?"

"No," he said. "This just sucks."

May noticed that his skin was flushed and he'd stripped off his sweatshirt, so he probably wasn't kidding. Pete tried to turn on the radio, but the stations drifted wildly every time he turned the steering wheel, so he had to switch it off.

"I think my car's possessed," he said. "And I just finished paying it off, too."

"Didn't your parents buy it?"

"Yeah, but I've been paying them back. It was fifteen hundred bucks."

"I didn't know you were working."

"Yeah, I am," he said, running the back of his hand over his forehead. "I work for this place in New Hope that rents theatrical equipment. Lights and stuff. I only help out when they're busy or behind, so it's really off and on. I need something more regular for the summer. More hours."

They stopped talking for a minute to lean out their windows and catch a breath of air.

"So, that's your uniform?" Pete asked, glancing over.

May looked down at the mass of maroon that was herself. She was so used to wearing her uniform now that she forgot how strange it had to look to other people. It was kind of severe—a plain, straight skirt with a single pleat, a white oxford-cloth shirt, maroon kneesocks, and loafers. The blazer, which she had tossed into the backseat, completed the look, which was kind of a cross between a stewardess and Thelma from Scooby-Doo.

"It's ugly," she said.

"No. It's . . . I've just never seen you in it," he said. "It says *academy*, you know? It's kind of serious looking."

"It's kind of polyester."

"Okay . . ."

"Sorry. I'm just irritated. And hot." She leaned out and took another breath of air. "Is it ever legal to kill your sister? If you had a really good reason?"

"I guess it depends. What's the reason?"

"Forget it. It's too annoying to even discuss."

"Brooks or Palmer?"

"Really, forget it."

"I'm guessing Brooks."

"Camper . . ."

"Ve can fix zees problems, you know. Ve hav ways of fixing ze peoples."

"Camper," she said sharply, "forget it. Where are we going anyway?"

"I'm psyched. I found the perfect place."

The perfect place turned out to be a deserted housing development still under construction. The roads were just laid, there were backhoes and cement trucks parked against the shiny new white curbs, and the streetlights weren't on.

"It's dark," May said, squinting.

"There's some light."

"From the moon."

"Driver's ed by moonlight." He grinned. "Come on—that's cool."

"I guess. It's your car."

May spent about fifteen minutes going over all of the controls in Pete's car. It wasn't that they were hard to understand, but she was nervous about practicing with his most valuable possession. She tried to relax and get the news about Brooks out of her head, but that didn't really work.

"So," Pete said, rubbing his hands together, "I guess you should just start driving around."

"You want me to just . . . drive? Around? What, in circles?"

"No, just normally. Like this was a real street. Just for practice. Let's see what you need to work on. We'll try the three-point turn, parking, all of that."

The first discovery they made was that May only seemed able to drive at five miles an hour or fifty—and she usually alternated between the two rather abruptly. The second was that she seemed to think things were much closer than they actually were. As a result, she drove down the center of the road.

"A little closer to the curb," Pete said, looking out the window.

"I'm going to hit it."

"No, you're not. Ease it in a little."

Pete watched for another minute.

"A little closer, May," he repeated.

"I just moved it closer!"

"We're still in the middle of the street. A little more."

May pushed harder on the gas.

"Not faster," Pete said. "Closer."

In frustration she slammed on the brakes, sending them both pitching forward. She ran her hands through her hair and grabbed two big handfuls.

"Okay," Pete said, pushing himself back off the dashboard. "So, I guess we'll kind of start at the beginning."

"I think I need to get out for a second." May sighed and wiped some of the perspiration from her face. She put the car in park and turned off the engine. They both got out of the car, leaving their doors hanging open to air it out. May sat on the brand-new curb and rubbed her eyes.

"How did you learn how to drive?" she asked.

"My dad. And driver's ed."

"You passed the first time, didn't you?"

"I had more practice."

Somehow May didn't think that was it.

"Things come easier to you," she said.

"I'm not even going there," he replied, shaking his head.

"What?"

"You know what."

"School stuff doesn't count," she said.

"Since when? I've always been way behind you. This is the only thing I've done better at first."

The flattery lifted May's spirits a bit, but she didn't want this to show.

"The only reason I have to learn is because my mom has all

these jobs she needs me to do," she said.

"That doesn't matter," Pete replied. "The best part about driving is that you can just sit and think or play music. Whatever you want. You're totally on your own."

May turned to him. He was too tall to sit with his knees tucked up, like hers were. He had to stretch them out.

"I want that," she said seriously.

"So, come on. Back in."

The car was slightly cooler when they got in, but this didn't last long.

"I've got an idea," Pete said. "We're going to play 'let's pretend we're in England.' This is how it works: You drive on the left side of the road. That way you can see how close you are to the curb."

"So I watch out the window?"

"Bloody right."

Pete was using the same strange voice that he'd been trying out on Saturday.

"We're going to do this without the accent, okay, Pete?"

"You got it," he said, again with the accent.

It took about an hour of going back and forth between the left and right sides, but she eventually managed to drive on the correct side at the correct distance from the curb. But an hour in the punishing heat of the car drained them both, and they turned around and headed back to May's house.

"So, what do you think?" he asked. "Want to do this again?"

"Yeah," May said. "It was good. I think I almost got it."

"You did get it. You were fine."

"So what's the catch?" May asked.

"Catch?"

"I'm just waiting," she said. "I know you have something planned. I know I'm walking into some plot of yours."

Pete snickered. "Just wait and see."

"Yeah," May said, getting out of the car. "I can hardly wait."

3

One of May's ultimate pet peeves was when people said to her, "Your dad's in a better place now." Like he had moved. May always wanted to say, "Yes. He loves it in North Carolina." Or, "He says Spain is amazing."

May resented the idea of anyone else thinking they knew where her dad had gone. She didn't know where her dad was. Not even physically. His body had been cremated, and the ashes were being stored somewhere. She had never asked where because she didn't want to know. As for the spiritual part (which was what the "better placers" were talking about), she got the impression they were talking about a heaven where he was floating around in the clouds, consorting with famous dead people.

The other thing they seemed to be saying was that death was a great thing. That was probably the part that made her so angry. It was like they were telling her she should be happy that her father had dropped dead because he ate too much fat and didn't exercise enough and clogged up his arteries. That was what her mom had explained to her, anyway. She said it could have been heredity or stress, but May had seen her father eat enough chili cheese dogs to know the truth.

On some level, she blamed him for it. He'd been a big guy to start with, and he'd just let himself get bigger. Mike Gold was definitely not a dieter. He was the kind of guy who just liked to let things go and have a good time. That was probably why he'd liked Brooks most of all and allowed her to do whatever she wanted. That Brooks was lazy, that she did the minimum amount of work at school or at home—her father never seemed to notice. As long as she could hit a ball with a stick, she was a wonderful human being. So Brooks coasted by, and May picked up her slack or dealt with the consequences.

For example, here May was at five thirty-five on Thursday morning without a single pair of clean underwear to her name. And why? Because in the week and a half since Brooks had quit the softball team, she had yet to actually complete any of the newly assigned chores that their mom had given her, including laundry. This meant May had to sneak into Brooks's room (she didn't make much effort to be quiet) to try to find some clean underwear.

Under ideal conditions, the ride from the Northeast Philadelphia suburbs to Girls' should have taken only half an hour. But May's bus served another private school on the edge of the city, so there were other stops to make, and there was rush-hour traffic to take into account. In the end, she had to be at her bus stop just after six.

As her bus rumbled through downtown Philadelphia, over the Schuylkill River and down into University City, past the dignified stretches of the University of Pennsylvania buildings, May was fast asleep with her head against the window. Her bus hit a huge pothole at Thirty-third and Chestnut, causing May's head to smack into the window, waking her. She didn't mind. She counted on that pothole to be her alarm clock.

Linda Fan, May's best friend and her constant companion

since day one of her freshman year at Girls', was sitting on the stone bench by May's bus stop, where they met every morning. Linda lived twenty blocks north and a few tree streets over from Girls', in a condo on Locust Street. She usually just woke up a half hour before school, threw on her uniform, and hopped on the subway.

Linda's parents could afford to live where they did because they were both doctors at Jefferson Hospital and Linda was an only child. She never had to worry about having enough underwear in the morning, because her family had a woman who came in three times a week to straighten up the house and take care of the chores, like the laundry. The only bad part of the deal was that her cousin Frank was living with them while he went to Drexel University, which was very close to their house. Frank was an engineering student with five pet snakes. Unfortunately, snakes terrified Linda, so she missed a lot of sleep.

"I'm dead," Linda said as May approached. "Very, very dead. I'm not even done with my history paper. I'll have to finish it and print it out at lunch. I would have gotten it done last night, but Frank was letting Harvey out for his weekly crawl, so I couldn't even think."

"Which one is Harvey?"

"The Burmese python," Linda said, getting up. She was almost a full head shorter than May, so May always had to look down when they were talking. It was an unusual experience since May was the runt of the Tall, Blond, and Wonderful family. "Anyway, I had ten minutes on the subway this morning to work, but Aubrey had to re-create this entire conversation she had with her boyfriend last night so I could analyze it. You know, because I'm a licensed psychologist, right? Do I wear a sign on my back that says Overshare with Me?"

"Yeah. A really little one."

"I thought so," Linda said. "So, do you have any personal information you want to share with me?"

"I'm wearing Brooks's underwear."

"Again?"

"She's supposed to do the laundry—but it's been over a week. You know Brooks. She doesn't do anything."

"Is she still seeing that guy?"

"Dave?" May said. "Yeah. More than ever now."

They walked up the front steps and in through the ornate doorway of the school. Herds of maroon-suited girls hurried in all directions.

"What about you?" Linda asked.

"What about me?"

"Aren't you getting lessons from Pete?"

May nodded.

"So?" Linda said. "How's that?"

"We've only gone once, a week ago on Monday. It was fine."

"You haven't complained about it at all. You always complain when you see Pete."

"He's behaving."

Linda hmmmed.

"Don't do that," May said.

"Do what?"

"Make that noise."

Linda smiled innocently.

"Anyway, I don't even know what's going to happen when I do get my license," May went on. "We only have the one car, really, and it's not like I'll suddenly have this amazing life even if I *can* drive."

"*When* you can."

"Whatever. The only reason I'm getting my license at all is because my mom can't count on Brooks to do things. We can't afford the extra insurance right now."

"But it will help," Linda said, "with getting a life."

"How do you get a life?" May asked. "I mean, does it just show up someday?"

"Getting outside of your house for something other than school or work is probably a good place to start."

"Well, that isn't going to happen," May said.

Palmer was happy out on the field, with the dirt, the grass, the blinding sun. Heat, cold, sweat—no problem. Outside, it wasn't quite so obvious that every part of her body was weirdly *long*, like she was actually a short person who had been stretched out of shape. It didn't matter that she had no chest or that she had the gangly walk of a girl who really only knows how to run. On the field these were advantages. On the field she was the pitcher—the star.

Here in the locker room, though, with the gels and lotions that smelled of peach and coconut, the body buffs, the blow-dryers, the exfoliant scrubs, the intense conditioners—this was where it all fell apart. This was where it was all too clear that Palmer was fourteen and flat, with perennially oily hair, chewed-up nails, and skin that was always either windburned or sunburned. In here, Palmer was just a gawky freshman. It had been different when Brooks was here. Brooks had always been so popular, so loud. She was the shortstop and the talker, and Palmer was the quiet, intense pitcher. That was how Palmer liked it.

Now she was just Palmer, naked, struggling to pull a scratchy towel around herself. The towels she brought were always too small, so she had to hunch to cover herself up.

Diana Haverty was sprawled out over most of the bench behind Palmer's locker, wrapped snugly in the thickest red towel Palmer had ever seen. She was examining her toes, which were tiny and cute. Her toenails were painted an Easter-egg blue.

"I don't know if I like this color," Diana said to no one in particular.

"I think it's nice." Emma, the third-base player, turned from her locker to join in the examination of the adorable digits. "Who makes it?"

"Hard Candy."

"Stila makes a color kind of like that, but it's a little glossier."

"Really?" Diana said. "I need to pick something for my prom pedicure, and that's what I want: a light gloss, but sort of like this."

Palmer looked down at her own big feet. She quickly threw on her grocery-store flip-flops and hurried to the shower with her little basket. She preferred being the first one in and out. As she dripped and flip-flopped her way back, she stopped short when she heard Diana say Brooks's name.

"Is she really dating Vatiman?" Emma was asking.

"That's what I heard. I don't know. She doesn't call me anymore."

"Isn't Vatiman a dealer?"

"Something like that," Diana said. "That girl Jamie I always see them with . . . psycho. Seriously. I had four classes with her last year. She's a total head case."

"I heard that."

"But you know Brooks," Diana said. "It was just a matter of time."

One of them mumbled something. Palmer knew instinctively that it must have been about her.

"I know," Diana said. "It's a shame. I really wish I could help."

Palmer stood there, unsure of what to do. It wasn't like she could just turn around and leave. Quietly she came back over. As she'd expected, Diana and Emma pretended like nothing had been going on. Diana looked over as Palmer tried to dry herself without removing the towel.

"That was an amazing curve today, Palmer," she said. "Really good. Are you going to a pitching coach?"

"No," Palmer said.

"Your arm is getting stronger."

"Thanks." Palmer hastily pulled on her shorts and her fleece top. She pulled her wet hair back into a heavy ponytail. Within a minute she was hefting her bag over her shoulder, ready to go.

"See you tomorrow," she said softly.

"Do you need a ride today?" Diana asked.

"No." Palmer shook her head. "My mom is coming for me."

"Hey," Emma said. "Palmer."

Palmer stopped and turned around.

"Is Brooks really dating Dave Vatiman?"

"I guess."

Diana and Emma exchanged a look.

"I have to go," Palmer said.

Her mother was waiting for her in the parking lot. Palmer climbed inside the minivan, roughly tossing her bags into the backseat. She didn't speak for the first few minutes of the trip, prompting a few quick glances from her mother.

"What are you going to do?" Palmer finally asked.

"About what?"

"About Brooks."

"What about Brooks?"

"About softball."

"What do you want me to do, Palm?" her mother asked. "I can't make her play."

"So you're just going to let her quit?" she asked.

"She's old enough to make that decision."

Palmer turned and stared out the window.

"May's at work right now," her mother said. "She'll be back around seven. You can either warm up something when you get home, or you can wait and have dinner with her."

"Fine."

"Don't get upset, Palm."

Palmer had every reason to be upset. Every reason in the world. And the fact that her mother didn't understand why made it even worse.

In Palmer's eyes, Brooks had given up everything and left her alone.

As she hung up her apron in the storage room after finishing her short evening shift, May's eyes fell on her name tag. It read *Lirpa*. She'd been wearing it for three hours and hadn't even noticed.

She pulled the apron back down and went into the shop. Nell was leaning against the counter, eating her dinner, which consisted of painfully pungent kimchi and large squares of wiggly tofu.

"What's this?" May asked, holding up the tag. "I just fixed it."

"It's April, spelled backward." Nell grinned, pinching up a clump of cabbage with her chopsticks. "Have fun finding the label maker again."

May tried to smile, because this was supposed to be funny. She returned to the storage room and deposited the apron. While she was there, she couldn't resist looking around for the label maker. It was no use. Nell had probably bricked it up in the wall or something. When she emerged, she found Pete leaning against the counter, already immersed in a chat with Nell. He didn't seem to mind having her talking into his face with her tear-inducing kimchi breath.

"Tech," Nell was rambling. "That's cool. I'm really into tech. Technical stuff is so important in theater. So many people don't realize that—they think it's all about the actors."

"Yeah," Pete agreed. "That's true."

Pete was wearing an open long-sleeve shirt over a T-shirt for Grant's recent production of *Brigadoon*.

"You do, what, lights?"

"Lights and sound," Pete replied. "Mostly lights. Some construction, too."

"I act," Nell said. "I did a lot of shows in high school. I've done some Shakespeare and some modern plays and some plays that my friends and I wrote."

"You wrote some plays?" Pete asked, looking impressed.

"Yeah." Nell nodded. "I had two years of playwriting classes in high school. I've written at least twelve or fifteen short plays and three full-lengths. They were all pretty experimental. We did them in alternative spaces. We did this kind of political play in the men's bathroom once. . . ."

"You didn't go to Grant, did you?" Pete asked.

"No." Nell laughed. "I went to the Albert School."

May turned around to roll her eyes. Pete stood up and wiggled his fingers at her.

"My girl Lirpa." Nell smiled. "I guess she's ready to go. You two have a good night."

There was something unbearably irritating about the way Nell said this. May gave her a stiff smile, then pushed Pete out the door.

"We're going to go parking," Pete said as he and May got into the car. "Let's just say it and get it out of the way. *Parking.* I know I feel better. How about you?"

"Where are we going to do this?"

"I was thinking here. You can just practice going in and out of spaces."

"Maybe we can do it on the other side of Pet Mart?" May offered, wincing. "I'd rather not have Nell as an audience."

They pulled around Pet Mart, on the far side of the parking lot, and switched positions.

"I heard Brooks quit softball," Pete said, moving his seat back and putting his Pumas up against the glove compartment.

"News travels fast," May said.

"Is that what you were mad about the last time you drove?"

"Probably," May said. "It's hard to remember anymore."

"Why'd she quit?"

"I don't know," May said, starting the engine and timidly backing up. "She's a mystery."

"That's kind of a big deal for her."

"No kidding."

"So she's not doing anything now? Is she working?"

"No," May said. "She's not doing anything. That's why I'm wearing her underwear right now."

Pete cocked an eyebrow.

"What, do you rotate?"

"Yeah." May smirked. "It's just something we like to do."

"If I guess what color they are, can I see them?"

"Just forget I said it."

"Give me one guess."

"Can you tell me what I'm supposed to do?" May asked.

"Pull into spaces, back out. We'll work on your turning angle."

May's turning angle was absurdly wide. She found herself heading into her space at a wild diagonal.

"So you don't know why she quit?" Pete asked.

"I told you, I don't know."

"A little less to the left," he said. "Here . . ."

As he leaned over to demonstrate, Pete snagged the waistband of her pants with one finger, pulling it down just enough to reveal the elastic of the famous underwear. Startled, May jerked away and in the process accidentally hit the gas. There was a great heaving under them. A grinding noise. And a heavy bump. May screamed and stopped the car.

"Oh my God . . ." May clutched at Pete's arm in panic. "What did I just do?"

"It's okay," he said, although his eyes had widened. "Hold on."

He was out of the car for about a minute, walking around the front and the back and taking a quick peek underneath. May sat perfectly still the entire time, like a rabbit, quivering and listening for signs of danger. Pete leaned in.

"You just . . . a concrete divider is there."

"I broke your car," she whispered.

"It's probably fine," he said. "This thing is a tank. We're just on top of it."

"*Probably* fine?"

"Here," he said, indicating that she should get out. "I'll do this."

As Pete eased the car over the divider, May took a look for herself, although she didn't know what she was looking for. There were no wires hanging down. There were no loose pieces of metal. Those seemed like good signs.

May quietly got in on the passenger's side.

"It's fine," Pete assured her. "We didn't even get started. Why don't you try again? Well, not *that*, but parking."

"I can't," she said. "Sorry."

May mused over what she should do for a finale as they drove home. Maybe she could tell him that when they'd taken pictures of him naked last year, her little sister had mentioned that she thought he wasn't very well hung. Of course, Palmer had no idea what she was even talking about, and they had no visual proof one way or another, but the mere suggestion that a thirteen-year-old girl found him inadequate would really make his evening complete.

"Forget it," she said. "Let's just forget all of this. I can't be taught."

"It was my fault. It wasn't anything you did. It's not—"

"Don't say it wasn't a big deal. Please. Just let it be. I screwed up. I am a screwup. Tell your mom you're not teaching me anymore because I drove your car up a wall. You're off the hook."

May could hear herself rambling but felt powerless to stop the rush of self-criticisms. Pete evidently knew that there was no point in trying to stop her either. He was being irritatingly patient, which only made her crazier.

"Camper!" she finally yelled.

"What?"

"Why aren't you saying anything?"

"What am I supposed to say?"

"That I suck!"

"You suck!"

It didn't make her feel better.

It took May a few minutes to realize that it actually hadn't been her fault. It had been Pete's. Instead of teaching her, he'd been his usual asinine self. But because May had been the one behind the wheel, she had mistakenly thought she was to blame.

She looked over at him slouching down in his seat. He glanced over.

"You're mad now," he said. "Aren't you?"

"A little."

"Thought so."

It was still early when they pulled back up in front of the Gold house. The garage door was open. Palmer was probably practicing out back.

"Look," Pete said, "we're good, right? You're going to try again?"

"I don't know."

"I shouldn't do stuff like that," he said. "It's just . . . old habit. Sorry."

He really did look sorry. And they were pretty much even since she *had* ended up almost destroying his car.

"Fine," May grumbled.

"Just tell me something."

"What?"

"Are you really wearing Brooks's underwear?"

May nodded and opened her door to get out.

"Why?"

"It's a little game we play," she said. "Sometimes we make out, too. Good night, Camper."

As Palmer lay in bed that night, she felt her heart jumping—hiccuping. She pressed her fingers to her neck and felt the irregular beat. Quickly at first, then a pause, then two hard beats at once. The sensation seemed to lock off her breathing for a moment. She sucked in air as powerfully as she could, and her heart staggered harder. By then the pressure was everywhere, blocking her nose and her throat, pressing down on her lungs. The dark in the room got darker. It throbbed.

Her hands scrambled for the bedside lamp. Unfortunately, the light only caused everything to glow a heady orange, which made the walls look like they were leaning in. She was unable to move from her position, unable to call out for fear of wasting all the breath she had left. She bent over and pulled the blankets to her abdomen. She concentrated on her breathing. Her chest hurt.

The fearless side of Palmer rose up long enough to tell the rest of her to ride it through. She tried imagining being on the field or being at school. Something with daylight, people all around her. She tried to imagine the most boring place to be— the back row of her algebra class, stuck in line at the supermarket. Sometimes those images were the easiest to pull up. Anything to distract herself, get her mind to a good place.

The feeling of dread was impossible to shake. It was like a stench that clung to her clothes. She knew from experience that this would last for at least an hour. These night attacks had started about a month after her father had died. At first they'd happened about once a month. But she'd had one once a week for the last three weeks.

She went down to the living room and switched on all the lights. She switched on *SportsCenter* and wound herself up in an afghan. The worst part was still coming—the feeling that the world was permanently screwed up. That this crippling fear would go right into her bones and stay there. That the afghan would suffocate her.

She kicked it off and wondered if she was crazy. Probably.

"Jesus, Palm," May said, appearing in the living room doorway a few minutes later and squinting at the television. "Could you turn that down?"

"I couldn't sleep," Palmer said. Though she felt like she should barely have been able to speak, her voice came out very loud.

"Fine. So you can't sleep. Does it have to be so loud?"

Palmer turned the television down a few notches.

"Did Brooks come home?"

Palmer shook her head mutely.

"Whatever," May growled. "If she oversleeps, she oversleeps. I'm sick of this."

May turned and went back upstairs, and Palmer pulled her blanket tighter. This wasn't working. Even the living room seemed like a bad place to be. The dark plaid sofa and the green carpet made her feel claustrophobic. The bobble-headed baseball dolls on the top of the entertainment console seemed to be leering at her. And she needed more air. Someplace cooler. She would go get a flashlight and take a walk.

She threw her fleece on over her pajamas and headed out to the garage. As she was sliding alongside the Firebird to get to the shelves on the other side of the room, Palmer looked into the backseat. She barely noticed the car anymore, even though it took up most of the garage. There was something weird about it now. It seemed forbidden.

When she was little and couldn't sleep, her father would put her in the backseat, take the top down, and drive her around. Palmer would stare up at the sky, and before she knew it, she would realize that her father was carrying her up to bed.

She stared at the door and bit at her cuticles. No one had gone inside the Firebird since that day.

If it would help her relax, she didn't care. She carefully opened the door, released the front seat, and crawled into the back.

Even though the seat wasn't quite big enough for her to
stretch all the way out, it was still large enough for her to be
comfortable. She looked up at the black convertible top that
stretched above her. It wasn't like before, when she would look
up at the stars, but still, things didn't seem to be closing in as
much. She breathed in and out slowly, taking long breaths and
holding them in her chest. She ran her fingers along the stitch-
ing on the backseats that had always reminded her of the pattern on the front of a catcher's chest protector. Slowly she
started to feel a bit better. She actually started to nod off.

The next thing she knew, there was a horrible grinding
sound above her, causing her to jolt awake midsnore. The
garage door was rolling back. Palmer crouched down, but
Brooks was obviously going to notice the huge car door that
was blocking her path into the house. Sure enough, Palmer
heard the footsteps stop, and Brooks leaned down and peered
into the back of the car.

"What are you doing?" Brooks said, smirking.

"Nothing."

"You're sleeping in the garage now?"

Palmer didn't answer. She would just wait for Brooks to lose
interest and go away.

"You're getting freaky, Palm," Brooks said, tripping just a bit
as she went up the two steps to the kitchen door.

When Brooks was gone, Palmer gave up on her idea. She
went back into the house and curled back up on the sofa, keeping the television on mute.

4

At work the next night, Nell approached May as she was restocking the milk-and-sugar counter. May went right on working, stuffed sugar packets into their clear plastic box, even though Nell lurked there for a solid minute or so. She got close enough for May to get a good whiff of her clove shampoo.

"Did you want something?" May finally asked.

"What's your deal with Pete, Ape?"

"My deal? I don't have a deal with Pete."

"Yes, you do. You guys seem pretty tight."

"I've just known him for a long time," May said, pushing way too many napkins into the dispenser. "My dad and his dad were best friends."

"Were? Did they fight or something?"

"No."

"So they're not friends now?"

"They're friends," May said, not wanting to explain. "Is there a reason you're asking?"

"So if Pete's not your boyfriend, why does he always come here?"

"He gives me rides sometimes. That's all."

"So you don't have a boyfriend?"

It was a piercing question.

"Not at the moment," May said, reaching for another pack of napkins. She wasn't about to tell Nell that she had never had a boyfriend—but for some reason, she felt like Nell could sense that fact.

"I think that thing is full," Nell said. The napkin dispenser was now groaning from the pressure of May's overzealous packing. Nell's cool hazel eyes said it all: *You poor, sexually frustrated mess.* Yeah. She knew.

May stopped filling the napkin dispenser.

"I did this photography project once," Nell said, looking down at her nails. "It was a study on body markings. You know. Piercing, tattoos, stuff like that. But also natural stuff, like people who have extra skin somewhere or freckles. I like freckles. I liked your friend Pete's freckles. He would have made a good subject."

"He's got enough of them."

"You brought your bike today, didn't you?"

Automatically they both turned their glances out the window and focused them on the Brown Hornet, which was bathed dramatically in a pool of parking lot light. It was U-locked to one of the parking signs, and it slumped rather pathetically against the pole.

"So he's not coming to get you?"

"No."

"Oh," Nell said casually. "Too bad. Why don't you give me his number?"

May cocked her head, unable to accept what she'd just heard. Nell carefully pulled one of the napkins from the dispenser, produced a pen from her pocket, and pushed them over to May. May stared at them.

"You just said there's nothing between you guys," Nell said. "Right?"

May could only nod.

"Does he have a girlfriend?"

This was something May had not asked Pete, but it seemed very clear that he didn't. She shook her head.

"So . . ." Nell tapped the napkin.

It was true. There was no reason May could give for not handing over the number—at least, not one that made sense. She couldn't really say, "No, if you and Pete come together in any kind of romantic or sexual way, nature will rebel and the entire fabric of the universe will collapse. All will perish."

Nell was looking May right in the eye now. As calmly as possible, May wrote out a number she had known all her life. The first phone number she had ever learned, in fact, after her own.

She pushed it over to Nell.

As May was wheeling the Brown Hornet across the front lawn a half hour later, a car came up directly behind her. It pulled up so quickly that May actually shrieked and put her hand up to her chest, damsel-in-distress style.

"Sorry," Pete said, stepping out of his car. He was dressed all in black—black T-shirt, black jeans, black sneakers.

"Were you at a ninja club meeting tonight?" she asked.

"I ran the lights at a show. We have to wear all black."

"Oh."

"I got home early. You should have called. I could have driven you home."

May almost cringed. If Pete had taken her home tonight, she would have been able to witness Nell asking him for his number in person. That might have caused her to have a seizure.

"I don't mind riding," May said. "It's the only exercise I get."

"Exercise is good."

The black outfit made Pete look thinner and taller than normal. They'd always been the same height when they were younger, then suddenly one day he was six feet tall (even taller with the hair) and she was half a foot down. It was weird to have to look up at him all the time.

"My mom asked me to bring something over, and I saw you go past on your bike a minute ago, so . . ."

May eyed him skeptically as he went back to his car and pulled a shrink-wrapped case of dozens of ramen noodle packets out of the backseat.

"That's a lot of ramen," she said.

"I know," he said, looking at the package critically.

"Let me just put my bike inside and I'll take it."

May reached into her bag and pushed the remote control for the garage door. It squawked hideously as it rolled up on its track.

"I think that thing needs a little oil," Pete said, watching it rise. "Want me to do it?"

"You're not our servant."

May ducked under and wheeled the bike into the darkness. Pete followed with the noodles.

"Your friend called me," he said.

"Do you mean Nell?" May replied, trying to sound casual. "What did she say?"

"She kind of asked me out."

"Kind of?"

"Well, she did. She asked if I wanted to do something with her sometime."

"Oh," May said.

"I wanted to see if you were okay with it."

"If I'm okay with it? What does this have to do with me?"

"Well, you know her."

"I work with her," May clarified quickly.

"I was just wondering what you thought. You don't really seem to like her."

"Does that matter?" May asked.

"No, but . . ."

"Well, what did you say when she asked you?"

"I said okay."

May shrugged, indicating that the matter seemed settled.

"I haven't figured out what to do yet about the prom," he said. "It's in the first week in June."

There was a long pause while May elaborately secured the Brown Hornet. She hadn't seen this one coming. She should have, of course. Brooks had been talking about the prom. For some reason, she hadn't connected Pete to the idea, even though he and Brooks were in the same class.

"Who are you going to ask?" she finally said, having run out of things she could do with the bike.

"I don't know."

"Oh," May said breezily, slipping between Pete and the Firebird and making her way out of the garage. He followed her and waited again for the horrible groaning and creaking of the garage door to stop. He shifted a lot, moving the lightweight box from arm to arm.

"Are you saying you want to take Nell to the prom?" May asked. "Is that what I'm supposed to get from this?"

"Well, maybe. I don't know. Like I said, I don't really . . ."

Pete sighed loudly and rolled his head back on his shoulders. May relieved him of the load of ramen. He used his free hand to start pulling on the collar of his shirt. May didn't even know what they were talking about anymore. Whatever it was, though, it was making her ill.

"Just ask her," May said. "I'm sure she'd go, especially if you sneak up on her with that smooth crouching tiger move."

"Right," Pete said. "I thought you'd say something like that."

Palmer watched May and Pete talking through the blinds on the living room bay window. It was hard to tell what was going on. May was doing a lot of shuffling and staring at the ground. Pete looked happy but not as animated as usual, and he was carrying a big box of something.

Palmer had a great interest in Pete. Unlike May, she had always found him amusing. (She had never been the direct target of any of his jokes.) He was kind to Palmer, and he liked to make her laugh. Plus he had his own car, and he always seemed to have some cash.

Palmer watched as May took the box from Pete and turned back toward the house. She came into the living room a minute later.

"What were you and Pete doing?" Palmer immediately asked.

"Ballroom dancing," May said, setting the box of noodles on the recliner. Palmer examined the package.

"Are you guys going out or something?" she asked, digging her fingers into the shrink-wrap.

"That's sick, Palm."

"He's always here now. And he brings stuff."

"You're right," May said. "You caught us. We're dating. That's why he brought me all this soup."

May jogged upstairs. Palmer listened carefully. She could read her sister's mood from the sound of her walking above, since her room was right above the living room. May was particularly stompy tonight, dropping her bag heavily on the floor and then throwing herself onto her creaky bed.

Palmer knew she wasn't going to be able to sleep again tonight—she'd known this the whole day. To spare herself the trouble of having to find something to do to relax, she'd already come up with a plan: She was going to go through the boxes and bins she'd seen stuffed under her parents' bed.

She waited about half an hour for May to fall asleep (May usually read in bed for a while), then crept up to her mother's room. Her mother, Palmer noticed, wasn't as tidy as she used to be. The bed was unmade. A camisole and shorts were on top. A black bra hung from the bathroom door handle. A pile of dirty scrubs lay on the floor.

Palmer lifted the cream-colored dust ruffle and evaluated the stash. The first thing she pulled out was a red expanding file full of drawings, tests, report cards, and notes from each of the girls. Each pocket was marked with a name and an age. From Brooks, age eleven: three certificates from various sports, a drawing of a dinosaur, a math quiz that she got 100 percent on (a rarity). From Palmer, age eight: a handprint in brown paint that had been drawn on to look like a turkey, a Little League certificate, a Valentine's Day card. May, age ten: a science fair ribbon, a report on koalas, a poem about ice cream, and a carefully written note on heart-studded stationery that made a passionate but well-structured case for a family dog.

Other things were under there. A cigar box brimming with concert ticket stubs, a few pairs of cleats, some rolled-up posters in a tube. She was in the process of trying to pull these out when she heard a car drive up. She hastily shoved everything under the bed and quickly left the room.

There were voices downstairs, very low voices. It sounded like there might be a few people in the house. Palmer came down the dark stairs and slipped along the hall past the living room, heading back into the kitchen.

A figure was leaning against the refrigerator in the dark. It took Palmer a minute to realize that it was actually two people, Brooks and Dave. They were the same height, and when they wound around each other, they seemed perfectly matched. Dave was on the outside, and Brooks's back was pressed against the door. She had her arms down low inside his jacket and was pulling out his shirt. Dave was mumbling things to her, nuzzling his head into her neck, kissing her.

It wasn't like Palmer had never seen anything like this before—she'd just never seen anything like this in her kitchen. With her sister. Against the magnetized frames that held the photos of their cousins in Maryland. Dave was pressing his one palm flat against their fridge now. Brooks turned her head in Palmer's direction and opened her eyes. She jolted upright.

"Oh my God, Palmer," Brooks said, her face full of disgust. "What are you doing?"

"I heard something," Palmer said.

Dave eased himself back against one of the kitchen chairs and laughed.

"How long have you been standing there?" Brooks demanded.

Palmer was thankful for the dark. Her face was flushed with embarrassment and she suddenly felt perverted.

"Like a minute," she replied angrily. "Not even. I heard you come in. You're loud."

"Go away," Brooks said. "Go back to whatever it was you were doing."

"Fine," Palmer said. "Whatever."

Palmer was a little too spooked to go right back to her explorations. She went back into the living room and switched on the television instead, trying hard to quickly lose herself in *SportsCenter*. After a minute or two, Dave passed by the living room door and grinned at her on the way out. Brooks stalked past a moment later and went right up the stairs.

Palmer had to wait another twenty minutes or so for Brooks to go to bed before she could slip back into her mom's room to put everything back as carefully as she could.

5

On a bright, warm morning a week later, Brooks landed her fist on her alarm clock. She was dismayed to discover that apparently she'd been eating paste all night. Her mouth felt like it was full of it. There was a dull, grinding pain on the flesh of her brain that sent shocks along her eyebrows. She slid one of her legs out from under the blankets and sent it on an exploratory mission to the floor.

Day? Probably a Saturday or a Sunday, since she was hung over. No . . . it was Friday. The night before, she'd been at the opening night party at the pool—the Memorial Day opening.

She wiped the film from her eyes and focused on the clock. Seven-fifty. She was supposed to be at school in fifteen minutes. She swung out of bed and felt the first full shock of cold air. Everything hurt. Even the carpet hurt her feet.

The house was quiet. The sun coming in through the window was cold and white. May and Palmer's things were gone. Her mom's keys were on the key rack. She could take the minivan to school. She opened the refrigerator and surveyed the contents. The only thing that appealed to her was half a lemon.

Five minutes later Brooks stood in a hot shower, leaning against the wall and sucking on the lemon. She tried to work up the energy to reach her hands over her head to wash her hair. That wasn't going to happen. The fragrance of her shower gel as it got caught up in the stream overwhelmed her. The transition from the warmth of the water to the cold air almost shattered her, and the rough towel grated her skin.

She went back into her room and grabbed a pair of jeans and a shirt from the chair next to her bureau. It made no difference to her what shirt it was. She put the clothes on, stepped into some sandals, and made her way downstairs to go to school.

There was a moment right between second and third period when Brooks thought she might be sick. She was walking past the art room, and a strong scent of spray mount came wafting out. Then she turned and looked at the putty-colored lockers, and the combined effect did her in. She ran for the nearest girls' room, where she spent ten minutes sitting in front of a toilet with her head resting against the side of a stall.

She delivered herself to study hall ten minutes late. The moderator was angrily fiddling with her laptop and didn't notice. Dave looked up in surprise to see Brooks hunched over, pale and sweaty. She put her head down on the table.

"From last night?" he asked quietly.

"Kill me," she said.

"Come on." Dave hoisted her up and grabbed her bag.

"I'm fine," she mumbled.

"Come on."

He took her up to the desk at the front of the room.

"I think she's sick," he said, pointing his thumb at Brooks's slumping figure. "Can I walk her down to the nurse's office?"

The moderator pounded on her enter key and glanced up at the two of them. Taking one look at Brooks's face, she nodded her assent, then continued slapping her disobedient machine.

Dave put his arm around Brooks's waist and eased her down the hall, joking with her the whole way. When they reached the door to the nurse's office, he put her bag over her shoulder for her.

"You'll be fine," he said, stroking back her long blond hair. "Tell them you have stomach flu. They'll send you home."

"Today's really bad."

"Drink some water. Take some aspirin."

"My dad died a year ago today."

She'd never mentioned much about her father before, except to convey the general information that he wasn't around.

He ran his finger along the line of Brooks's chin very softly. The sensation momentarily cut through the racking pain she felt. She set her head down on his shoulder for a moment, and he rubbed her back in small circles. She could have stayed like that all day, but he gently pulled her upright and looked her in the face.

"Go home," he said with a smile. "Sleep."

"Right."

He kissed her once on her lips and once on the forehead, much more gently than he ever had before. For a moment Brooks almost thought the sickness was worth the sensation. She looked up at him, and he gave her a broad smile, showing off the gap between his teeth.

"Go," he said, pointing at the door. "In."

"Okay," she said.

Dave started walking backward, watching her until she was inside the office.

"You all right, Palmer?"

Diana had pulled up to Palmer and was looking up at her

from the driver's seat of her car. The day was long over. Practice had been finished for half an hour. Everyone else was gone except Palmer, who was standing at the edge of the field, her bag over her shoulder.

"Yeah," Palmer said, eyeing the road. "I'm fine."

"Need a ride?"

"No." Palmer shook her head firmly. "My sister's coming."

"Brooks?"

"Yeah."

"You want me to call her?"

"No. She's coming."

"If you're sure . . ."

"I'm sure."

Palmer wasn't sure at all. Brooks could very well have forgotten. Brooks forgot everything. This wasn't the first time she'd been left waiting. Brooks's incompetence embarrassed her. She preferred to cover it up.

With a nod Diana drove off, leaving Palmer staring out at the empty brown field and the expanse of surrounding trees. The sky was heavy, prematurely dark. A wind was kicking up. She set her messenger bag down in the dirt along the side of the clubhouse and started digging through the contents, finally producing a small address book and a handful of change. Enough for two calls. There was a pay phone at the front of the school. It would take her ten minutes to walk all the way around. If Brooks came while she was gone, she'd be stuck. She jingled the change in her hand and stared up the driveway. Then she took out her algebra book and put it in her lap. Then she stared out at the road again.

Fifteen minutes later she was still staring.

No one was in front of the building by the time Palmer made her way around. Somewhere, deep in the bowels of the building, there were probably meetings or detentions going on, but outside there was only the phone, a concrete bench, the flagpole, and Palmer. She took one of the two coins, dropped it into the phone, and dialed her house. No answer. She dropped in the second and dialed the work number that May had given her. An unfamiliar voice answered the phone, and she asked for May.

"Brooks zoned," Palmer said when May got on the line.

"What?"

"She forgot about me."

She heard May sigh into the phone.

"Just stay where you are, okay?" May said. "Someone will be there for you soon."

"Who?"

"I'll figure it out. Just don't worry about it."

Palmer hung up the phone. Undoubtedly Pete would be sent, since he suddenly seemed willing to run or fetch or roll over at May's bidding. In response, May was going out of her way to make it clear that she didn't notice this—until, of course, she needed him to do something. It was an annoying little game they played. Even if he was being dispatched to pick her up like a FedEx guy, a ride home with Pete was still a good thing. He was one of the few people who might actually make her feel better today.

Palmer sat down on the bench and stared out at the road, waiting for Pete's car to turn into the parking lot.

*   *   *

As May hung up the phone, she noticed Nell had fixed her with a curious stare.

"Was that Pete?" she asked.

"Yes."

"Who called before?"

"My little sister."

"She's stuck at school?"

Nell seemed to have no desire to hide the fact that she listened to other people's phone conversations.

"Yeah," May said. "She's stuck."

"Pete's going to get her?" Nell asked. "You know, we went out on Wednesday."

No. May did not know that. However, this was probably the best day to get this news. Listening to the story about Pete and Nell's date—as nauseating as it was sure to be—would at least shift the focus away from her.

Not only was it kind of ironic that her father should have died over the Memorial Day weekend, it also made it easy for people to remember when it had happened. That morning it had seemed like everyone in homeroom was watching May out of the corners of their eyes. Linda had shadowed her all day, constantly asking if she was all right. Her English teacher had quietly mentioned that May was exempt from her homework for the weekend. The guidance counselor had pulled her aside to ask her how she was doing.

Today had reminded May, with shocking clarity, of what the first few weeks had been like last year. Constantly being watched. Constantly being asked if she was all right. Having conversations stop when she walked by. Facing that strange collage of forced smiles and concerned expressions at every single turn. Repeating the mantra "I'm fine" over and over again until it lost all meaning, and she had no idea what fine was anymore.

So this was really a perfect time for Nell to be her normal rambling self and allow May to fade into the background. Unfortunately, she decided to act completely out of character and paused and took a good long look at May's face.

"You look kind of weird, Ape," she said. "Are you sick?"

"No," May said, rattling a coffee mug full of tiny flags that sat by the cash register.

"Maybe you're a little toxic."

"Toxic?"

"From dairy. Your vessels could be clogged up."

"Vessels?"

"Dairy is harsh on the digestive system. So is meat. Do you know that it takes seven years for a piece of meat to leave your system? It rots in your body. Maybe you should do a cleanse. You should get some psyllium husk. . . ."

"Yeah . . . so you were about to say? About Pete?"

"Oh, right!" Nell smiled brightly and pulled herself up on the counter. "Pete collects movies, did you know that? We watched *The Fearless Vampire Killers*, which is just classic. We're really alike."

May doubted this but made no objection.

"And this you will not believe, Ape. He asked me to his prom. How hilarious is that? We didn't even have a prom at my school—we had 'The Collective Experience,' which was like an all-night thing with music and poetry readings and then we all went swimming at like two in the morning. So now I have to get a *prom dress* and *prom shoes* and a *manicure*, and all that. Seriously, how funny is this?"

"That's . . . funny."

"Know what's cool, Ape? Pete's got freckles on his eyelids. So when he closes his eyes, you can barely tell where they are. It's like they're camouflaged."

May suddenly felt a throbbing along her left temple and a pressing need to get out of Presto immediately.

"You know, I really don't feel well," May said. "I think I have to go across the parking lot to get some aspirin from the drugstore. I'll be right back."

When she arrived home four hours later, May was less than thrilled to see Pete's car sitting in her driveway, right behind the minivan. She looked at her watch. It was almost nine o'clock. He'd picked Palmer up over three hours before. It made no sense for him to still be here.

She dismounted, wheeled the Brown Hornet into the garage, and slipped in quietly through the kitchen. The first strange part was the silence. No blaring TV. Then the faint laughter. May followed the sound until she reached the doorway to the living room. She paused for a moment and listened. Palmer and Pete were talking. And laughing. Her appearance stopped them both cold.

"You're still here," she said.

"Oh . . . yeah." Pete glanced between Palmer and May. "We were just talking."

"Where's Brooks?" May said, looking up and around the room as if her sister might be clinging to the ceiling like a spider. "I have to kill her."

"She's sleeping," Pete said. "She seemed kind of sick today."

"Pete and I were talking," Palmer said suddenly. She looked at May with a decidedly unfriendly expression.

"Okay, then . . . ," May said. "I'm starving. I'm going to make something to eat. Anybody want some dinner?"

"We ate," Palmer said.

"We?"

"Pete and I."

"You went out?" May asked. "The two of you?"

"Yeah." Palmer almost looked defiant. "We went out. To the T.G.I. Friday's near the mall."

Pete was not contributing to this part of the conversation, May noticed. Instead he seemed to be asking himself whether or not the two sides of his body quite matched up. He looked at his hands side by side. Then he grabbed the zipper of his sweatshirt and began pulling it up and down.

May flicked her eyes in his direction and he glanced away.

"Okay . . . ," she said. "Well, I'll be in the kitchen."

A minute later, as she dug around the icy, uncharted territory in the back of the freezer, May heard someone come into the room. She retracted her head and peered around. Pete was standing in the kitchen doorway.

"You took Palmer to dinner?" she asked. "What, was she complaining about my cooking again?"

"No. She just seemed kind of lonely."

"Oh," she said simply. "That was nice of you. I'll pay you back for whatever you spent."

"Don't worry about it."

May disliked the thought of Pete giving them money, so she

left the freezer door open and reached for her purse anyway.

"No, really," he said, more insistently this time. "She was just upset because of today."

"Oh, right," May said. Pete pulled out a chair and sat down. May pried a frozen dinner from a pack of unidentifiable meat and shut the door.

"Brooks really looked kind of bad," Pete said.

"She was out last night."

"She looks like that a lot."

"She goes out a lot."

Palmer turned on the TV, and the kitchen wall began to shudder. May deposited the frozen lump on a baking tray.

"I got a call about this summer job I applied for," Pete said. "It would be really cool. It's at a golf course, just inside the city, about fifteen minutes from here."

"That's great."

May shoved the snowy brick into the oven. She could feel Pete's eyes on her as she did this.

"My dad . . . ," Pete said slowly, rubbing at his chin. "I don't know if you heard this, but he's sponsoring a bench at the softball field, the one over by the middle school. It'll have your dad's name on it."

"A bench?"

"I know," Pete said. "It's just a bench. And it's going to take them four months or something to install it—don't ask me why. But just so you know . . ."

"Thanks." May nodded.

"How are you?" he asked.

"Me? I'm fine."

"Are you guys going to be doing anything?"

"No," May said. "You know us, we've never been religious or anything."

"I thought you might have a dinner or a service or something."

"We're not a dinner-and-service kind of family."

May had nothing more to say about this. She looked down at the floor. There was a blotch of something dark and sticky by her foot.

"So Nell tells me that you two are going to the prom," she said.

"Yeah. I . . . you know. Asked her."

"I figured that."

Neither one of them seemed to want to push this subject any further, either.

"Monday still good for a lesson?" he asked.

"Monday's fine."

"I guess . . ." Pete looked down the hall. "I should go."

"Okay. Thanks again."

After he'd let himself out, May spread her books on the table. She hastily flipped through a four-page biology lab report that she had to complete. She felt like she had lived this moment a hundred times over—making dinner for herself in the middle of a messy, empty kitchen with a pile of homework on the table. Feeling the walls rumble from the television. An endless, deadly cycle.

"Turn it down!" she yelled to Palmer.

The volume went up.

Before, she could just as easily have walked into the living room and found her dad sitting on the edge of his recliner, yelling at the screen. Part of her almost wanted to try it to see if this was some kind of very long dream. Maybe he would be sitting there in the stretched-out navy blue T-shirt he always put on when he got home. He would laugh and apologize for "disturbing the professor," and he would turn it down. He always called her that—the professor. May could never tell if it was a joke or a compliment, but she assumed it was a joke because Brooks would laugh, and Brooks *got* everything their dad said, and May didn't. So it had to have been a joke.

She felt herself getting angry, like she wanted to go in and have an argument about something that hadn't been said with someone who couldn't possibly be there. But only insane people did things like that, so the argument twisted and stewed inside her with nowhere to go. She wanted to scream, but she just threw one of her pens against the refrigerator. It bounced off and rolled under the lip of the dishwasher. She felt stupid. She got up and retrieved it.

There was a burning smell coming from the oven. It needed to be cleaned.

And the volume just kept going up. For once, though, it had a useful effect. When it was sufficiently loud enough to cover her sobs, May sat down on the floor, put her head in her hands, and cried.

june

Firebird, golden

Gold family entrances associated with

1. Site of Brooks's conception. Occurred at the Vince Lombardi rest stop off the New Jersey Turnpike, just outside New York City, on the way to a game at Yankee Stadium. (Not something I asked to know. I overheard my dad talking about it to Mr. Camp at a picnic.)

2. Impromptu ambulance used to rush my mother to the hospital when she went into premature labor with me. My dad ran four red lights trying to get there and was eventually pulled over. The police escorted us the rest of the way. (I figure I can say "us"—I mean, I was there, right?)

In the past, the arrival of June had always been treated like a major holiday in the Gold house because June meant summer. June was when school ended and the Golds could turn themselves over entirely to the Baltimore Orioles and the summer leagues. A balanced meal suddenly consisted of hot dogs burned nice and dark on the grill, with a pile of fried onions and coleslaw on the side. Dinner was either in front of the television or out in the backyard, with the radio tuned to the sports station. There would be beer for the adults and fudge Popsicles or Mister Softie for everyone else. The Camps and various softball teammates of Palmer and Brooks drifted in and out, the phone rang constantly, May complained that she didn't have anywhere quiet to do her homework (until she got her ice cream cone), and a happy chaos reigned. The main concerns were how Baltimore was doing and when Brooks or Palmer was playing.

All of that had changed last year.

For a start, Mike Gold's funeral had been on the first of June— an overcast and unseasonably cold day. The service at the funeral home had been short and simple. Since his body had been cremated, there was no trip to the cemetery. There was an informal lunch in the back room of a small local restaurant, during which the Gold sisters sat in a corner, mute, ordering soda after soda and looking numbly out on the crowd of people, many of whom they barely knew. Their mother, who had been medicated by this point, made hollow conversation with whoever sat next to her.

Their father's parents had come out from California and stayed for the entire month. When that set of grandparents had gone, their mother's parents, the Dreijers, had come over from Holland for a week. The Camps made daily visits. It was strange to have this endless company—this steady stream of people who seemed hell-bent on distracting them all. Whenever Brooks tried to retreat to her room, someone would come knocking.

When Brooks finally got tired of sitting at home and returned to work at the pool in mid-July, her bosses gave her the easiest and most boring assignment—checking tags at the gate. People got quiet when they passed her. Even members of the pool who were complete strangers to her seemed to know that she was "that poor girl who had just lost her father."

This year, June came in on a decidedly more positive note. Brooks was concentrating on the details of her junior prom. It had taken a while for Dave to get around to asking her, but two weeks before, he'd finally done it. Casually, of course. In study hall.

Even though the Gold family budget couldn't really cover Brooks's expenses, destiny had already decided that she should go to the prom in a certain amount of style. Magically, people started coming forward with all kinds of items. A neighbor had recently been in a wedding, and she had a spare dress—satin, basic black, with removable spaghetti straps. A nurse who worked with her mom lent Brooks a choker. Another had the right size feet and an amazing pair of black heels. The nurse manager had a gift certificate for a free manicure at a local salon that she was never going to use, having permanently lost her thumbnail after getting her finger caught in a car door.

The topper was a two-hundred-dollar check made out to Brooks from their grandparents in California, who had correctly guessed that funds were running a little low. Of course, with all of the donations, this was just gravy. It went toward the limo, her hair, an eyebrow wax, a deluxe pedicure, ten minutes of shiatsu shoulder massage, and a black henna tattoo (the Chinese character for *party*) on the small of her back. She had just enough left over for all of the odds and ends.

Brooks had started reading fashion magazines to get ready. She'd ripped out an article called "The Ultimate Prom Preparedness List," which she tucked into the side of her mirror. (When May had seen this, she'd simulated vomiting. Brooks took it down and folded it into a notebook.) On the night before the prom, Brooks stopped into the huge drugstore across from Presto Espresso to do a little shopping.

She wandered the sterile aisles, examining the cotton balls and cold remedies. She picked up a box of medicine that Jamie swore cured hangovers. She grabbed bobby pins, dry-clear deodorant, clear nail polish, safety pins, a small pack of tissues—everything on her list. As she walked past the alcove near the pharmacy, something caught Brooks's eye. There, between the nonprescription eyeglasses and the incontinence supplies, were the condoms. Brooks stopped and stared at them for a moment. Then she turned her back on them and pretended to be deeply engrossed in the task of picking out baby formula.

Condoms were not on the prom preparedness list. But maybe they should have been.

The one thing that had been eating at Brooks recently was the fact that—no matter how obvious it was—Dave had yet to say that he was her boyfriend. Brooks had tried to bring the subject up, but it always seemed to fall by the wayside.

Brooks was a virgin. No particular reason—it was just that she hadn't seen the right opportunity yet. This, she realized, was the right opportunity. If she were ready at the prom, with Dave . . . it would be hard to evade the subject after that.

She turned back to the display and tried to figure out where to begin. There were about fifty different kinds— ribbed, thin, sensitive, flavored, colored, extra strength, non-latex, nonlubricated, spermicidally lubricated, extra pleasure, large. . . . After a quick examination, she grabbed the pack that seemed the most average—something that offered protection yet came wrapped in a green package that looked kind of fun (it featured a dancing cucumber). She shoved the pack under her other purchases and headed for the checkout.

There were two registers open at the front of the store and only one person waiting in line. As Brooks stepped behind, she saw that one of the cashiers was a girl from her Spanish class. It wasn't someone Brooks really knew, but still, she didn't want someone from school ringing up her stuff. She went to the back of the store, to the pharmacy line. There were eight people in this one, but Brooks joined it anyway.

"Are you waiting for a prescription?" the woman behind the counter called to her.

"Uh . . ." Brooks dug into her basket. "No."

"Then go up front. There's no line up there."

Brooks couldn't really demand to wait in the longest line, so she reluctantly turned and went back to where she had just been. Now Brooks was the only person waiting.

"I can take you."

Of course it was the girl from class.

The girl gave Brooks a glance and an I-know-you-slightly nod. Brooks nodded back and started unpacking her basket. Bobby pins . . . tiny hair spray . . . pack of tissues . . .

"You're in Keller's Spanish class," the girl said. "Right?"

"Yeah," Brooks said.

Nail polish . . . deodorant . . . morning-after effervescent medicine . . .

"Are you taking Spanish IV?"

The girl's name tag read *Tammy*. She didn't even know this girl Tammy. Why was she trying to get the lowdown on Brooks's academic future?

"I don't know yet," Brooks said.

The basket was empty now except for the condoms. She wondered if she should just drop them to the ground. Forget about them. Or come back later.

"I am," Tammy was saying. "I'm thinking about taking Keller again."

No, Brooks thought. Why should she care if someone she barely knew saw her buying something that she had every right to buy? Brooks reached in one last time and set the condoms on the counter, sliding them as far under the pile of stuff as she could.

"Except that I want to take AP history, which is at the same time," Tammy said. She wasn't even looking at the stuff. She reached over blindly, grabbed each item, and held it up to the scanner. Maybe she wouldn't even notice.

"Oh."

Everything but the condoms had been rung up. Tammy

looked down, as if to ask, "Is that all?" and spotted the condoms on the counter. If Brooks had blinked, she would have missed it, but Tammy shot her a curious look, scanned them, ran them over a separate sensor, and dropped them into the bag.

"Fifteen seventy-five," she said, not looking Brooks in the eye.

Brooks handed over her last twenty dollars of the two hundred. Tammy pushed back the change.

"See you in class," she said.

"See you," Brooks replied.

As she hurried out into the parking lot, Brooks made a mental note to herself: Avoid Tammy like the plague.

Palmer was on her way out of the locker room when she heard her name being shouted. She turned around to see her coach waving her into her tiny office, off on the far side of the gym. Palmer went over and peered into the room, with its mint-colored cinder block walls. Her coach, Mrs. Grady, was ducking in and out of various file cabinet drawers. Mrs. Grady never sat still.

"I want to ask you something, Palmer," she said, throwing a pile of manila folders to the ground.

"Okay."

"I'm running a July session this year," she said. "It's the whole month, four hours every weekday morning. I have a pitching coach come in for part of the time. We'll also be playing a few sample games for some scouts. It's very competitive. We're taking people from all over Pennsylvania, New Jersey, and Delaware. I'm not even taking too many people from our team."

Palmer tangled her fingers in a nearby volleyball net, wondering where this was going.

"I think you should come, Palmer. I think we could do some good work."

"When's the tryout?"

"You don't need to try out," Mrs. Grady said, dumping the contents of a very fat file into a recycling bin. "I'm accepting you."

Palmer didn't know what to say. This was almost too good. But camps cost money.

"I have to ask my mom," Palmer said. "I don't know if I can."

Mrs. Grady stopped file purging for a moment.

"I need an assistant," she said. "If you help out with the equipment and the paperwork, you can come for free."

"Free?"

"Do you want the job?"

Palmer nodded, trying not to look too eager. She didn't really succeed. She also didn't question why the coach seemed to know that money was a problem. That was fine. If it meant that she could go to the summer session, Palmer didn't care what she knew.

"So," Mrs. Grady went on, "if you want to, talk to your mom about it and let me know by the end of this week."

"I'll come," Palmer said.

"Check first. Make sure that you can."

"I'll come," Palmer repeated. "I'll check, but I'll be there. I'm just telling you."

"Good." Mrs. Grady nodded. "We start the first of July."

As she left the building, Palmer felt a lightness she hadn't experienced in a long time. Tonight she just might get some decent sleep.

7

The next morning May gazed miserably into her locker, trying to make some sense of the mosaic of self-stick notes that covered the door. Why did she write incredibly obvious and non-specific things like *study Tues.* or *bring book*?

"You're mad about something," Linda said as May yanked down three identical notes that read *paper due*.

"Brooks's prom is tonight."

"You're mad about Brooks's prom?" Linda asked.

"I'm not mad about her prom," May said, shutting her locker door with a loud bang. "I'm mad because she gets everything she wants. I work so I can buy a laptop and save some cash for college. Brooks does nothing, and people like *leap out of the bushes* to throw money and stuff at her."

"Bathroom," Linda said. "With me. Come on."

They turned into the bathroom by their homeroom door. Girls' had been built over a century before as a club for male students. The bathrooms were huge, intricately tiled places with historical plumbing and six inches of paint on the walls. May leaned against one of the old pedestal sinks and played with the cold water knob. Linda went over and sat on the high marble windowsill, pulling her long hair from behind her back and piling it on top of her head in a huge black coil. This was her thinking spot.

"So," she said. "The prom."

"I know what you're thinking," May said. "That's not it."

"I'm just asking. Could you like him?"

"Pete? He's *Pete*. . . ."

"Let me get this straight," Linda said. "Pete gives you driving lessons and he drives you around. He shows up whenever you need him and even when you don't. You want to know what this means?"

"Not really."

"You're in denial."

"I am not in denial."

Linda smiled, as if she had just heard a little voice in her head that was telling her a private joke.

"I am not in denial," May repeated. "Seriously. Pete is just a big-haired freak. He's like a brother to me. It's like asking you if you could date Frank."

"But he's *not* your brother."

"I said *like* a brother," May replied.

"Right," Linda said. "But Frank is *actually* my cousin, which makes it illegal as well as repulsive. You are not related to Pete in any way."

"After a while, it's almost like I am. He's like my common-law brother."

"You should work in an excuse factory," Linda sighed. "It doesn't occur to you that he's only dating Nell because you pretty much told him to? And that it's possible for him to date Nell and like you at the same time?"

"Stop. Seriously."

"You won't admit it."

"There's nothing to admit," May said. "He's teaching me to

drive because his mom made him, and he's going out with Nell because he feels like it. He was nice to Palmer because it was a serious thing. That's it. End of story."

Linda considered this as she reached into her bag and pulled out a small white candy, which she unwrapped and popped into her mouth.

"My grandmother keeps giving me this ginger candy," Linda said, her face contorting into an agonized spasm. "And I really hate it. It burns. But I can't stop eating it."

"Is that supposed to be some kind of parable?"

"No," Linda said, sucking in air to cool her mouth. "Do you want it to be?"

May turned the ancient tap on one of the sinks a bit too roughly, and water came gushing out and covered the front of her skirt. She brushed it away. The one good thing about her uniform was that it was made of indestructible polyester, impervious to stain or spill.

"It was always the big joke," May said, "when we were kids. Our parents always used to say that Pete and I were going to end up together. My dad said it all the time. He thought it was hilarious."

Linda fell into the wide-eyed silence that always cropped up whenever May accidentally mentioned her dad. It was a guaranteed conversation breaker. May was obliged to continue speaking so that Linda could see that it was okay to keep talking about the subject.

"Pete is that person who wiped his nose on my ruler in fifth grade," she went on. "I still can't eat bologna because of him. . . ."

"Is that a bad thing?"

"The point is," May said, "I just don't understand why Nell would date *that* guy."

"Because Pete's not that guy anymore."

"Quit it with the deepness."

"I'm serious," Linda said. "Things change."

"They don't change that much."

"Yes, they do," Linda said. "Are you saying that you're the same now as you were when you were eight?"

"I'm not talking about when I was eight. I'm talking about last year."

Linda made a thoughtful noise. May looked up at her.

"What? That's a Dr. Linda sound."

"Why did you give Nell the number?" Linda asked.

May shrugged.

"I had to."

"Had to? Oh, I get it. Nell's scary, impressive assistant manager's credentials got to you. You were blinded by her power."

"It doesn't matter," May said. "I don't even care."

"Yes, you do. You care a lot. Will you please stop saying you don't? It's annoying."

"I just think it's weird," May said. "I can't figure it out. Pete was the most annoying person I knew, and just as he was becoming normal, he gets together with the person who took his title."

"Okay, two things," Linda said. "One, don't try to figure out why people pair up the way they do. Perfect example: You know Dash?"

"Frank's girlfriend?"

"Right," Linda said. "Pep squad girl. Father owns a paper

company in New Jersey. Painfully dumb, but really good looking. She's got the hair and the scrawny body and the nose-job button nose—everything. And she's dating *Frank*? Four out of five experts would never have seen that one coming."

"Well," May said, "Frank's kind of smart. . . ."

"He has five snakes and he just dyed his hair purple," Linda said firmly. "He laminated his Mensa card. Dumb blond paper heiress—insane, snake-loving engineer. There's no logic behind it. Don't try to find any. And don't try to figure it out with Pete and Nell."

"Okay," May said, reaching up to pick at some flaking paint by the mirror. She looked at her reflection as she did so. She was scowling. She looked a lot like Palmer when she scowled—all chipmunk cheeks and round, maniac eyes. Very attractive.

"Second thing," Linda continued. "Don't get involved in the details of other people's love lives, because the details are always creepy."

"Trust me, I'm not getting involved."

"I'm not saying you would want to. I'm saying it might happen, and you have to avoid it."

"Huh?"

"Here's an example. Just last night Dash comes over to dinner. So I have to listen to her rambling on at the table for half an hour about how she's so excited to be eating actual Chinese home-cooked cuisine. We were having little crab cakes, which she obviously thought were dim sum fish balls or something. But I can let that go. She's from Jersey. It's a handicap."

Linda reached into her bag and popped another candy into her mouth.

"Anyway," Linda went on, waving her hand in front of her mouth again, "after dinner she tries to bond with me. She comes up to my room, sits on my bed, and tells me that she's been shopping. She pulls this pink silk gown out of her bag and asks me how I like it. This gown is about five inches long and covered in lace—it's disgusting. I don't want to see this. So I tell her it's nice, thinking she'll go away. But she just agrees with me and starts explaining to me how sexy it looks on her."

"We should get her together with Nell," May said. "They could start an I'm-comfortable-with-my-own-body club."

"It gets worse. Then she starts asking me if I think Frank will like it, as if I study my cousin's turn-ons. She was going to try it on and show it to me, but someone called her from downstairs and she left."

May wrinkled her nose in sympathy.

"But you see what I mean," Linda said. "People will try to open that window sometimes and give you a little look. Don't let them. Unless, of course, you have some personal interest in the relationship."

It was said innocently enough, but May understood what the pause meant.

"What am I going to do?" May asked, sagging against the sink.

"I don't know," Linda said. "Can you talk to Pete about it?"

"No." May shook her head. "It would be too weird."

"Then try not to watch," Linda said. "That's really all you can do."

*   *   *

That night May could barely be coaxed out of her room to take the obligatory photos of Brooks stabbing Dave Vatiman in the heart with a small boutonniere pin.

"Palmer!" her mom was yelling up the stairs. "Come down here and look at Brooks."

May sniggered as she laid the photos out on the coffee table. *Yeah, Palmer,* she said to herself, *come see the leaning tower of Brooks.* Brooks had mastered walking in her heels on the driveway, but the living room carpet was presenting a whole new challenge, and she was listing precariously to the left.

Palmer came halfway down the stairs and stared at Brooks, as directed.

"Doesn't your sister look great?" her mom prompted.

"Uh-huh." Palmer was chewing on something very loudly.

"Instamatic," Dave said, reaching for May's camera. "Cool. Can we take this? Do you have more film?"

"No," May said, automatically retrieving the camera and tucking it under her arm. She didn't know Dave that well, but her every instinct told her that she didn't want him getting his hands on her precious Polaroid.

"Isn't Brooks's dress great?" Her mom was still needling Palmer. "Doesn't she look nice?"

"Yeah."

May gathered up the photos and went into the kitchen. Brooks pigeon-toed behind her and cornered her by the refrigerator.

"We need a camera," Brooks said pointedly.

"Buy a disposable. You have the cash."

"I'm out."

"Well," May said, dropping the still-developing photos into Brooks's purse, "at least you have that nice tattoo."

Brooks hadn't actually mentioned the tattoo to May—May had heard her describe it over the phone. This silenced Brooks, and she did her funny little walk back into the living room, this time with an angry little hustle.

May smiled in a rare moment of complete satisfaction.

The feeling lingered up until the time May arrived at Presto Espresso, but it fled at the first whiff of elevator jazz she heard as she walked in. It didn't help that it was a gorgeous, warm Friday night in early June. And this was where she would spend it. The only good thing about it was that for the first time, she would work alone. There had been no one available to share the shift. At least she could get something done.

May spent an hour attempting to read *Pride and Prejudice* for her English class, but her attention kept drifting. She kept looking out the window or just staring into space. As she tried to turn her focus back to her book one more time, she noticed Pete's car pulling into the far entrance of the lot. Without any time to wonder what Pete and Nell were doing there, she dropped into a casual pose and tried to look as engrossed in her book as possible.

Nell flounced—and that really was the only word for it—out of the car and into the store, striking the skinny heels of her shoes hard against the red tile so that her every step could be clearly heard by all.

"Like it?" Nell said, twirling for May.

"It's great." May nodded. It *was* great. It was black and very

long and clingy, run throughout with a gold threading. Nell
had piled her hair on top of her head and tied it into a shaggy
lump with a leopard print scarf. It was the kind of thing May
could never, ever pull off.

"It's Betsy Johnson," Nell said proudly, coming closer so
that May could feel the velvety material. "I got it online for
forty bucks. Vintage."

"Wow."

"This," she said, holding forth her hand and revealing a silver bracelet that was linked to a silver ring on her middle finger
with a small chain, "is my new slave bracelet. Like?"

"It's beautiful."

Pete came in quietly. He wore a slate gray suit, which May
recognized from her father's funeral. It was probably the only
one he had.

"You going to be okay by yourself here tonight?" Nell said,
taking a sudden concern in the running of Presto Espresso. On
any other day the roof could have caved in and she would
hardly have noticed.

"I'll be fine," May said. "Nothing's happening here."

Pete saw Nell and May conferring.

"I'm going to"—he looked around—"go to the bathroom."

He sped off toward the back. Nell nose-whistled.

"I already traced a star on the side of his neck," she said.

"You what?"

"The freckles," Nell explained. "They make a star pattern
on his neck. On the right side. I already told him that he
should get the outline tattooed."

"Oh."

The rather eerie image of one of Nell's slender fingers playing along the side of Pete's neck leapt into May's mind. She could see it quite clearly. Nell leaning across the front seat of Pete's gray tank, her short, ruby-colored nail stroking the coppery freckles. Linda was right. Nell was already opening the window and letting the creepiness come pouring in. She really didn't want to know these things.

While May was musing, Nell jammed her hand down the front of her dress and busily adjusted her bustier.

"I have this wire that's making me crazy . . . ," she mumbled. "And the front keeps getting stuck on my . . . Ow. Ow. My rings are . . . Oh, I think I may be bleeding."

May struggled for something to say.

"I don't know if he really likes them," Nell managed as she rummaged around in her bustier.

"Likes what?" May asked as the horrifying image of Pete examining the knocker knockers leapt into her brain.

"Tattoos."

"Oh." May sighed. "Right. Tattoos."

"I'm totally caught here," Nell said as she pulled a napkin from one of the dispensers and plunged it down into the depths. "I'm seriously stuck."

Do not expect me to help you, May thought. *You are on your own.*

"This *always* happens." Nell groaned, rummaging and pulling like crazy now. "But with studs it would even be worse, you know? I . . . oh. Got it. Thank God."

She tugged the bustier up and arranged herself. Pete emerged from the bathroom just as Nell's performance was complete.

"You look nice," May said in her clearest this-is-a-sincere-yet-obligatory-remark voice. But he did actually look nice, even though the sleeves of the jacket were a bit too short. The gravity of the suit really made him seem adult, something she'd never thought possible with Pete.

Pete stared down at the suit, unbuttoned the bottom button, then quickly rebuttoned it. He must have seen the extra space at the ends of his sleeves in the process, because he jammed his hands deep in the jacket pockets.

"I guess we should go," Nell said. "You're sure you're going to be all right?"

"I think I'll manage."

"Here are my keys," Nell said, pulling a Hello Kitty key chain out of her bag. "And don't worry about doing the bank deposits. Someone will do them tomorrow."

"I never do them anyway. . . ."

"And if you have any problems, you can call Ann on her cell. Mine's going to be off."

With that, Nell skittered off in the direction of the door. Pete turned to follow, smiling a good-bye at May.

"Have fun," May said.

"We will," Nell said, grabbing Pete's arm and pulling him along.

May walked over to the window when they were far enough away and watched Pete's Cutlass disappear through the line of shrubs that separated the shopping center from the road. The parking lot was nearly deserted. A big white moon was just coming into view in a lavender evening sky.

It was only seven thirty. She would be here until eleven,

engulfed in the odor of overroasted coffee and the chill breeze of the air conditioner, guarding her empty tables and doing homework. May pressed her hand against the window and left a soft print that quickly faded away. She rubbed at the spot with the edge of her apron and stared across at SuperDrug. She remembered that whenever she'd go in there with her dad to pick up soap or bleach, he'd always have to buy something by the front counter, like a pack of mini–Snickers bars or some barbecue potato chips. Or they'd stop and get a double-dip cone from the ice cream stand ("they're only open three months a year"). There was always a reason, some little celebration, some splurge. He seemed to see every day as a special event.

May turned away from the window. This night was bad enough without dragging up any of *that*. She went back behind the counter. At the very least, she could use the time to try to search for the label maker and fix her name tag. At least that would be constructive.

The ladies' room in the catering hall was divided into two parts—the stall-and-sink room and the bizarre "ladies' parlor" area. This was overstuffed with silk flowers, plush pink carpeting, beaded glass light fixtures, and prints of shy ballerinas waiting to go onstage. There were two marble-topped mirrored makeup tables, a full-length mirror, and several chairs in this antechamber, inviting all users of the rest room to recline and breathe in the overwhelming fragrance of woodland rose potpourri and listen to the cascade of flushing toilets. Brooks and Jamie had taken them up on this generous offer several times this evening.

"Okay," Jamie said, shuffling through her red silk draw-string bag. "Anyone coming?"

Brooks cracked open the door and peered into the hall. Nothing but the lingering smell of sterno and a staff member pushing an empty coatrack into the lobby.

"No. We're good."

"We got Jack. We got Jim. Who do you want?"

"Jack," Brooks said.

"Jack." Jamie nodded, pulling a tiny bottle of Jack Daniels from her purse. "Here you go. I'll take Mr. Jim."

"How did you get all of these?" Brooks asked.

"My dad is a frequent flyer," Jamie said, breaking the seal on her little bottle. "Ready?"

Brooks unscrewed the cap and nodded. On Jamie's nod they tipped the small bottles back and sucked down the contents. Jamie quickly passed her empty over to Brooks, who had a dis-posable hand towel ready and waiting. She wrapped up the evi-dence and shoved it deep into a small pink trash can next to her chair, taking a moment to carefully rearrange some of the other discarded towels and tissues over it.

"Okay," Jamie said, taking another look in her bag. "So, Jim Beam I can do without a chaser, but I am not drinking straight gin. That's disgusting. Ooo . . . teeny, tiny Absolut vodka."

She held up a small bottle, grinned, then plunked it back into the bag.

"I swear to God I had a little Grey Goose in here, but I think Dave swiped it. Oh, well." Jamie rose unsteadily on her open-backed heels and turned to the mirror to rearrange her tight, Chinese-style red cocktail dress. Brooks watched her for a moment, then reached for her own evening bag and emptied the contents onto the dressing table.

"Look," she said.

Jamie looked down at the small pile of makeup, keys, and wallet. Brooks pushed the objects around until she revealed a small square of green plastic. Jamie laughed and picked it up.

"Did you just buy these?" she asked. She held on to one edge and dangled the three condoms from her fingertips.

"Yesterday."

"Are they for tonight?"

"I don't know," Brooks said, staring at them. "I was thinking tomorrow night, at the party, when we stay over at Dave's. Here."

She opened up her bag, and Jamie dropped in the condoms.

"Look at you." Jamie grinned. "All prepared."

"I don't know if I can get up," Brooks said.

Jamie reached over and presented her carefully manicured hand. Brooks accepted the help out of the chair.

Back in the main room, about half the people were on the dance floor. The others were huddled in conference around tables. The inseparable couples were in each other's laps. Brooks looked at one of the tables near the door. Pete was there, deep in the throes of telling some story, obviously. He had taken off his suit jacket and rolled up the sleeves of his shirt. He was waving his arms wildly at some girl in a tight black dress who was laughing hysterically.

For some reason, Brooks found the sight very amusing.

"Oh my God," Brooks said, pulling Jamie to a stop. "That's Camper."

"Who?"

"Camper. Peter Camp. Don't you know him?"

Jamie shook her head.

"He's a friend of ours."

"Who's he with?" Jamie said, leaning in close to Brooks. "Is that Ani DiFranco? All she needs are the dreds and maybe a little more body hair."

"I have no idea. I thought he was stalking May. I *have* to say something. Come with me."

Arm in arm, they approached the couple. Pete stopped his gesticulating.

"Pete!" Brooks screamed. "What's going on?"

Jamie laughed politely into her fist, as if coughing.

"We're sitting," he said. "What's going on with you, Brooks?"

"Who's this?" Brooks asked.

Nell narrowed her eyes a bit.

"This is Nell," Pete said.

"Nell. Oh, *Nell.*" This was much too loud. Brooks had lost her sense of volume. "You work with May, right?"

"Yes." Nell nodded. "You know her?"

"She's my sister."

"May's your *sister?*" Nell said. She carefully looked over the very tall, very blond, very drunk thing in front of her.

"Pete," Brooks said, throwing herself down in the empty chair on his other side, "have you seen Dave? We're looking for Dave."

Brooks dropped her head onto Pete's shoulder and began to laugh a loud, snorting laugh, grabbing the front of his shirt for support. Her head began to slide down, and she left a long smudge of black mascara across his chest.

"Who's Dave?" he asked.

Brooks picked her head up and smiled.

"You want a tiny Absolut?" she said. "Show him, Jamie. Show him."

"You're kind of falling out there, honey," Nell said sweetly, pinching the front of Brooks's dress and tugging it up an inch. "You might want to get off your hem."

Brooks looked down. Her dress was pinned under the leg of the chair, and it was pulling down the entire front.

"Come on," Jamie said. "Let's go find them."

"We have to go," Brooks explained as she stood up and steadied herself. Then, somewhat mysteriously, she added, "Good luck with everything."

"That's why I don't drink," Nell said as Brooks and Jamie stumbled off across the floor. "Nothing. No alcohol, no drugs. Not even taurine. Is that really May's sister?"

Pete nodded, watching as Brooks tried to regain a steady gait.

"That's really her sister," he confirmed.

8

The next day Dave's parents left town for a Jimmy Buffet Parrothead convention in Key West to drink tequila and sing "Margaritaville" for four days.

Brooks had spent the day in bed, recovering from the prom and resting up for the evening. She'd worked out a cover story about staying at Jamie's, so everything was ready. In the late afternoon she showered and dressed, then tore through her closet looking for the most feminine outfit she owned. This was tricky, since she mostly wore jeans and T-shirts. Of these, she chose the most flattering. She finally chose a blue baby tee that just hit her waistline and her darkest jeans, which made her legs look even longer than they already were. It wasn't that much of a switch from what she normally wore, but it was a nice combination.

She used some of the makeup she'd purchased for the prom. Brooks never wore makeup, so the sensation of having stuff on her face was a little distracting. She could smell the foundation (it reminded her of glue) as she rubbed it into her skin with her fingers. She applied a bit of the blush, then stood back to check the effect. It wasn't even noticeable. She tried again, streaking the brush along her cheekbones up past her eyes.

She took the condoms from her prom purse and considered them, unsure of where they should go. In the end she put two of them in the front pocket of her backpack. The third one went in the pocket of her jeans, in case she couldn't get to her things when she needed them.

As she came down the stairs, Palmer glanced over and grinned.

"Hey, Ronald," she said. "Blush much?"

Brooks ran back up and practically sanded down her cheeks. The force of her rubbing only made them redder, until she couldn't tell what was natural and what was cosmetic. After a minute, though, the redness faded, and Brooks was satisfied with the result. Her eyes stood out more. Her lips were pink and slightly wet looking, which was exactly the effect in the ad that had prompted her to buy this lipstick in the first place.

Brooks stayed in her room until Fred arrived at seven to get her. He was on his way back from a beer run. It was a strange sensation, riding along with Fred, making idle conversation over his stereo, knowing what was about to happen to her tonight. This was it. She would walk in a virgin and out—not so much.

Dave lived in a massive new house in a development by the mall. A dozen or so speakers shook the thin, new walls. The noise echoed down the newly paved street of mostly vacant houses. The ground actually had a pulse. There were cars in every available space along the entire length of the road.

"I guess people are here," Fred observed.

He parked on the next street and didn't seem to worry about being caught carrying two cases of beer to the house. It was crowded already. Some of the people Brooks recognized; many, she didn't. Fred squeezed through a crowd by the door, hoisting the cases over his head. He continued on through the living room, straight out to a back porch. Brooks was on her own. There was nothing for her to do but go in and wander around until she found Dave or Jamie.

She'd been to Dave's a few times before, but it was a big enough place that there were many parts of it she hadn't really seen. There was something strangely impersonal about the inside of the house. Brooks felt as though if it were destroyed during the course of the night, Dave could just pick up the Pottery Barn catalog and have it back in order within a day.

Every room had its own wonders. The tarp from the swimming pool was stretched over the living room floor, and a keg sat in the middle. There were flaming Dr. Pepper shots on the enclosed porch. The blender was going in the kitchen. A bit of towel stuck out from under one of the bedroom doors where the potheads had barricaded themselves. There was a girl in a vintage eighties prom dress standing on the back deck and shouted the name Gary into a cell phone.

Brooks wound her way down to the furnished basement. It was very dark, and the music was mellow and guitary. There were a few candles burning. This was a more refined group. People sat in all corners of the room, close together, talking. Jamie was there, sprawled out on a piano bench, sipping from an enormous round glass of blue liquid. She was perched above a group of what looked like college guys in retro-chic nerd gear—sweaters, T-shirts, thick glasses—and they were all talking in very deep and sober tones about some band that Brooks had never heard of.

Jamie had taken the opportunity to pull out all the stops. Her black hair was chiseled sleekly behind her ears, she had long drags of black eyeliner carefully smudged around her eyes, and she wore tight black pants made of some leather-pleather-vinyl-plastic-wrap amalgam.

Brooks looked down at herself. So tall, so plainly dressed. Her muscles, though still well developed, had melted a bit since she'd given up her daily workouts. She did have some glitter on her T-shirt, and she was wearing makeup . . . but it wasn't the same. Jamie had a perfect, barely tinted glaze on her lips; Brooks's were a childish pinkish red. And she still had a backpack on her back.

"You look great!" Jamie said. "Sit down! Drink." She pressed her glass into Brooks's hands. Brooks studied the glass. Jamie didn't even drink unfashionably.

"I found that in a cabinet in the dining room," Jamie explained.

Brooks nodded, taking a sip of the blue liquid. It was a harsh combination. All raw alcohol.

"I've been here since five. Dave's here somewhere," Jamie said, waving her hand and indicating the entire house. "He's making the rounds."

As if on cue, Dave strode in with a bottle of Johnny Walker Red in his hand. He had kept his tuxedo from the night before and was wearing the jacket and shirt with a pair of jeans. He hadn't shaved, so his face had a shadowy cast. Seeing Brooks and Jamie, he gathered them up, one under each arm.

"My ladies!" he said. "Come with me."

Brooks and Jamie headed off on the parade route with Dave, and it soon became apparent to both of them that he had started early. He leaned on them heavily, and he kept accidentally knocking the bottle into Brooks, where it made contact with her clavicle with a hollow thump. Jamie was too small to offer any support, so Brooks ended up doing the lion's share of the work.

He dragged them from group to group, all people Brooks had never really met before. He did most of the talking, since these people regarded Brooks and Jamie as bits of human architecture. They exchanged amused glances across his chest and passed the bottle back and forth. They wound up their tour by kicking a few people out of the master bedroom and dropping onto the bed. It was covered in a thick, obviously expensive, and very ugly comforter. Brooks put her backpack down to the side and threw her legs up on the bed somewhat gracelessly. Try as she might, she still moved like a jock. Jamie stretched out as well. Dave reclined between them.

Brooks tried to meet Jamie's eye to signal her to leave. Jamie leaned heavily against Dave and wrapped her arms around his chest. Brooks leaned on his other side and crossed her legs in his lap.

"What do you say?" he asked, drawing them both in to his shoulders. "We're all here. . . ."

"You have to be kidding," Jamie said with a laugh.

"Worth a try." He shrugged amiably.

Brooks smiled at both of them but was a bit confused as to what was going on. Jamie was clearly out of it—she had buried her face in Dave's neck and seemed to be going to sleep. Dave rummaged around in his pocket.

"Okay," he said. "Let's play a game."

"I like games," Jamie said, her muffled voice taking on an affected little-girl tone.

"Me too," Brooks said, surreptitiously grabbing one of Jamie's fingers and tugging on it, trying to get her attention.

Dave held up a quarter.

"Jamie is heads. . . ." He balanced it on his thumb. "Brooks is tails. Here we go. . . ."

He flicked the quarter into the air, then slapped it down on his wrist.

"Heads!" he said.

And with that, he passed the Johnny Walker to Brooks and rolled over on top of Jamie. Within seconds they were fully engaged.

Brooks sat there for a moment, holding the bottle, trying to process what she was seeing. She had just been lost in a quarter toss. She stared at her reflection in the television, took a sip of the Scotch, and then quietly slid off the bed. She watched the two of them for just a moment before leaving, waiting to see if this was some kind of joke or if they would try to stop her. But they were both too busy.

She set the bottle down on one of the dressers and left the room. Outside, everything still pulsed. Brooks walked back downstairs. A large guy with a goatee was sitting on the sofa with a bug sprayer at his feet. He regarded it proudly, like it was his pet. As Brooks passed, he held up the nozzle invitingly.

"Close your eyes and open your mouth," he said.

Brooks eyed the sprayer doubtfully.

"It's okay," said a girl who was now suddenly standing beside Brooks. "I did it. It's good."

The girl seemed like a bit of a Gap victim, a walking, talking display of khakis and white cotton shirt. But she seemed somewhat sober and certainly sincere. It was enough of an endorsement for Brooks. She leaned down and closed her eyes, and a fast shot of grain and juice washed down her throat.

"Good?" he asked.

She nodded. He looked pleased.

"More?"

She nodded again and received another spray. Thanking him in a thick voice, Brooks continued across the room and out the French doors onto the patio. She pulled a beer from the outside cooler and sat down at the empty wrought-iron umbrella table to collect her thoughts. Somewhere, deep in the back of her mind, she knew that she was devastated by what she'd just seen. It should have torn her apart that he was lying on top of Jamie right now, and that Jamie had been so willing, and that this had all happened *right in front of her.*

But she was just drunk enough to momentarily accept this as part of the reality of the party. Instinct told her that if she drank more, it would become less and less of a problem.

Brooks drained her beer and began peeling off the label.

Suddenly the girl in the prom dress who had earlier been making her repetitive appeal to Gary threw herself down in the chair next to Brooks, put her head down into her hands, and started sobbing uncontrollably. She looked up for a moment and saw Brooks staring at her.

"I hate him!" she screamed. "He said he would call!"

Presumably this was Gary she was talking about. Not that Brooks really cared. Her brain was too busy making mental movies of what was going on in the bedroom.

"I waited," the girl continued, dribbling rivulets of eye

makeup soup all over her dress. "But he didn't call, and he wasn't picking up, and he was on the phone with her the whole time, and—"

"Shut up," came an annoyed male voice from somewhere on the opposite side of the patio.

"You want me to shut up?" the girl asked.

A chorus of affirmative noises. The girl threw a knowing glance at Brooks. Brooks held up her hands to the group, indicating that she had no connection to the matter.

"Okay." The girl sniffed angrily. "Okay. I'll shut up. I won't say another word. I'll just . . ."

With that, she started slamming her cell phone into the wrought-iron table. Everyone else on the patio backed away from their corner.

"Fountainhead's doing it again," Brooks heard one guy mumble as he retreated behind the grill.

The girl made a low, animal-like grumble. She started banging other bits of the table to try to make more noise. She beat the phone on the chairs and on the hollow umbrella pole. Then she started a little chant to her own rhythm.

"This . . . is . . . me . . . shutting . . . up . . . this . . . is . . . me . . . shutting . . . up. . . ."

"I have to go," Brooks explained to her, quickly getting up. The girl was too absorbed now to care whether Brooks was there or not, and she said nothing as Brooks headed for the patio doors.

Sprayer Guy was happy to have a repeat customer.

"It's good, huh?" he said as Brooks took another hit of the punch. She nodded, swallowing hard. The alcohol burned her throat this time.

"Tell your friends!" he called to her as she walked away.

Brooks made her way through the people on the basement floor, the people on the stairs, the people in the upstairs hall waiting for the bathroom, down to the bedroom door. She had made a decision. She would see what was going on.

The bedroom door was closed. She put her hand on the knob and leaned her head against it, trying to hear what was going on inside. Everyone else in the hall was being too loud—laughing too much. She couldn't hear anything. She gently tried the knob.

It was locked.

She was surprised to feel her eyes filling with warm tears.

Brooks backed up and leaned against the opposite wall. She looked down at herself again—the jeans, the stupid T-shirt. Her hair smelled like smoke and her lipstick had eroded. She suddenly wanted out of this place, to get away from all of these people.

"Hey . . ." A girl had grabbed Brooks by the arm and was pointing to the bathroom. "Where's the puking sink?"

"What?"

"The *puking . . . sink?*"

The girl kept falling forward, almost hitting her head against the wall.

"It's in there," Brooks said, pointing at the bedroom door and walking away. "Just keep knocking."

While this was going on, May was at the wheel of Pete's precious Cutlass Ciera, headed right for the center of Philadelphia, which loomed on the horizon, like Oz. She wasn't happy about this, nor did she mean to be here.

It had probably been a mistake to leave her house in the first place, as she was intently studying for her finals. She had taken over the kitchen completely over the course of the last week, writing papers, making flash cards, shifting from subject to subject. But she did have a lesson scheduled with Pete for that night, and she felt like she needed a short study break. He'd shown up and made the observation that highway driving was easier than driving on little roads—that the lines of traffic were neat and well divided and all you had to do was go straight. That had sounded good to May, so she'd agreed to turn onto I-95 and try to go a few minutes up the road.

What Pete apparently hadn't taken into account was that it was eight o'clock on a glorious Saturday night in June. The sun was just setting over the skyline, the air was balmy, and thousands of people were racing toward the downtown area. May found herself surrounded by tailgaters and weave-arounders who trapped her on the road, forcing her to drive all the way downtown. Or at least, that was how it seemed to her.

"Okay," Pete said. "This turns into an exit lane. We'll loop through the city and turn around."

"Loop through the city?" May cried. "Are you nuts?"

"It's either that or keep driving forever," he replied. "Besides, you just got off."

May looked up and found, to her horror, that he was right. She was on a ramp now, about to merge with fast-moving traffic on the Vine Street Expressway.

She screamed.

"Just keep right," Pete said firmly. "You're fine."

May turned the wheel hard to the right, and an angry honking came from behind her.

"Uh . . . that's okay," Pete said, glancing from back to front quickly. "Maybe use the mirror next time. Good. Now. Merge."

"What?" she said, stepping on the brake. More honking.

"No!" Pete yelled. "Go! Go! Now!"

May stepped on the gas and the Cutlass narrowly slipped in front of a truck and into the right-hand lane of the expressway.

"Okay," he said, wiping his brow and pointing straight ahead. "First exit. Right up there. Turn."

This resulted in a near-death experience on a hairpin turn that wound 270 degrees and landed them on a tightly congested road near City Hall.

"Okay." Pete sighed. "We can stop. I'll look for a parking space."

"No, we can't!"

"Why?

"There are too many cars coming for me to stop!"

"Just find an empty space—"

"Shut up! I'll figure something out," May mumbled.

They drove deeper into the city, into historic downtown Philadelphia, where the streets were as wide as twin beds. Cars were parked all along the side of the road, making it difficult for her to pass through. She gripped the wheel with such force, she felt as though she might snap it to pieces, like a pretzel.

May looked at the lunchbox-size spaces between the cars on the side of the road. She looked in the rearview mirror and saw the endless stream of cars behind her. All she could do was drive on and on, deeper into urban traffic hell, onto streets that she imagined only got smaller and bumpier and had even more trolley tracks to catch the wheels on and more drunken bystanders wandering into them.

And this had all been Pete's idea. He sat there, in his bright red T-shirt, his hair wild in the intense humidity, the fringe around his face almost covering his eyes—like some overgrown talking rag doll that spouted nonsense about driving when you pulled its string.

"Come on," he said. "There are two spaces right there. Just pull over and I'll do the rest."

"I won't fit."

"Yes, you will."

"*No*, I *won't*. Have you seen this car? It's about fifty feet long. Just shut up for a second, okay?"

Cars were now crowding her out on her left. Why were people trying to make these streets into two lanes? She screeched in anguish.

"All right," Pete said, speaking slowly, "at the next red light, put the car in park and I'll slide over and drive."

"The light's not long enough for that!"

He leaned back against his seat and put his hands over his eyes.

At the height of her despair, May had a burst of inspiration. She knew, from the occasional trips she took into the city with her parents, that there were parking garages where attendants parked *for* you. It would be expensive, but it was better than crashing the car or running someone over.

"Look in my purse," she gasped. "In my wallet. Open it up. See how much money I have."

He gingerly picked up May's straw purse and poked around inside.

"Three bucks," he said.

On her right May saw a sign with a big *P* on it and an arrow pointing left. She made an abrupt turn onto one of the narrow, cobblestone streets that she feared so much. There, in the bottom of some kind of warehouse, was the opening of a garage. She pulled the car up to the attendant and came to a jerky stop. She laboriously rolled down the window with a shaking hand.

"Do you, like, park the cars for us?" she asked.

"Yeah," the man said, ripping a ticket in two and putting half under a windshield wiper.

"Okay." May nodded. "What do I do?"

"You get out."

May reached for the door release.

"Park," Pete said quickly, his hand flying for the shift.

"Oh. Right. Sorry." May slipped the car into park, collected her bag, and exited. Pete was already standing off to the side, looking a little weary.

"So," May asked the man, "how much?"

The attendant, who was gazing at May with unconcealed disgust, pointed at the huge wall sign with the times and amounts.

"Do I pay now or—"

"When you come back."

"Oh, right." She laughed. "Because that's how you'll know how long I've been gone. Okay. Great. Thanks."

So what if her pride was shot? Her sense of relief at being out of the car was immeasurable. She suddenly understood those stories of ship captains who dropped to their knees and kissed the sand once they hit shore.

"What are we doing?" Pete asked, looking down at her through his curly fringe. He was slouching a little more than usual.

"I have to go find an ATM to get some cash," she said.

"Why didn't you say so? I have some cash. Let's just get the car back."

"No," May said as she started walking briskly. "I'm not borrowing."

"Come on." Pete groaned. "Don't get like that."

"It's your fault we're here."

"*My* fault? You wouldn't park!"

"'Straight line on 95!'" May mimicked. "'It's like the *easiest thing in the world.*'"

May walked ahead, and Pete followed, somewhat grumpily. The area was fairly desolate since all of the office buildings, squares, and historical sites in the area generally emptied out at five or six. There seemed to be a thousand shadowy nooks behind trees, low brick walls, and deep doorways. Independence Hall loomed up on their right.

Okay, maybe this *was* her fault. But it wasn't so bad.

"Look!" She held up her hands. "Free field trip."

"Uh-huh. Maybe America's first ATM is in there."

"Look, I'm sorry, okay?"

Pete stared up at the side of Independence Hall and attempted to whistle. All that came out was a strange sputtering sound.

"They have blinds in the windows," May said, stopping and pointing up. "That seems wrong."

Splutter.

"I was just trying to keep your car in one piece. You can't blame me for that."

He switched over to humming.

They walked around Independence Square, which was filled with construction equipment. One lonely park ranger stood against the barricade that surrounded the area. He turned orange, red, and purple as the huge spotlight that sat on a tall building just beyond Independence Hall threw its light down on him. At the end was the Liberty Bell pavilion, a small glass structure that housed the world's most famous defective noisemaker.

"Remember coming here in grade school?" May asked as they looked across the square at the building.

"Yeah. I think we went about twelve times."

"I always thought they'd keep it someplace bigger . . . and look at this," she said. "It's a *shed*. And it's just a bell. It feels like such a rip-off."

"It *is* kind of a rip-off."

"Then why does everyone get so excited about it?" she asked.

"I have no idea."

"A lot of things seem like that," she said. "They build you up and build you up, and it's . . . a bell in a shed."

They examined the bell and its housing critically.

"So," May said, giving him a sideways glance, "speaking of big buildups, you haven't told me about the prom. Was it good?"

"It was all right."

"So are you and Nell *dating* now or something?"

"I don't know." He shrugged.

"How do you not know something like that?"

"We might go out again," he said. "But I haven't really dated anyone since Jenna."

"Jenna?" May said, throwing him a puzzled look. "You dated Jenna? Jenna Cazwell?"

"Yeah. All last fall."

Jenna Cazwell was an unrelentingly perky girl with huge boobs and an amazing singing voice. She had been in May's elementary and middle school classes.

"How did I not know this? How did that happen?"

"We worked on some shows together." Pete shrugged again. "Things happen when you do shows. And we liked a lot of the same stuff—same bands, same shows, same movies. She was really into movies, like me. Really specific stuff, too. Like we both like bad shark movies. She had *Jaws 4* and *Deep Blue Sea* on DVD. She even had *Shark Hunter*."

"Jenna Cazwell collects *shark movies*?" May said. This seemed about as likely to her as finding out that Jenna collected human bones.

"I know. I couldn't believe it either. She seemed perfect—but she was so—"

"Chestually blessed?" May offered.

Pete was wise enough not to reply to this.

"Jenna always reminded me of a stewardess," May said coolly, "with that creepy smile. And she was kind of dumb."

"Yeah, well, we're not all geniuses."

"What's that supposed to mean?"

"I didn't get a 200 on the PSATs like you did," he said,

looking just a little irritated. "I mean, I didn't think she was dumb."

"Two-oh-five . . . ," May mumbled automatically before catching herself. "It doesn't matter. So what happened?"

Pete didn't reply right away.

"We kind of . . . stopped calling each other."

"You stopped calling each other? That's it?"

"Kind of," he said, pulling on his watchband.

"That's weird."

"It happens that way sometimes," he said.

"God," May said, finding herself inexplicably annoyed by this new knowledge. "You're like crush boy. Nell, Jenna, Diana . . ."

She started walking again, a little faster this time. There was a strong horsey smell here, which was emphasized by the heat. May picked her way through the numerous knee-high concrete thumbs that had been planted all along this stretch of sidewalk, presumably to keep cars from crashing into the square, or maybe just to make life *that much* more difficult for people searching for ATMs in a historical zone. "That's not a lot," he said. "It's just that someone's there, so you date them."

May raised an eyebrow. She wasn't sure what this meant, but he seemed to be *saying something*.

"What about you?" he asked.

"What *about* me?"

"Do you . . . like anyone? I mean, you never mention it."

"All-girls' school." She smirked. "It's not happening."

"What about work?"

"It looks like you're already dating Nell. That totally breaks my heart."

He stopped moving for a moment. Pete was one of those people who had to freeze completely when he was turning something over in his mind.

"It's so hard for me to share her with anyone," she clarified quickly. "Come on. I guess we should be looking for the ATM."

Brooks managed to bum a ride home from the party, and she arrived home at the pathetic hour of nine o'clock. Only Palmer was home when she got there, and she was glued to the television as usual. Brooks sat alone at the kitchen table in the dark, looking down at May's books and notes, which were spread everywhere. She felt the dryness setting in. She needed hydration. She got up, threw open the refrigerator door, and eyed the empty water-filter pitcher.

"Does that thing *always* have to be empty?" she muttered. "Is it the *law*?"

There was nothing cold enough to drink. There were a few cans of warm soda, but the ice cube trays were also empty. She got some water from the kitchen tap, but it seemed to make her throat even scratchier. Her stomach was tumbling lightly now. She knew this was only a sign of the turbulence to come.

The Dave and Jamie movie was still playing on all screens inside her head, and now, as she thought about it, it was all getting weirder. She had shown Jamie the condoms. She had told Jamie her plans for the night. And what had Jamie done? Vamped herself up in bondage pants and planted herself in Dave's lap. In fact, Jamie had moved in before Brooks could do anything.

Jamie had screwed her over. She had done it intentionally.

Brooks drummed her fingers on the table. Then she got up and started pacing the kitchen. Her head was going to explode.

A glint across the room caught her eye. The key to the Golden Firebird hung from the key rack on the kitchen wall. The pewter key ring embossed with the logo, the key with the three colored triangles at the top . . .

She knew why no one had touched the car. It had never been said, but it had never needed saying. It was Dad's car. The car was where it had happened. The car was frozen in time—left, like a museum exhibit, commemorating the worst moment in all of their lives. Through the warm haze of grain punch, beer, insecticide, and whiskey, Brooks saw the absurdity of this. Dad wouldn't have wanted the Golden Firebird kept that way. He had loved that car, and the thought of it rotting away would have made him miserable.

It was her *duty* to take it out.

She grabbed the key, then lunged in the direction of the garage door.

The long fluorescent lights blinked on in segments and sizzled a bit before lighting completely. There it was—all dull, heavy gold, a beast from a different time. There was the black vinyl top. The headlights that reminded her of frog eyes. The huge backseat where she and May used to sit and have kicking wars.

As she approached the car, she had the weird sensation of breaking through an invisible barrier, like an electrical dog fence. The shock was internal, very deep. It repulsed her and charged her at the same time. The Golden Firebird had been waiting here for a long time, wanting to take her wherever she wanted to go. It had been sleeping.

Brooks crossed around to the driver's side. The door was unlocked. She opened it slowly but waited a moment before getting in. This was *the place*. The actual spot where he had passed from living to dead . . .

She couldn't think about it that way. Besides, years of athletics had hardwired one fact into Brooks's brain: On the field, you don't hesitate. You decide, and then you do. So she had decided, and now she had to act. If she stood there and thought about it all night, nothing would ever happen.

She dropped down into the driver's seat. It was very far back. (Her dad had been six-foot five, after all.) She reached around the side of the seat and found the crank that moved it forward. The inside of the car seemed a bit strange to her now, after an absence of a year. It was a world of cream-colored vinyl. It had ashtrays and a bench seat. Nothing aerodynamic or sleek about the inside of this monster. The radio was ancient, ridiculous. Nothing digital. Huge knobs for the lights. Cold bits of metal. There were some things of her father's on the floor—his gym bag, a plastic container that must have held his lunch, a newspaper. She used her foot to push them a little farther under the shadow of the dashboard.

Brooks looked at the key in her hand and the outstretched wings of the embossed Firebird on the key chain. Her father had always told her it was good luck to touch the key chain, so before games she would always "pet the birdie."

She stroked it once and put the key into the ignition.

Nothing.

She tried again. Still nothing.

Luckily her father had at least taught her something about

the car. She got out and reached under the front bumper for the hood release, then popped it to have a look. The problem was, fortunately, one she'd been taught how to identify—corrosion on the battery terminals.

When she looked up, Palmer was standing in the doorway. She didn't speak.

"What?" Brooks spat. "I'm fixing the car."

"Why?"

"Because," Brooks said, as if the point were self-evident, "it's got stuff on the battery."

"Why are you fixing it now?"

"Go watch TV."

Palmer didn't move.

"Or just stand there," Brooks said. "I don't care."

Palmer stood there. Brooks retrieved a can of cola from the supply shelf. She cracked it open and poured the contents over the terminals.

"Why are you pouring soda into the car?" Palmer asked. Her round face was pulled into a very dark scowl. Her hair was pulled up in a lopsided ponytail. She cocked her head, as if it were weighed down by the imbalance.

"I told you already," Brooks said, leaning down and keeping her eyes on the battery. "Go take a shower or something."

"I took a shower. . . ."

Brooks grinned as the corrosion bubbled away. She closed the hood and jumped back into the driver's seat. After waiting a moment she tried the engine again. This time there was a growling, grumbling noise. The engine seemed to be in the process of deciding whether or not it was going to fully engage.

Brooks felt it rumbling under her, alternating between a steady purr and a dying cough. Suddenly there was a familiar if alarming smell, and a steel gray cloud of fumes came seeping up from the back. Life rippled through the Firebird, and the engine became loud and steady.

"Okay," she said, wincing, "I'm never drinking that again. . . ."

"What are you doing?" Palmer shouted over the engine.

"Nothing. Go back inside."

"You're drunk."

"I'm fine," Brooks shouted. "Go inside!"

After snapping on her lap belt, she took hold of the thin steering wheel, adjusted the rearview mirror, and slowly began backing the Firebird out of the garage. The wheel turned stiffly, and the sheer length of the car's back end was intimidating. You could *feel* this car.

Palmer stood in the open doorway of the garage, watching her go.

When Brooks started down the road, the acceleration pushed her against her seat. The Firebird seemed to despise low speeds, and it became easier to drive whenever she went a little faster. No wonder her dad had felt so manly driving this thing.

She reached for the radio dial and switched it on. The signal was weak, just long silences broken by deafening crackle. Single words boomed out of newscasts. Jolting snatches of songs. Frustrated, she gave the knob a hard spin and got a weird range of feedback. She held the car steady on the road with one hand as she worked the tuner furiously with the other. Scratches of noise—blips. A little more pressure from one finger . . . carefully. It required absolute precision, like safecracking. Minute turns now. Microscopic.

A horribly loud *whooping* sound filled the air. Brooks jumped back and let go of the dial. Punishing static noise blasted through the car. She slapped at the knob to turn the thing off. As she did so, she caught a swirling vibration of light out of the corner of her eye and jerked her head up and looked into the rearview mirror. There was a police car just a few feet behind her, and it was the one making the unpleasant sound.

Pete drove on the way back from the city. As if trying to exact some revenge for what he'd been put through on the ride through the city, he spent the entire return trip talking like Yoda. He seemed to enjoy watching May flinch with every "Annoyed you look" and "Irritating you, am I?" After the first fifteen minutes she got the impression that he wasn't even doing it consciously anymore—that he had just gotten stuck and couldn't stop himself.

"Hear me can you?" Pete asked as he turned off 95.

May flicked him on the shoulder with her finger. Pete switched on the radio and adjusted a nickel that he had taped to the face of the dial.

"Works this does. Ask me why do not."

May concentrated on the music until they pulled up in front of the house and he spoke in a normal voice.

"That's weird," he said.

"What is? Talking like a human?"

"Palmer's out front."

Sure enough, Palmer was sitting on the low, flat step in front of the screen door. May felt her nerves tingling. There was something very not right about this. Palmer got up and walked over to meet the two of them.

"Brooks," she said.

"What about her?"

"She took the car."

"What?" May shook her head, not understanding. "Mom took the car."

"No," Palmer said, pointing to the empty garage. "The Firebird."

May got out of Pete's car and walked to the garage as if to prove to herself that the Firebird was really gone. She stood in the space that it had occupied for the last year. The void was weird, almost mesmerizing. The garage was suddenly huge.

"Where did she go?" May asked.

"She said she was just going to get some Gatorade."

"She took the Firebird for Gatorade?"

"She poured soda into the engine, too," Palmer added, pointing to the case of generic cola on the shelf behind May.

"Probably for the battery," Pete said, coming up behind them and looking around for himself.

Both Palmer and May turned and stared at him as if he had suddenly started speaking in Portuguese.

"Coke can loosen things up," he explained. "Get rid of buildup on the battery nodes."

"How long has she been gone?" May asked.

"About two hours."

"Two hours?"

"She was drunk," Palmer said. "I'm pretty sure."

May exhaled heavily and paced the room. She plucked a

canister of WD-40 from one of the shelves and shook it violently, listening to the little metallic rattle.

"I can go look for her," Pete offered. "Drive around."

"There's no point," May said. "Two hours. She could be anywhere."

She continued to walk around the room, seemingly looking for something that would explain it all—where Brooks was, why she had committed this insane act of treachery. Something that could put the Firebird back just as it was, just as it had been for the last year. But nothing was there but half-used containers of car cleaners, a few tools, some rags in a bucket, some shelves of old junk. Palmer lingered by Pete's side, keeping about a foot away but moving whenever he moved, as if he were a magnet pulling her around. She looked at him searchingly, but since he had no explanation either, he could only shrug.

"Okay," May finally said, "I'll give her another half hour. Then I guess we can drive around and look. She's probably over at Dave or Jamie's or something. . . ."

A car approached the house. It pulled in behind Pete's Cutlass, under the heavy shadow of the Starks' oak tree. May could see that there was writing on the door and sirens on the roof. A large man in a dark uniform got out of the front seat.

"No," May said, almost to herself. "There's no way. . . ."

Palmer shot off in the direction of the car. May and Pete followed, almost cautiously. With every step the scene came into clearer focus, and May's fears were confirmed. The car was a police cruiser, and Brooks was being unloaded from the backseat. She had no handcuffs on. Her makeup was smeared.

A husky officer was standing by the door, watching May and Pete approach and basically ignoring Palmer.

"Are you her brother?" he asked Pete.

"No." Pete shook his head. "I'm—"

"I'm her sister," May offered, pulling herself up straight. "What's going on?"

"Your mother is on her way," he said. "Is your father home?"

"No. He's . . . no. Not home."

"She's been processed," the officer went on. "Will you both be here until your mom gets home?"

By both he seemed to be indicating May and Pete.

"Yes." May nodded. "I will. . . .'"

The officer looked to Pete.

"Sure," Pete said. "I'll be here."

"All right. Here are your forms." The officer passed Brooks a number of pink and white papers. "Call that number on Monday morning."

Brooks took the papers silently.

"Where's the car?" May managed to ask. "Our car?"

"It's at the police lot," the officer explained. "One of your parents can get it out tomorrow. I circled the address on that yellow sheet there."

"Right," May said.

"Wait here," he said to Brooks. He walked back around and got in his car, leaving the door hanging open. He spent a few minutes talking into his radio. All four of them stood silently, listening to the muffled codes and chatter from inside the car. Brooks stared at the ground. Then the officer climbed out and leaned over the roof.

"We're good," he said. "You'll stay here, Brooks, with your sister and—"

The "and" was Pete. Palmer was still invisible.

"Okay," Brooks said.

"Remember what I told you."

"I remember."

"Okay."

Without another word, he got back in his car and pulled away.

"What was that?" May asked, even though she felt like she probably already understood.

"I'm going in," Brooks said.

"It's a DUI." May sighed. "Isn't it?"

"I'm going in," Brooks repeated, heading toward the house. Palmer trailed along behind her.

When they were gone, May looked around and saw curtains being drawn back discreetly in the house across the street. The Stark boys were standing in their screen door, unabashedly staring. Once again, she realized, the Golds were the neighborhood show. She walked over to Pete's car and slid down the side to the ground, leaning against the tire, where she couldn't be seen. Pete came over and stood with her, pushing his hands deep into the pockets of his long army green shorts.

"It had to be a DUI," May said. "She gets that look when she's drunk. Kind of glassy."

"Is she drunk a lot?"

"A couple of nights a week."

"What do you mean by a couple of nights a week?"

"Two, three. Maybe more."

"Does she have some kind of problem?"

May stared at Pete as if she didn't understand the question. Asking her if Brooks had a problem was kind of like asking her if rain was wet.

"Does your mom know?"

"I don't think so," May said. "Brooks leaves after she goes to work."

"Did you ever tell her?"

"My mom's got enough problems," May said, picking up a twig and snapping it into several small pieces. "What am I supposed to do? She hates working nights as it is. Do I tell her that Brooks gets wasted all the time and that Palmer stays up all night watching TV? Great. She can feel even worse."

"She's going to know now."

"This is just what Brooks is like," May said, her exasperation growing. "Everybody knows it. You know it. My mom knows it, but she doesn't want to deal with it. Besides, no one yells at Brooks. Probably not even this time."

May listened to the cicadas chirp for a moment and stared at the yawning space in the garage, the spot where the car had been.

"I must sound pathetic," she said.

"What?"

"It's just that this is it. This is my life. I go to school, and I go to work. Someone has to be the good one, you know? I'm the good one. Which pretty much means I'm the boring one. No boyfriend. No life. Nothing."

She exhaled deeply and turned to look at him. She noticed that his nose was just slightly crooked. It had been broken twice when he was younger—once when he'd played Superman and tried to fly down the steps and again when he'd ridden a shopping cart through the grocery store parking lot like a skateboard. He had a personal understanding of stupid behavior and its consequences.

"I'm fine with it," she continued. "It sounds really sad now, I know, but I have a plan. College. I can do fun stuff in college, when I don't live here. I just have to get in and get a scholarship."

"So you can't have fun now?" he asked.

"I have fun," May clarified. "I just don't have as much fun as some other people, like Brooks. And Palm's happy as long as she's playing softball. She doesn't even notice anything else."

"I don't know," he said. "Palm always noticed things. She's really aware of stuff—what people are doing."

"Well, yeah. She listens in on conversations when you don't want her to. But she's still a lot like Brooks. She's clueless. Like she'll spill her soda everywhere and just stare at it. It doesn't occur to her to wipe it up. Things don't *occur* to my sisters because it was always different with them. My dad would yell at me for taking too long in the bathroom, but if Brooks burned the house down, that would be okay. He'd probably get some marshmallows or something. Everything she did was great as far as he was concerned. Brooks was like the son he never had."

As she was speaking, May felt herself getting angrier and angrier. The Firebird's absence was starting to give her an actual ache. She pulled her knees tight into her chest. It was a minute or two before she noticed that Pete was holding her hand. It wasn't a dramatic gesture. He was sitting cross-legged, leaning forward on his elbows, looking at her. It took her another minute still to realize that she didn't mind and that it actually made her feel a bit better. She didn't, however, want to call attention to the fact, so she just went on as if she was unaware of it.

"Anyway," she said, "I just wanted you to know that I'm consciously pathetic. It's all part of my plan. My escape-to-college plan."

"You're not pathetic," Pete said, somewhat unexpectedly. May didn't know what to say to that. A silence settled over them for a few minutes.

"I'm sorry you had to be here for this," she said. "Sorry for the drama."

She felt his grip on her hand tighten slightly.

"What is this *processing*?" she said. "'She's been *processed*.' I guess that's police-speak, but what the hell does it mean? She's not cheese."

May heard a car spinning around the corner. They both looked up and saw the minivan racing toward them. She casually took her hand from Pete's, as if sitting in the driveway holding hands was something she did every day, then rubbed her face and got up.

"Here we go," she said.

"I guess I should leave."

Before Pete could make his getaway, however, the minivan screeched to a stop in front of the house. May's mom, clad in pink scrubs, raced across the lawn. She went right to the opening of the empty garage, looking as confused as May had been. Pete froze in his tracks, looking unsure about his next move.

"We can get the car in the morning, Mom," May said quietly. "And she's been processed or whatever."

Her mother didn't answer—not in English, anyway. Whenever May's mom got really mad, she started speaking in rapid-fire Dutch to herself. She never told anyone what she was saying, but May was pretty sure that it was some seriously unrepeatable, melt-the-paint-off-the-walls swearing. The Dutch was flying freely now, all *j*'s and hocking sounds.

Pete backed up a few feet and gave May an I'm-going-to-go nod.

"Pete." May's mom finally noticed that Pete had been there the whole time. "This is . . ."

She shook her head and paced in the driveway.

"What happened?" May asked cautiously. "What was she arrested for?"

Before she could answer, Palmer came down and joined the group.

"Brooks is in her room," she reported. "I think she's still pretty drunk."

With the Dutch still trailing from her lips, their mother headed inside with a determined stride.

"You're still here," Palmer said, staring at Pete.

"I was leaving." He walked around to the driver's side of his car. He gave May another nod, and she acknowledged this with a nod of her own. Palmer observed this silent exchange, then watched as Pete drove away.

"What were you guys doing?" Palmer asked, cocking her head like a little kid.

"Talking."

"About what?"

"What do *you* think?"

"You guys were holding hands."

May felt her face flush.

"God, Palm," she said, heading for the door. "What's *with* you?"

"Well, you were," Palmer replied to her sister's retreating figure.

When May had gone inside, Palmer stood for a minute on the lawn and looked up at the house, wondering why all activity always seemed to stop whenever she came near.

9

Brooks's sentencing took place late on Tuesday afternoon, in the middle of a torrential downpour. She sat in the court, carefully dressed in a turtleneck (May's) and a pair of khakis. The room, to her surprise, was just a small, plain space in the middle of a huge office building. It had no windows, and everything—the walls, the judge's bench, the seats—was made of the same dark wood. No imposing columns or marble, no paintings. Her mother sat next to her, stony faced.

The memory from the bedroom still stung her, even now, as she faced the bench. She could still see their reflection in the dark television—the three of them. Dave rolling over so easily, Jamie so willingly. The last two days at school Dave had been amazingly evasive. He didn't even show up to study hall. Every time Brooks saw Jamie, she had somewhere to be, immediately. She'd never had much to say to Fred, and the rest of Dave's friends were strangers to her. So she was alone.

A bailiff came in and ordered them all to rise.

The judge walked into the room, and then they all sat down. She took a few moments to shuffle through some papers in front of her.

"Brooke . . . ," the judge read. "No. Brooks? Is it Brooks, with an *s* on the end? Is this right?"

The stenographer paused. Brooks and her mother nodded.

"*Brooks* Gold," she repeated.

Brooks steeled herself, then walked to the small podium that the bailiff pointed her to.

The process took little time. Charges were read. When asked, she pled guilty to underage drinking and driving under the influence, as the family attorney had advised her to do. She hadn't thought you were just supposed to plead guilty. On television everyone always fought or entered some crazy reason that all the evidence has to be thrown out. But Brooks had nothing to say in her own defense. She'd been speeding. They'd done a Breathalyzer. She was underage. End of story.

The judge was not going to care that she'd just seen her boyfriend cheat on her from two feet away—with her best friend. It didn't matter that she hadn't hurt anyone or that she'd just wanted to take the Firebird to get something to drink. That it had been hard to take the Firebird, but she'd done it. She'd liberated it. Now anyone could drive it. May had even taken it for a test run to the store with her mom.

Nope. The state of Pennsylvania did not care about any of that.

Her license was immediately revoked for the year. She was remanded to a counselor who would evaluate her substance abuse. She would be referred for treatment. She was fined three hundred dollars. She was directed to check in with the court clerk on her way out.

Brooks had known this was coming; the lawyer had advised her that this was the likely sentence. It meant no driving until November, so the summer was shot. All the money she'd earn at the pool would pay for the fine and the treatment. She could deal with that, but Dave and Jamie . . .

The judge banged her gavel. At least that seemed authentic and final.

May watched the rain that flooded the parking lot outside of Presto.

"So I was on top of him, right, and then we heard the door open. . . ." Nell paused. "Do you know how Pete's house is laid out?"

May nodded, defeated.

"Okay, so we hear his parents, and they're coming up the stairs. Then we remembered that I'd hung my shirt on the doorknob before we shut the door, so my shirt is like hanging in the hallway, like a flag. . . ."

For the last half hour Nell had been pouring out every clinical detail of the events of the previous night. Apparently quite a bit had happened since the conversation she'd had with Pete on Saturday, during which he hadn't even seemed sure that he'd see Nell again. Whatever pet theories Linda had had about Pete holding out for his one true love . . . they were out the window. Pete was waiting for nothing.

May didn't particularly need this news right now. For three days she'd been listening to the wailing and crying and slamming doors that had echoed through the house since Brooks's arrest. In the last two days she'd been dragged through her German, history, and trig finals and had finished her English paper on three female British novelists. She still had to finish getting ready for the most terrifying exam of all: the biology exam, which she would be taking in the morning. She'd barely gotten any sleep. And now she knew the unabridged biblical truth about Nell and Pete's relationship.

In short, she was in hell.

"So Pete completely freaks out. He jumps out of bed and puts his boxers on. . . ."

Sheets of rain battered the windows. May wanted to run out into the storm, swinging something large and metallic over her head until the lightning got her and frizzled up her brain, wiping all of this information away forever.

". . . and jumps for the door and just manages to grab the shirt. It was hilarious. Can you imagine his mom catching us like that?"

"No," May answered honestly.

"It's good that you're so cool about this," Nell said. "I mean, it bothers some people to hear about their friends dating. Some people get so weirded out."

"It's fine," May said as she watched the pansies in the flower box outside getting crushed by the torrent. "Why would it bother me?"

Later that night May bunched herself into a corner of her bed and tried to imprint the following sentence into her head: *The Krebs cycle, also known as the citric acid or the tricarboxylic acid (TCA) cycle, is the second of three steps involved in carbohydrate catabolism.*

"He said he'd call when he could, but it's been three days . . . ," Brooks was saying.

For the past year Brooks had more or less shut May out of

her personal business. She had chosen this moment to break her silence, as her exams weren't for another week—not that May was expecting her to do much studying then, either. She had stationed herself at the foot of May's bed and had been talking nonstop for the last fifteen minutes.

The Krebs cycle, also known as the Dave-has-not-called cycle, is the second of three steps involved in my going insane if she doesn't shut up. Oh my God . . .

"Three days," Brooks went on, rocking back and forth slightly. "What does that mean? Three days? What do you think I should do?"

"I don't know," May said, keeping her eyes trained on the page. "Call him, I guess."

"You think I should?"

"Um, yeah. Sure."

"It's that thing with Jamie," Brooks mumbled, chomping at her nails.

"What?" May asked.

"I didn't tell you about that."

May gripped the edge of her book. One more tangent and she would definitely go down a full grade.

"Brooks," she said with a sigh, "I do care. I really do. But do you see this?" She held up the book. "I am going to be up all night. I have an exam at nine in the morning. Could we maybe talk tomorrow?"

Brooks looked shocked, as if she'd just been slapped.

"God, you're so selfish."

"*I'm* selfish?" May shook her head. "You didn't just say that."

Brooks slid off the bed without comment and stalked out of the room, slamming the door behind her.

When May emerged from her room two hours later, she saw Brooks sitting on her bed, listening to her CD player and staring at the wall. (Brooks had blue-and-white-striped wallpaper, which, though much cooler than May's pink ponyland paper, gave her walls the unfortunate appearance of bars on a jail cell.) Brooks looked up as she passed, and May felt obligated to stick her head in.

"Did you call him?" May asked after Brooks slipped off her headphones.

Brooks didn't reply.

"Are you okay?" May asked. "What happened?"

"I called Jamie," Brooks said, her voice raspy.

"What did she say?"

"They're dating now."

"Dave and Jamie?"

Brooks nodded and pushed the advance button on her CD player a few times.

"I'm sorry," May said, running her finger along the edge of the door frame. "What happened?"

"Jamie says that he and I were never dating," Brooks said. "Not officially."

"Not officially? What does that mean?"

"We never said it. *He* never said it." Brooks smirked. "It wasn't official. So it was okay for him to sleep with Jamie."

"Dave slept with Jamie?"

"That's what he said."

The logical side of May's brain was sending her urgent

messages, telling her that she didn't have time to stop and talk to Brooks right now, that it was partially Brooks's fault that she was so behind. But the sight of her sister slumped up against her headboard, her hair hanging limply over her shoulders, looking as defeated as May had ever seen her—it seemed bad enough to merit taking a few minutes away. May came over and sat at the foot of Brooks's bed.

"Do you want anything?" May asked quietly.

"No."

May heard a gentle plunking sound. She glanced over to see water dripping down into a trash can in the corner of the room.

"Your ceiling's leaking again," she said, looking at the yellowing spot that the water was coming from.

"Why do you think I put that there?"

She was cranky as ever, but May could see tears welling up in Brooks's eyes. She got up and moved to where Brooks was sitting. Aside from the funeral and when they were small, May had never seen Brooks cry. It was a little bizarre. May reached out to put a hand on her sister's shoulder, but Brooks turned to her with a decidedly unfriendly expression.

"Just go, okay?" she said.

"I was just—"

"Go."

"Fine," May said. She felt a little stung. Only Brooks could make her feel bad for something like that.

Brooks put her headphones back on and May got up and left. Back in her room, the television roared up from below. May rubbed her eyes and kept reading.

*   *   *

May took a minute to buy herself a soft pretzel and a soda for breakfast from a cart on the corner of Thirty-fourth and Chestnut, right around the corner from school. It was a sharp, crisp morning with a bright blue sky. Because she had only slept for a couple hours the night before, she was overtaken by that strange trembling and hyperawareness that comes from pulling an all-nighter.

She saw Linda coming down the street from the direction of the subway. She looked just as exhausted as May. She had on her thin, rimless glasses instead of her contacts, and she walked quickly, pulling her sweater tight against her chest.

"You sleep?" Linda asked as she approached May.

"An hour and a half."

"I think I slept two," Linda said, accepting a piece of May's pretzel.

"Brooks was having a crisis," May explained as they walked down Walnut through the throngs of Penn students hurrying to their morning classes.

"About her court thing?"

"No. About her boyfriend. That guy Dave."

"What's going on with him?"

"He dumped her," May said. "And she has to go for counseling, starting tonight."

"Not a good time to be Brooks," Linda said, reaching for May's soda and taking a long sip. "You're still coming over to my place afterward, right?"

"I'm thinking about moving in."

"Fine by me," Linda said. "I could get rid of Frank that way."

*   *   *

The biology exam was twenty-two pages long and included five diagrams and three essay questions. May worked until the very last minute, furiously scribbling out her final sentences. It was an extensive, somewhat painful test, but May had known all of the material. The only problem was time. If she'd had four or five hours to finish it, she would have been a lot more content.

Linda stumbled up to May's seat.

"I think I just got my Ph.D.," she said.

Dazed, they headed out of the building, toward the subway.

Linda's house, one of the only ones on the block built after 1776, was in a small gated area called Independence Mews. Each floor had only one or two rooms. The kitchen and laundry room took up the whole basement level. The living room (with the wood-burning stove that May loved) was on the first floor. The bedrooms were on the next two floors. Everything was cozy and compact.

Since they were both completely exhausted, they headed right up to the third floor, where Frank and Linda's rooms were.

"Is Frank here?" May said quietly as they passed his door. She had never actually seen Frank—he was kind of like the Easter Bunny to her.

"No," Linda said, pushing open her door. "He's doing some kind of big experiment with gasoline today. Maybe he'll blow himself up."

Though it was extremely tiny, Linda's room always awed May. One of her walls was a bright violet, and the other three were cream. Her slender window was guarded by purple blinds, and a large round paper shade covered the overhead light. The bed was in a metal frame and covered in a thick cream-colored duvet. Aside from her desk chair, the only place to sit was in a pile of multicolored cushions in the corner. Linda set herself down in these.

"I'm seriously going to die," Linda said. "You can take the bed. I'll be fine here. I sleep here all the time."

Linda leaned back on the cushions. May kicked off her shoes and climbed up the metal rungs. Linda's cream-colored duvet was very thick and soft, and May sank into it appreciatively.

"So," Linda said, "it's over."

This should have filled May with elation, but for some reason, it didn't. School gave her life some structure. She didn't want to think about another long summer stretching out in front of her.

"Have you seen Pete?" Linda asked.

"Not since Saturday," May said, burrowing into the thick folds. "But I've heard about him. Ask me how much I've heard."

"You sound bitter," Linda said, propping herself up. "You got details, didn't you?"

"Kind of."

"Bad?"

"I feel . . . unclean."

"Unclean? Or jealous?"

"The weirdest part is that I got this feeling like it wasn't even the first time," May said. "He's been dating her for what, not even a month? I mean, what the hell?"

"He's sleeping with her? Who told you? Pete or Nell?"

"Nell."

"Are you sure she's not lying?"

"I don't think so," May said. "She described the inside of his house."

"They had sex inside his house?"

"Maybe we should talk about this later," May said. Before, when she'd found this out, she'd just thought it was weird. Now that the exam was over, the facts were starting to sink in, and they were immeasurably depressing.

"May?"

"Yeah?"

"You're bummed, aren't you?"

"Kind of."

May rolled to the side of the bunk and looked down at Linda.

"The other night," she said, "when Brooks got busted—Pete stayed with me. He sat with me and . . ."

"And?"

"Well, he just held my hand. But it was weird. It felt kind of huge."

"Huge?"

"Yeah," May said, hanging her head over the edge. "Sucks, doesn't it?"

"No," Linda said. "He likes you. You like him."

"If he likes me so much, why is he sleeping with a girl I work with?"

"It could be that he thinks he has no shot with you."

"I guess that's one way of handling rejection. . . ."

"Think about it," Linda said. "Before you knew that he dated this other girl and that he was sleeping with Nell, you never seemed to think of him like he was a guy. Now you seem to. So maybe it's good."

"Good how?" May grumbled, rolling onto her back and propping her feet against the ceiling. "Good for making me feel jealous and pathetic?"

"Talk to him."

"And say what?" May asked. "I can't compete with Nell. I'm not ready for that yet."

Linda fell silent. May listened to the traffic passing by out on Locust Street.

"If it really bothers you, maybe you should stay away from him for a while," Linda suggested. "I mean, if you're not going to do anything about it, why torture yourself?"

"Stay away?" This hadn't occurred to May before. "I'd have to stop the lessons."

"It sounds like you're almost ready anyway."

"Maybe you're right," May said, closing her eyes. "Maybe I need to do this one on my own."

Palmer was completely alone in the house that night. She didn't mind. She planned on taking advantage of that fact to conduct her most thorough examination of her mother's room yet—she was going to do the top shelves of the walk-in closet.

She started by carefully removing her mother's shoe boxes and sweaters, arranging them on the floor exactly as they'd been set up on the shelf so she would be able to put everything back as it had been. As she had expected, she hit a gold mine. There were yearbooks, photo albums, a heavy crate of vinyl records. She spread herself out on the bed and took a long look through everything.

The most interesting items could be found in the photo albums. These were early ones, from when her parents had started dating. She spent a good two hours paging through them. There was her mom in leather pants and ripped shirts and Halloween-like makeup; then there she was in her nursing school uniform, looking demure. There was her dad, with the same goofy face he made in every picture—his huge eyes popping open and the strange grin that obscured his bottom teeth. There he was with his college roommate Richard Camp at a toga party. There he was, eighteen years old, posing in front of the Firebird, which he had just purchased.

These pictures fascinated Palmer. The idea that her parents had had lives before she and her sisters had come along—totally different lives—was hard for her to believe. The pictures had been taken in front of bars, in dorm rooms, in hallways at parties. Her dad with a beer in one hand, his other arm wrapped all the way around her mom's tiny waist. She could see the slow change as she flipped through. Her mother cut back on the makeup; her father grew a little larger. There were pictures of them in cutoff jeans and T-shirts (her mother's pregnant belly proudly popping out) getting Brooks's room ready. Then there was May, with the head of red hair she'd been born with. And then the picture labeled *Me and Peach*. That was her father holding her when she'd just been born. She looked incredibly tiny in her father's arms; he practically had her resting in one of his hands.

After a couple of hours, Palmer started packing up. As she replaced the items on their shelf, she realized the shoe box she was holding was very heavy. She took off the lid. Inside she found a bronze canister, shaped like a vase. In small block letters along the bottom was an engraving that read *Michael Scott Gold*.

For a moment Palmer thought she'd found a strange trophy. Then it hit her. These were the ashes.

Time stopped moving for Palmer for about ten minutes.

Palmer took the canister from the box and willed herself to walk over and set it gently against the pillows on her father's side of the bed. She stared at it. She couldn't put it back, not up there in a shoe box in the back of the closet. It was impossible.

No. She had to take care of the canister. It was her job now.

She hurriedly replaced all of the other items in the closet, including the empty shoe box. When everything was as it had been before, she plucked the canister up and quickly took it to her room.

10

Without the burden of having to study, May had no problem sleeping in on the first few days of the summer. She had to be at Presto at three, so she lay in bed until eleven, basking in the cool breeze from her clickity oscillating fan.

When she came downstairs, she found her mother sitting at the table in a pair of black running pants and a black T-shirt. There was a box of doughnuts on the table. May eyed them. Her mom must have picked them up on the way back from dropping Brooks off at the pool for work. Her mother never bought doughnuts unless she had something unpleasant to tell them.

"Doughnuts?" she said. "Okay. What's going on?"

"Well," her mother said, casually piling up a stack of laundry detergent coupons, "the Starks offered us something."

"One of their boys? Say no. We don't have any Ritalin to give them."

"Their RV. It turns out they rented a spot at a campground in Ocean City, Maryland, for a few days, starting on the first of July, but they can't use it."

RV? May's mind tried to connect these letters to an object, but the only thing she could come up with was one of those extremely large trailers.

"A what?"

"Like a Winnebago. They keep it at Bonnie's mother's house."

"But that's so soon," May said.

"I know."

"I have work," May said, sitting down with her coffee. "Brooks has work, and she has her alcohol awareness classes. And Palmer has her softball camp. We can't go then."

"You can take off. Brooks can take off, and we can work around her class schedule. Palmer can miss a few practices."

"But why?"

"We need to spend some time together," her mother said, peering at the coupons. "I think we need to regroup a little."

"But we've never been camping," May said slowly, taking a chocolate doughnut from the box. "I mean, we don't even know *how* to camp."

"I know how to camp. I went camping when I was younger, and your father and I used to go."

"You used to *camp*?"

"Sure." Her mom nodded. "Why do you seem so surprised?"

"How did you keep your hair spiky in the woods? Did you have to use maple sap or something?"

"It wasn't that spiky. And I just used to tie it back under a bandanna."

"Punk-rock nurse in the wild, using her hair to trap small animals . . ."

"New wave, not punk," her mother corrected. "Anyway, you'll love it. We'll camp right on the beach."

"We're going to park a huge RV on the beach?" May asked. "Won't it . . . sink?"

"The park is next to the beach. It's paved."

Palmer passed through the kitchen and grabbed a doughnut

from the box. She was about to leave, but her mom caught her by the sleeve of her shirt.

"What?" Palmer growled.

"Just explain that it's a family emergency," her mom said to May.

"But it's *not* a family emergency."

"What's not a family emergency?" Palmer yawned and took a bite of her doughnut.

"Going to Maryland in an RV," May said.

Even Palmer couldn't ignore something like that. "Mwhuh?" she replied as she chewed her doughnut.

"On July first," May added.

"Mhwha?"

"To Maryland! They have crabs there!" their mom suddenly jumped in, as if the presence of crustaceans would transform the prospect of spending days trapped together in a parking lot into a living dream.

"Mom," May said, "RVs are enormous. They're like houses. How are you going to drive something like that to Maryland?"

"It'll be fine," Mom said. "They explained everything to me. And it's gorgeous. They took me through it. It has a bathroom, and a shower, and a TV, and everything."

"That's when my summer session starts," Palmer finally said. "I can't go."

"I'm not asking you, I am telling you. We need some time together, and we are going. It's up to each of you to get yourselves ready to go."

"I'm supposed to take the driver's exam . . . ," May said.

"You'll take it when we get back. Or take it before you go. It will be fine."

Palmer leaned against the counter, chomping furiously on her doughnut. When she was finished, she left the room without a word.

Palmer stalked into the backyard. It wasn't a great idea to go and exercise with a fat doughnut still sitting in her stomach, but she had to do something.

She bent her knees just slightly and hung herself down over her toes until she could easily straighten out her legs and put her palms on the ground. The grass was already dry and warm, and there was a fat bee buzzing around nearby.

She knew perfectly well that the girls who got on the professional teams, the Olympic teams, and the good college teams all went to camps and had personal coaches. She was way, way behind. Her dad had known all about this. You needed to be serious about it; otherwise, you were just another girl with a pile of worthless school trophies and a few pictures in the sports pages in the yearbook. Brooks's entire dresser was filled with trophies—what had they gotten her? Now the only thing Brooks did was lifeguard at the pool. It was pathetic.

As she hung upside down, she saw her mother coming out the back door with her cup of coffee in her hand. Palmer gracefully moved her right foot back into a lunge and pretended not to notice her.

"Do you have a second, Palm?"

"No," Palmer said, reversing her feet and stepping back with her left.

"You seem mad."

Palmer deepened her lunge and concentrated on stretching out her inner thigh.

"It's only a few days. And I thought you liked the beach."

"I start summer session then," Palmer said simply.

"You'll only miss three days."

"We play our first game for the scouts on the sixth," Palmer said.

"We'll be back by then."

"But I won't have time to get ready!"

"It's just a game," her mom said. "You know how to play. You'll be fine. Then you can start the session on Monday."

"Why do we have to go now?"

"Because that's when the Starks have the space," her mother said. "They're doing us a favor."

Palmer shook her head. Her mom just didn't get it.

"I'm going to go run," she said.

"Our lives don't revolve around softball, Palmer," her mother said, irritation creeping into her voice. "I'm sorry if this doesn't fit your schedule the way you'd like, but that's not the only thing we have to consider."

Palmer walked away from her out of the yard. As she passed through the house, she saw May still sitting at the table.

"I don't really want to go either," May said.

"It won't hurt you," Palmer spat. "You'll just miss work."

She continued on her way to the front door and headed out to the street.

The day before the trip May was in the basement, staring down into a laundry basket full of her sisters' dirty underwear and listening to the rhythmic thumping of the load she had just put into the dryer. There was a heavy fabric softener smell in the air, and she realized that she had forgotten to clean out the lint trap.

It was nine o'clock at night, and she'd just gotten off an eleven-hour shift. To compensate for the time she would be gone, May had managed to squeeze in fifty hours at work over the last four and a half days. Technically, this wasn't legal, but she'd managed to quietly swap out with people on the side. She had only "officially" been there for thirty-two hours; the rest of the time she'd entered someone else's work code into the cash register. During her absence some of her shifts would be covered in the same way.

The overtime meant that even if she'd wanted to, she'd had almost no time to see Pete. She hadn't even spoken to him in almost two weeks. He had called several times, but she'd never called back.

The idea, of course, was that this separation was going to make things easier for May. In reality, it made things much worse. She'd found that it was becoming harder and harder to listen to Nell talking about him. There was no way to deny it. She missed him, and not being around him was weird.

She stared at the bits of broken elastic zinging up from the waistband of one of Brooks's blue thongs.

"Why I am doing this?" she suddenly said out loud. "This is Brooks's job."

She grabbed the basket, marched up the basement steps, and went into the living room, where Palmer and Brooks were silently watching a baseball game. She dropped it to the floor.

"You do this," she said.

"What?" Brooks said, not looking over.

"This is your job," May said. "You do it."

"We've already done our stuff," Brooks said, turning to May. "We had to clean out the garage and get all of the dishes and chairs and beach stuff ready. We're done."

"But this is *your job*, remember? I've been doing it for weeks because you haven't."

"Like I said, I'm done."

"Well . . ." May kicked the basket in her direction. "I've done the first two loads of stuff. Now I guess it just depends on how much you want underwear for the next five days."

She walked away, feeling a strange adrenaline rush. She went upstairs to her room, closed the door, sank down on her shaggy rose-colored carpet, and picked up the phone. Before she could think it over, she dialed Pete's number. He answered and was clearly surprised to hear her voice.

"I have to get out of here," she said. "Seriously. Can you—I mean, are you around?"

"I'm here," he said. "I can. I was supposed to meet Nell after work, but . . ."

"Oh," May said quickly. "Never mind."

"But it's not a big deal. I can get out of it. You sound kind of burned out."

"I am," May admitted. "I just need to not be here."

"Sure," he said. "No problem. Give me fifteen minutes?"

May got off the phone.

She changed into her favorite T-shirt, a blue camouflage print. She squirted on some freesia body spray and let her hair down. Maybe it was the light (or the lack of it, since the blinds were down), but May actually liked the way she looked tonight. She pulled her hair around her chin. With her widow's peak, this gave her face a heart shape. The blue shirt made her eyes seem even greener.

Brooks and Palmer were still watching the baseball game when she went back downstairs. The laundry still sat in the middle of the room.

"Where are you going?" Palmer said, glancing over at May.

"Out."

Brooks and Palmer watched in amazement as May sailed out the door.

May was waiting on the front step when Pete pulled up. The humidity had frazzled his hair a bit, and he was wearing his standard-issue cargo shorts and a T-shirt that read I Ate the Whole Thing!

"I called you," he said as she got into the car. "You haven't called back."

"Sorry," May said. "It's just been a weird couple of weeks."

"Oh."

"Can we just go away from here?" May asked. "Can we just drive?"

"Sure." He nodded, pulling back on the road. "Anything wrong?"

"Just stir-crazy. And I have to go away tomorrow."

"Away?"

"Camping on the beach for a few days. I'll be trapped with Palmer and Brooks."

"I have an idea," he said. "I think you'll like it."

They drove for about ten minutes. May noticed that they were heading for the edge of the city, to the northeast. The houses got closer together as they approached the city line. There was a high wall of fence and trees. Pete pulled into a hard-to-spot opening, which led to a vast, empty parking lot.

"What is this?" May asked as Pete stopped the car in front of a small white building. She then noticed a line of white golf carts next to the building, just behind a cyclone fence. "Is this where you work?"

"Yup." He nodded. "The world's crappiest golf course."

"What do you do here?" she said, looking through the fence at the expanse of shadowy lawn.

"I'm a cart boy, but really I'm sort of an unofficial greenskeeper. I mow lawns, dig holes, collect the pins at night. And I sometimes accidentally lose control of the carts and chase golfers into the rough. Stay here a second."

He walked up to the door of the building and let himself in. A minute later he appeared on the other side of the fence. He unlocked the gate from the inside, let her in, and locked it again. He walked to the first parked cart and pulled off the seat, revealing the engine underneath.

"Here's another lesson," he said, pointing at the mess of

parts. "This is the governor. It regulates the speed. And this is how you disengage it." He produced one of the tiny scorecard pencils from his pocket, pulled back a spring, and jammed the pencil in as far as it would go.

"Now this," he said, replacing the seat, "is a much-improved golf cart. Hop in."

"Won't people get upset?"

"This is a public golf course. No one cares. My boss definitely doesn't. Come on."

With a quick look around May carefully got into the cart.

"Aren't there cameras or anything?"

"Nope."

"Or guard dogs?"

"No. It's really simple. Accelerator. Brake. Wheel. Put your foot on the brake."

May did so. Before she knew what was happening, Pete put in the key and started up the engine.

"That switch by your leg flips it from forward to reverse," he said. "You have to come to a full stop before changing direction, or it'll make a really ugly sound."

May nervously glanced down by her leg.

"Drive wherever you like. Just be careful not to go too fast on the declines, especially near the water. Not that that even matters much. It's only a foot deep. But you might flip the cart."

"What?"

"And don't push the brake too hard, or it will switch to an emergency brake. If that happens, just tap it again and it should release."

"Oh my God . . ."

"Okay," he said. "Go!"

"What about you?"

"I'll be right behind you," he said, pulling the seat off the next cart. "Go on."

The thing was chugging underneath her. She put her foot on the accelerator, and the cart started rolling forward. Though there were a few floodlights scattered around the perimeter, they barely illuminated the ground. She saw some slight dips, bits of sand and grass, but mostly just murk. Pete shot past her a moment later and waved her on. She hit the accelerator and the cart rumbled along a little faster.

Puttering through the dark at ten miles an hour wouldn't be exciting to some people, but to May it was kind of like having a private amusement park. Sometimes she trailed along behind Pete, and sometimes she just drove off whichever path she liked and he would come along and find her. Then they would race for a minute.

After about an hour, when she felt she'd had enough, she rode up next to him.

"How do I stop it?" she yelled over.

"What?"

"You said if I hit it too hard, it would turn on the emergency brake! So I don't know how to make it stop!"

He stopped his cart and jumped out. Then he jogged alongside her and hopped into her cart.

"Excuse me," he said, reaching over her and putting his foot on the brake and his hands on the wheel. This meant that he was somewhat on top of her, which was a weird sensation. The cart eased to a halt. He turned off the engine and retracted himself.

"Sorry," he said.

"No. Thanks. I would have been riding around all night."

"Or until it ran out of gas," he said, putting his feet up on the dashboard (which was also the hood). May followed suit and gazed around at the course.

"Your hair is getting longer," she commented.

"Oh, yeah. I haven't cut it in a while. I know, it's—"

"It looks good. You should keep it." She nodded.

"You like it this long?"

"Well, it was longer when we were kids, but then it just made you look crazy."

"And it doesn't now?"

"You still look crazy. But it suits you. You don't scare me as much as you used to."

"You thought *I* was scary?"

"You *were* scary," she said. "You're *still* scary. You're just not *as* scary."

"Me? You used to flick me on the head with a pencil every time I looked at you."

"Self-defense."

"No, it wasn't." He laughed. "You were *always* trying to kick my ass."

"You must be thinking of Brooks."

"No. That was you."

They were shoulder to shoulder now. She could actually feel his heart beat by leaning against him. There was something comforting about being here—it was open, yet it was dark and quiet. Nothing they said here would be heard by anyone.

"Are you mad at me?" he asked.

"What do you mean?"

"You know what I mean."

May slapped a mosquito on her leg and flicked it away. She didn't reply for a moment. She didn't know what she was feeling.

"I'm not mad," she finally said. "I think it's really weird that you're dating Nell. I know both of you. It's just weird when two people you know are together. And I've known you forever. . . ."

A bat flew out of one of the trees next to the course and zipped past them. May jumped. She was edgy now, and a deep curiosity was burning inside her.

"Was Nell the first?" she asked.

"First?"

"First person you slept with."

"Um . . ." Pete stared around at the dark trees. "No. There was Jenna."

"Oh." May nodded.

Okay, it really bothered her. It was like she'd swallowed a drill, and it was boring a hole through her insides. Now she felt like she was somehow way too unsophisticated for him—for Pete, *her* Pete. The whole thing was just humiliating, and it hurt.

"Great," she heard herself saying. "Good for you. Go, Pete."

Pete kept unbuckling his watch, taking it off, and putting it back on again. His face was serious.

"With Jenna, it was kind of weird," he said. "She had a lot of problems. Her parents put a lot of pressure on her. I know she looked really happy all the time, but she was on antidepressants."

"Jenna was?"

"She used to have to talk to me or be with me all the time.

She was always really emotional, constantly, but especially after we would—"

He grabbed his mouth, as if he had just caught it speaking out of turn without his knowledge. He thoughtfully drummed his long fingers against his lips, debating how much more to say.

"Have sex?" May asked.

"Right."

"Intense."

"Yeah."

"So what happened? You said you stopped calling each other."

"*We* didn't stop calling each other," he said slowly. "It's just that she always needed me. Always. And if you have sex with someone and then they always start crying afterward, you start to wonder about yourself. It's sort of not what you hope for."

May caught herself smiling at that, even though it didn't seem appropriate.

"So we didn't stop calling each other—I stopped calling her. I didn't know what to say to her anymore or what to do."

In the last minute or so, it seemed like the world had utterly transformed in May's eyes. The perfect Jenna Cazwell was depressed. Pete had done something a bit cruel, but also pretty understandable. His confession lifted her sinking spirits. She felt the spasm in her stomach relax.

"It sounds like a dick move," he said dejectedly. "I almost told you before, when we were in the city. But I thought you'd hate me, you know, more than usual."

"I don't hate you. You're Camper. Nobody hates Camper."

"That's not true." He laughed mirthlessly. "I'm pretty sure Jenna does."

"But I don't," May said. "I know you're a nice guy. I mean, your mom makes you teach me how to drive and you don't even—"

"My mom never asked me," he said.

"What?"

"I lied."

"Why?"

"I don't know," he said. "Seemed like it might be a good thing to do. So I just offered."

It hung in the air between them for a moment.

"Why did you make up the part about your mom?" May asked.

"You looked suspicious, so I decided to say that my mom had asked me to. Sounded like something that could happen. Are you mad?"

The one thing May knew at that point was that she was definitely not mad. Instinctively she reached out to ruffle his hair to reassure him. She always whapped at his curls when they were kidding around. This time, though, instead of just giving the outer curls a quick shake, she actually let her fingers sink in. His hair was very soft, almost like baby hair. She could feel his surprise at the contact. He sat up a bit straighter.

She continued pulling her fingers through his hair, right down to the nape of his neck. His skin was cool, and she dragged her hand along it casually as she pulled her arm back. She pressed her fingers down into the soft fabric of his cotton shirt. A strange tingling spread through her body.

It seemed to turn her brain back on.

"We should probably drive back," she said, withdrawing her hand. "It seems kind of late."

Pete didn't get up right away, so she gave him a gentle push out of the cart.

When they pulled back up to May's house, they stared at the RV in the driveway. All twenty-six feet of it. Longer, actually, since the Firebird was latched onto the back. So more like forty feet. The chain holding the Firebird on seemed way too small, and the mess of wires and lights would be impossible to disentangle.

"So that's it?" Pete said.

"Yep." May nodded, getting out of the car. "Want to see?"

It was very dark inside the RV. Shadowy mounds covered the sofa, the table, and the floor. There was a light smell of mold in the air. May found a tiny battery-powered camping lamp on the counter and switched it on. It emitted a feeble glow.

"See this?" May said, grabbing a dish from the kitchenette sink. "We stopped using these dishes when I was five. All of this other stuff is just junk we haven't gotten around to throwing away. It's like we're taking a trip in a garage sale."

She sat down on one side of the bench-style kitchen table. Pete shut the door and sat on the other side of the table. May could barely even see him over the pile.

"This isn't going to work," he said. "I'm coming over."

"Okay," May said. "See you when you get here."

Pete came over to May's side and joined her on the bench.

"This stuff reeks," she said, cringing. "It's probably been baking in here all night. It's going to be unbearable tomorrow."

She reached up and pulled a box down from the top of the pile.

"Operation," she said, feeling the thick dust under her fingers. "We used to play this."

"I remember," Pete said. "I think I swallowed some of the pieces."

"That's right. I dared you, and you did it. What did you eat?"

"Definitely the Adam's apple. And the butterfly from the stomach. Maybe the funny bone."

"God." May laughed. "You would do anything. Brooks and I used to sit and think stuff up to get you to do. I'm glad we didn't kill you."

"You wouldn't have learned how to drive."

There was something very deliberate about the way he said it.

"Right," May said. "I guess you can't complain about having to teach me, you know, since—"

"I wasn't complaining. Like I said, I wanted to."

"Oh. Well, thanks. It's been . . . good. It's kind of weird not wanting to kill you. Much."

"Yeah."

They were shoulder to shoulder now, the box between them.

"This box is so filthy," May said. "Did I get dust all over you, or . . ."

And that's when it happened. It was almost too dark to see Pete's face distinctly, but May saw a shadow coming closer. Her first instinct was to brace herself in panic when she felt Pete's lips trying to find hers (he missed at first, catching her nose). But then she found herself reaching up to his face and wrapping her arms around his neck, and in a moment she was leaning back against the window. Pete was leaning into her, and she was sliding farther down on the bench.

And the panic was gone.

july

Vomiting on Gold family vacations
a brief history of

1. Mike and Anna Gold drive Brooks (age six), me (age five), and Palmer (age three) to Williamsburg, Virginia. Brooks throws my Barbie out of the Firebird on I-95. As cosmic retribution, she is seized by car sickness and hurls into a shopping bag from Baltimore all the way to the Virginia state line.

2. The next year the Gold family joins the Camp family for a trip to Florida. I get a very serious case of sunburn while riding in the back of the Firebird on the way there—one so bad that it causes me to barf non-stop. I spend two days in the motel being cared for by my mother while everyone else goes to Disney World. Pete brings me back the stick from his Mickey Mouse Popsicle as a present.

12

At seven o'clock the next morning, dressed in the same blue camouflage T-shirt, May carried a laundry basket full of food to the RV. She gazed down the length of the behemoth before climbing in. Even at this hour, it was already hot. The air was heavy and wet. When she stepped inside the RV, May felt herself explode in perspiration. She set the basket down and started loading up the kitchenette counter. Spaghetti. More spaghetti. Taco shells. Cereal. Ziti. Peanut butter.

It was going to be a starch fest.

When she was finished, she turned and stared at the spot where she and Pete had been the night before. The Operation box was on the floor. May quickly moved to pick it up, as if it were somehow incriminating. Once she'd picked it up, though, she was flooded with emotion. She held the box as if it were a love letter.

"What are you doing?" Palmer greeted her, pushing in with a waterproof sleeping bag.

"Nothing," May said, tossing the box back onto the stack. "This fell."

"Whatever. Move."

Palmer managed to knock over most of the groceries May had just piled on the tiny counter. She shoved her way back into the bedroom, which was one tiny space with two small beds. There was what looked like a large curtained shelf right above these beds; this was really yet another bed. This "room" was where the three of them would be sleeping (Palmer had already been assigned the shelf-bed). Brooks had brought her bags down the night before, and her things alone took up most of the tiny space. May had thrown hers on top.

"Where is my stuff supposed to go?" Palmer whined. "You guys took up all the space!"

"Snooze, you lose. We got down here first."

"I'm moving this crap out."

"You can't. Mom's sleeping on the pullout couch. You can't put it there."

Assorted grumblings from Palmer as she climbed over the bags.

"Where's my bed?" she yelled.

"Behind that curtain."

May heard the curtain being drawn back and Palmer's groan.

"How's it going?" Their mom was at the door, travel mug in hand, beaming over the entire disaster site.

"Palmer's complaining," May said.

"Uh-huh," she said, walking away from the door and toward the cab. "Make sure all of that stuff is secure. We're leaving in half an hour."

An hour and a half later, when Brooks had woken up, when the dishes were finally done, and the map had been reconsulted, the four Golds were ready to go. As she climbed inside the RV, May took one last quick glance at the huge load they were towing behind them—the Firebird dangling off the back like an uncontrollable tail that could wipe whole lanes of traffic clear off the road in mere seconds.

"We're going to kill everyone," she whispered to Palmer.

"Shut up," Palmer replied.

The driver's seat was the only uncluttered space, so the girls each had to find themselves a place to sit. Brooks was stretched out on one of the bench seats at the table and was already trying to go back to sleep, even though she'd only been in the RV for thirty seconds. Palmer nestled amid the sheets and towels on the sofa. May got the passenger's seat, which was completely surrounded by bags. She had to tuck her legs up.

"Listen to this," their mom said as she started the engine. "The Starks told me that all we need to do is fill a big container with hot water, our dirty clothes, some detergent, and a rubber ball or a sneaker. Then we stick it on the back of the RV, and it bounces around while we drive. It acts just like a washing machine. We can try it on the way back if you want."

She's lost her mind, May thought.

It took six hours for them to get there. Palmer and Brooks slept for most of it. Their mother listened to talk radio. May put her headphones on her ears and stared out the window. She didn't want to be going on this trip. It was so strange—for years, all she'd wanted to do was get away from Pete. Now the thought of being separated from him was more than she could take.

May replayed the scene from the night before in her mind. She would find that the memory worked well with one song, so she'd play it over and over until she got bored and had to search out a new song. Then the scene would come alive again, with different nuances. It was one thing to know someone in a sitting-across-from-them kind of way; it was another thing entirely to lie on top of someone. Everything she knew about Pete was different now.

Of the many varieties of pathetic she had been in her life, May was proud that she had never slipped into the I'm-obsessed-with-my-boyfriend kind—although this was largely due to the fact that she had never had a boyfriend. Now, she realized, she was already slipping into the behavior. She was going to be like one of those pathetic girls who had to call their boyfriends on their cell phone every two minutes, except that she didn't have a cell phone. Maybe she would start writing things like MG + PC = TRUE LOVE 4 EVER on her note-books. Then the transformation into Totally Pathetic Girlfriend would be complete.

Then again, she thought, she shouldn't be premature. The one useful life lesson that Brooks had taught her was that you shouldn't assume someone was your boyfriend without solid evidence. But this was Pete. And she knew Pete. And she felt pretty certain that was what he was thinking—that he should be her boyfriend.

She replayed the scene several more times, looking for clues on this subject.

After about four hours the memory started to wear a bit, so she tried to distract herself by reading the RV camping guide-book that she'd found in a pocket on the side of her seat, trying to get a sense of what was going on. Anything was better than looking up and seeing the trail of destruction she was sure they were leaving behind them.

"Okay," she read aloud, "gray water means the water from

the shower and the sink. And black water . . . oh God . . ." May put the guide down. "They have actual bathrooms there, right?"

"I'm not sure," her mom replied.

May sank lower in her seat.

When they arrived at the park, it took twenty minutes for their mom to steer around the narrow roads to get to their space. It took three people to guide them in, but the ride finally came to an end. Their mom hopped out, strangely energetic.

"We have to hook up the water," she said, "and the electricity, and I think maybe the air . . . or that might be with the electricity. I'll have to ask. Go down and look at the ocean. It'll take a few minutes."

"Where is it?" May said, looking around the lot.

"It's the ocean. You should be able to find it." She strode off in the direction of the park director's trailer, which they had passed (and, May would have sworn, hit) on the way in.

"I'm staying here," Palmer said, sinking down into a chair.

Brooks and May walked off without her and promptly got lost in the tangle of tiny roads. All the trailers looked pretty much identical to theirs, so they couldn't get their bearings. The same kids rode past them on their bikes four and five times in a row and started giving them strange looks.

"Maybe we should ask someone," May finally said.

"We're standing next to the ocean, but we can't find it," Brooks explained. "Imagine what that's going to sound like."

They kept walking in circles until Brooks spotted a small path lined with railroad ties that they hadn't noticed before.

They followed this through another campsite, this one filled only with tents, until they found themselves walking on some sand. They followed the sandy path to an inlet and the inlet to the ocean.

"There it is," May said. It was a beautiful view—a gorgeous, clean beach surrounded by a wall of enormous rocks along the inlet. People fished from these. Since it was getting late, people were starting to take down their umbrellas and chairs and head back to the park.

"Well, here we are," Brooks said. "Want to go back?"

On the walk back, they discovered that the entire trip actually took three minutes, not the forty they had spent getting there in the first place.

"We're going to starve," Palmer greeted them.

"What?" Brooks asked.

"Something's wrong with one of our cables or something. We have no electricity."

May and Brooks looked up at the dark windows of the RV.

"Mom's seeing if she can borrow one from someone else. She's going around to all the other trailers. We're supposed to find the grill. It's in one of these things." She pointed to the small hatches at the base of the RV.

"Don't we need keys for those?" May asked.

Palmer squinted at one of the hatches.

"Yeah."

"Did she leave the key?"

"No."

"The water's running, right?" May asked.

"No. We didn't have some kind of hose."

"Well," Brooks said, sitting down at the picnic table. "Who's having fun?"

The cables and hoses couldn't be found before dinner, so plans were made to take the Firebird back to town to pick up some fast food. But as May had anticipated, her mother didn't know how to detach the car from the complicated system of chains and lights that held it to the RV. Some neighbors came over and showed them how to do it.

It was almost eight o'clock before they were finally able to get out. They brought back a bag of hamburgers and drinks and waited for the man with the cables and hoses to arrive. The rest of the night was spent attempting to hook everything up.

By eleven they had electricity and water, but—despite the hours of sleep that most of them had gotten in the car—everyone seemed too tired to care. They all decided to use the bathhouse instead of the slightly frightening bathroom (especially since they weren't entirely sure that they had connected the water supply to the correct feed line, and the consequences if they had made a mistake were too dire to even imagine).

Washed, groggy, and annoyed, the Gold sisters piled into their "room." The beds were only a foot apart, and Palmer kept climbing in and out of her shelf, stepping on May and Brooks's pillows and heads.

"I don't get it," May said, trying to settle herself in her bed. "Mom said she'd been camping before. She said she and Dad used to go all the time."

"That doesn't mean anything," Brooks replied. "Remember

how she used to tell us that when she went to Amsterdam to see Aunt Betje, they used to like to go for coffee all the time?"

"So?"

"Dad told me that in Amsterdam a coffee shop is where you go for pot."

"Oh . . ."

"Mom smoked pot?" Palmer leaned down from her shelf.

"Mom did a lot of things," Brooks answered. "I think what she meant was that she and Dad went camping, and Dad put everything up."

"Makes sense," May said. "She doesn't lie. She's just—"

"Mom smoked pot?"

"It's legal there," Brooks said. "Go to sleep."

"Dad never told me that," May said.

Brooks turned her back to May and switched off her overhead light. May followed suit. A moment later something soft fell over her nose and mouth.

"Could you keep your socks up there, Palm?" she said, removing the sock from her face.

A hand came down and clawed up the sock. May closed her eyes and went back to the place in her mind where she and Pete were always kissing, and she stayed there until she fell asleep.

13

As far as May was concerned, the days at the beach were just days she had to kill as painlessly as possible so that she could get back home. She stretched out on the sand with her chemistry book (she'd already purchased her textbook for the next year, as was recommended for advanced students), trying to absorb the periodic table. When she couldn't focus on that, she tried to work through her pile of required summer reading books for English, all of which she'd checked out of the library and brought with her. About ten pages into *Frankenstein* she flipped over on her stomach and fell asleep. She accompanied Palmer to a batting cage and watched as her little sister stunned everyone by hitting every single ball with astonishing ferocity. She walked along the strip of shops in town with her mom and tried to work up an interest in coral necklaces and knickknacks made from painted seashells. She played cards with Brooks under the awning of the RV.

But her brain was filled with Pete. He walked into her every thought—all freckles and frizzing curls. When she walked past the old-fashioned photo place, she imagined them getting their picture taken. (He would look cute in one of those gangster outfits.) At night she counted up in her mind the dozens of secluded spots on the campground and the beach where they could be together.

On the third night her mom and Palmer decided to get

some dinner and go to a movie. Their selection held no appeal for May or Brooks, so they were dropped off at the boardwalk along the way. It wasn't quite dark out, and the crowd was still mixed. There were groups of elderly people and adults with kids, but the first of the night crowd had also arrived, taking their positions in front of the arcade or at the beachfront bars.

"I feel like a twelve-year-old." Brooks sighed, leaning against the boardwalk rail, looking out over the sand. "I hate getting dropped off."

May was gently pressing on her sunburn, watching the white fingerprints appear and disappear under the pressure. The time on the beach had fried her beyond recognition.

"What do you want to do?" Brooks asked. "Or are you just going to do that all night?"

"I might," May said. She leaned against the rail and put her back to the ocean to watch the slow boardwalk tram chug along at three miles an hour. "Why do they need a train for something called a board*walk*? Doesn't that kind of defeat the purpose?"

Brooks kicked a crab claw in the direction of an overflowing trash can and took a deep breath. The smell of beer and buffalo wings wafted over from the restaurant across from them.

"What have we got?" she asked May. "Two hours until their movie is over?"

"Something like that," May replied, making a happy face of white splotches on her thigh. "We can go back whenever we want. We can just walk."

"I guess we could go down to the rides," Brooks said, squinting at the brightly lit amusement pier, about a quarter mile up from where they were standing.

They walked along past the T-shirt shops with the throbbing speakers and the endless food stands. Brooks stopped and bought a soda. May bought a small bag of candy fruit slices.

"Palmer told me that you and Pete were in the RV for almost an hour the other night," Brooks suddenly offered as they continued toward the pier.

May almost choked on her orange slice.

"I was . . . showing him . . . it."

"*Were* you?"

"You know what I mean."

"Actually, I do," Brooks said.

May saw no point in trying to deny anything. Brooks would see right through her.

"Want me to shut up?" Brooks said.

"That's an option?"

"Come here," Brooks said, pulling May off to the side and taking a large Coke bottle from her bag. It was filled with a clear liquid.

"What's that?"

"Vodka."

"Are you nuts?" May said. "Where did you get this?"

"I had a bottle left over from before. Come on, we're on vacation. And I'm not driving. Neither are you."

"You can't have this! You've already been arrested."

"No one is going to find out," Brooks said. "Look around. We're on the board*walk*. We're *walking*, not driving."

May threw up her hands and walked over to the rail. She stared out over the sand. Brooks followed her.

"Come on," Brooks said. She smiled. It was an approving

smile, one that warmed May's heart. Brooks never smiled at her unless she had something horrible caught in her teeth or some piece of damaging information against her. "We've never gone out together."

This was a first—Brooks was actually trying to include May in something. Normally Brooks's idea of bonding with her sisters was shooting straw wrappers at May's face and snickering with Palmer.

"You have to be kidding," May said.

"What else are we going to do tonight?" Brooks asked. "Come on. It'll be fun. And I'll shut up about Pete."

There was something in Brooks's tone that warmed May. She really did appear to want to spend some time with her and include her. Brooks wanted to *party* with her. As much as she hated to admit it, she had always longed for this kind of approval from Brooks.

And really, what else *were* they going to do? Drinking might make the time go by a little faster.

May reached over and took the bottle.

"All right." Brooks nodded encouragingly. "This is how this works. You take a long sip from the bottle, then you gulp it fast and take a drink of the soda right away. It's got to be fast—the soda washes away the taste."

May sniffed the contents of the bottle and eyed the sweating soda cup.

"Okay," May said. "But you have to promise to keep quiet about Pete."

"My lips are sealed," Brooks said.

*   *   *

An hour later—was it an hour? May wasn't sure. Anyway, they were playing Skee-Ball.

May had always been the queen of the arcade when they were kids. She could roll those hard wooden balls down the lane, catch just the right amount of bounce, land them right in the middle rings, get loads of tickets. It was her one athletic skill.

Of course, she'd never tried the game after sucking back a huge bottle of extremely cheap vodka and Tang. Some of May's Skee-Balls made it into the rings, but many more made their way into other people's lanes, and she decided to leave after getting a few dirty stares. She wandered out of the arcade and into the crowd, past the Tilt-A-Whirl and the haunted house and the giant slide.

She looked out over the beach to the water. Kites. A whole lot of kites tethered to rails of the boardwalk, to poles in the sand, to . . . nothing? May hung her head over the rail and looked in wonder at the dark space below her, then she swung her gaze up to the kites. There was one kite in particular, an enormous dragonfly, that held May's attention as it cut through the air. It made crisp noises to demonstrate—just to her, she felt—that the air was there and real and tangible. You could slice into it with a soft piece of cloth and it would make a sound like a knife sliding into an apple.

The wind that propelled the kites blew strands of her hair into her mouth when she opened it, so she had to spend a few seconds extracting them from between her teeth.

"That's it," she said aloud to no one. "I'm going to do it. I'm going to call him."

After making this pronouncement, it took her a few minutes

to find a phone. It took a few more still to figure out how to make a collect call, even though there were clear instructions. But her trying paid off, and she heard Pete's mom answering the phone and taking the call.

"Hi!" she screamed.

"May?" Mrs. Camp seemed surprised to hear from her. "Are you okay?"

"Hi, Mrs. Camp! It's May! Is Pete there?"

"Um, hold on, May."

Some noise as Pete was found. May picked some chipping paint off the wall behind the phone.

"May?"

"Can you hear me?" she yelled. "Should I speak up?"

"No!" Pete yelled back. "No. I can hear you."

"Okay!"

"What are you doing?" he asked. "Is everything all right?"

"I'm on the boardwalk! I wanted to talk to you."

"Okay."

The dragonfly swooped down to the sand, then tore straight up again, dipping and swerving.

"It's just that . . . there's been a lot going on, you know?" May inhaled deeply and took in some of the warm salt air, the fragrance of hot fries, lemons from the lemonade stand, a sugary odor that floated on the cold blasts from the air-conditioning vent of the candy shop.

"Right . . ."

"Okay." She sighed. "So listen. The other night."

Silence as May watched a kid feeding cotton candy to a dog. The dog got confused when the candy stuck to his nose. He tried unsuccessfully to wipe it off with his paw. May considered setting down the phone to go help him.

"Are you still there?"

"Listen," May said, snapping back to the conversation, "I want to know if you're . . . mad at me or something."

"*Mad* at you?"

"Because now you might have some trouble. The whole Nell thing. I mean . . . I just wanted to call and say thanks."

"For what?"

"I mean, since my dad . . . It's all been so weird since then. Since we have, like, no money, and my mom has no time . . . You should break up with Nell."

Now the silence was on Pete's end.

"You should really, like, dump her and date me instead," May heard herself saying, all confidence. "I'm not as irritating. I mean, I'm irritating, but I'm not as bad as she is. And you know me better. Wouldn't that be funny? I mean, we've already hooked up, so we're good."

"We broke up," Pete said quickly. His voice was so bright that May could hear the smile coming through. For a moment she was confused.

"Who, you and me?"

"No. Nell and I."

"Oh . . ."

The meter in her brain clicked once or twice, signaling May that she'd probably said enough.

"I have to go," she said suddenly. "Okay? I think that's great. Cool. Okay. Gotta go now. Hey, Pete, I love you!"

There was a pause during which Pete should have said

something back, but May didn't hear anything. She assumed that he was gone, hung up the phone, and swaggered off back down to the boards. That was good. It was good that she'd had a talk with Pete. All she wanted to do now was let the warm ocean air run along her skin, let the breeze push her hair from her eyes, and walk around with people.

Brooks . . .

Her sister's name drifted through May's consciousness, but there was no urgency accompanying the idea of Brooks. Brooks was somewhere in this crowd, and if she walked around, sooner or later she would find Brooks or Brooks would find her.

She went down the steps to the beach and walked along the cool sand. The ocean was dark and thin and rolled off like a carpet until it hit the horizon. May walked toward it, noticing a strange, tumbling feeling inside, as if her stomach had switched into cement mixer mode. It all went south very quickly. May was down on her knees within a few minutes, gripped by a hideous wave of nausea.

Sand gets cold, she thought. *Cold sand seems to stick less.* Maybe the coldness of the sand could prevent vomiting. If she just focused on the coldness of the sand and nothing else, maybe, just maybe, she might not vomit.

Cold sand, cold sand, cold sand, cold sand . . .

Nope.

Her back arched, her insides convulsed, and nothing came up but air. She clawed into the sand. Nothing to grip.

She was alone, as alone as she could ever get, shuddering on the sand, looking out over the sea, in the realm of jellyfish and ghost crabs and rogue tidal waves and wayward Jeeps racing along the beach and potential rapists hiding under the board-walk—and she was in danger of just generally dying, unseen and unheard. Everything, including the entire ocean and horizon, was spinning.

I'm just drunk . . . , she told herself. *I'm not dying.*

She curled herself up into a ball, put her head on a pile of damp seaweed, and tried to breathe evenly and rest.

It took Brooks about fifteen minutes to realize that May was no longer in the arcade. She had been mesmerized by a group of guys trying to master Dance Dance Revolution, and when she'd managed to rip her gaze from their efforts, May had been long gone. At first she was unconcerned, thinking May had stepped out for air. But when May wasn't waiting outside or standing at one of the booths nearby, it began to dawn on her that she might have a problem on her hands. She looked down at the mile of boardwalk, the surrounding beach and water that bordered them on one side, and the entire shore town that was right at their heels. May could be anywhere in the mix.

She cased the boardwalk, walking at first, then loping into a slow jog. She was slightly drunk, so each step seemed to bounce her high, and all of the lights bounced up and down with her. She went all around the area, up one side and back down the other, peering in every shop, every arcade, every ride, every little offshoot. When the search of the pier turned up nothing, she went down to the sand. She looked under the boardwalk and the pier, then started combing the beach. The run on the sand was a slightly harder one, especially considering that there was a good amount of punch still sloshing around in her stomach. It was a smelly night at the ocean. The air was heavy with salt and decaying seaweed.

She found May a block or two away, sitting between six tethered kites, staring out at the water. Brooks sat down in the sand next to her sister. May smiled and coughed. Her eyes were badly bloodshot.

"I *didit*," May slurred.

"That's great, May," Brooks said, rubbing her temples. "Now, do you think you can walk?"

"*Warlk?*"

"Walk. Can you stand up and walk?"

"I can walk," May said, angrily smacking Brooks on the arm. "*Shuddup.*"

May lay back against the sand.

"No, no," Brooks said, tugging her back up. "No. Stay up. We're going to walk."

Brooks reached under May's arms and pulled her little sister up. Even though May was shorter and lighter and even though Brooks was very strong, May was total deadweight. It was a hard trudge over the sand. May's head rolled senselessly on her shoulders, and she mumbled nonsense at Brooks the entire way.

"It's all right, May," Brooks said over and over as she led May to the sidewalk. "You're doing fine."

It took about four blocks before May's feet actually started to move in rhythmic steps—but it was still a plodding, Frankenstein kind of walk. As they made their way along, a Toyota Tercel full of guys slowed next to them. The car was equipped with a subwoofer so powerful that two alarms went off as it passed. An Eminem wannabe in a bandanna and an Abercrombie and Fitch hat leaned out of the open window.

"Your friend need a ride?" he asked, smiling.

"No," Brooks said, dragging May along.

"Ri—"

"Shut up, May."

"She can sit on my lap," he said as the car slowly followed them along. "I got room for both of you."

Brooks ignored him.

"Come on," said the guy, leaning far out now, reaching for May with outstretched arms. "She likes me."

Brooks switched positions with May and increased their pace. May groaned.

"You don't like me?" The guy leered. "Your friend does. She's looking at me."

"Look," Brooks said, reaching deep into her pocket, grabbing her thick stick of zinc oxide, and pulling it out as if it were a canister of spray, "Feminem, how about you keep driving before I pepper-spray you?"

There was a roar of laughter in the car, and Brooks heard the word, "Dykes!" screamed from somewhere inside. The guy pulled himself back in, spitting on the ground near Brooks's feet before they skidded off. Brooks heaved a sigh and slipped the sunscreen back into her pocket.

"Jackass," she mumbled, continuing to steer May back in the direction of the camp.

"*Wooo*, Brooks is tough. . . ."

"Please, May. Just walk, all right?"

When they got to the convenience store halfway to the camp, Brooks set May down on a bench for a moment.

"Stay here," she told May firmly. "Got it?"

May's chin slumped down on her chest. She wasn't going anywhere. Brooks ran inside and bought a bottle of water and a bottle of Gatorade. Even though she was barely in the store for a minute, May had thrown up on the ground by the bench by the time she came out.

"Oh God," Brooks said, pulling her up and forcing some of the water down her throat. Tears of confusion were running down May's face. Her skin was damp.

"Come on," Brooks said, stroking back May's loose, damp hair. "Almost there."

May slumped, and her eyes began to close. There was no way she could walk any more. Brooks sat down on the bench next to her sister and looked at the passing traffic in despair. There was only one solution she could come up with. May would need to be driven, and that meant getting the Firebird, which was at the movie theater four blocks away. She didn't have the key, of course, and wasn't legally able to drive it. But she *was* sober now.

"May," she said, very clearly, "I want you to stay here. Got it? *Stay here.* I'm going to come right back. Don't move from here, and don't talk to anyone."

May had slipped out of consciousness. Brooks managed to get her up and pull her over to the side of the store, which at least kept her out of sight from the road.

Brooks stood up and pulled each heel up to the back of her thigh, stretching out her muscles. Four blocks. She could do four blocks in just a minute or two. With one final look at May, she took off.

The sidewalks were crowded with people headed up to the boards. She cut across the parking lot of a run-down hotel and headed down an alley parallel to the main road. Her arms pumped hard and even, and her footfalls were steady and fast. *One, two, three, four*—over a broken boogie board. Around a discarded cooler. Past three Dumpsters behind a pizza shop.

It took very little time for her to reach the theater, but once she was there, she faced another problem. Generally speaking, movie theaters didn't let people in unless they had money for a ticket, which she didn't. So she would have to get creative.

The guy at the door was about her age. He didn't look too inspired by his job.

"I need your help," Brooks said, running up to him.

"Huh?"

"Our car is in the lot, and my mom and little sister are inside. My sister's medicine is in the car, and I have to get the keys. Could you please let me in?"

He stared at her doubtfully. She wondered if she had alcohol on her breath. Then she remembered that vodka didn't have an odor.

"Look," she said, reaching into her pocket and pulling out her worn tiger print wallet. "Here is my wallet." She unsnapped it and handed over her worthless driver's license. "Here is my ID."

She held the card up to her face so that he could see that the image matched the reality.

"You can keep this. Keep the whole wallet. I will be in there for less than five minutes, I promise. I just need the car keys."

"I need to ask my manager."

"I have no time," Brooks said. "You have all my money. You

have my ID. I'm not trying to sneak in. Who leaves their wallet?"

The guy looked at the wallet.

"Please . . . ," she said, leaning in.

"Okay," he said. "Five minutes."

Brooks tore off down the hall. It was a little place, with only four screens, so the theater was easy enough to find. But since it was a holiday night, the room was packed. And, of course, the scene she walked in on seemed to be a suspenseful one—two people staring at each other significantly—so the place was dead quiet. She squatted down almost to a crawl and sneaked down the middle aisle, snooping on each row from a dog's eye perspective. Using this method, she finally found her mother and Palmer sitting about five seats into one of the front rows.

Palmer noticed her first and wrinkled her brow in confusion. Brooks tried to pantomime keys, but that had no effect. So she decided to try the whisper-down-the-lane method.

"Could you tell that girl I forgot my wallet," she whispered to the first guy in the row, who was staring at her strangely. "Can you ask them for the keys?"

He passed the message, though somewhat grudgingly.

Palmer turned and looked Brooks in the eye. *You are so lying,* her gaze said.

When her mother looked over, Brooks turned her pockets inside out, showing that she had no wallet. Then she pointed out, hoping this would signify the parking lot. She tried the key pantomime again. Her mother looked hesitant.

"Tell them I'll meet them out front when it's over," she said.

There was some shushing.

Once again the message was passed. Finally the keys were

passed back, but not before Brooks got a strange look from her mother and one final, withering gaze from Palmer.

Out in the lobby, Brooks ran up behind the guy at the door and threw herself over his shoulders.

"You're my guy," she said, plucking the wallet from his hands. "I'll remember you forever."

She kissed him on the cheek and ran out the door to the parking lot. She found the Firebird toward the back. She checked her watch. Nine-ten. The movie would be over in half an hour. She started the engine and pulled onto the road.

Her desire, of course, was to drive as quickly as possible. But her suspended license and the heavy traffic kept her crawling along. It took her five minutes to drive four blocks to the store. May was still there, thankfully, but lying on her side. Brooks loaded her into the backseat, which she lined with some bags she found in the trash, just in case May threw up again.

It took another ten minutes to drive back to the camp. The air was full of the smell of ocean, burning wood, butane, and barbecue. Normally it would have been pleasant, but any one of those odors might very well cause May to hurl again.

One of the neighbors, who was passing by with his dog, stopped as Brooks dragged May's limp figure out of the backseat.

"She okay?" he asked.

"Oh," Brooks said casually as May nearly slumped to the ground. "Yeah. Fine. Too much sun."

He looked doubtful but moved on. Brooks set May down on the tarp in front of the camper. May managed to get on all fours and crawl over to the picnic table. She put her head down on one of the benches and stopped moving.

"Why don't you try to be sick again?" Brooks suggested, making her voice cheerful, as if this was something fun May should do for old times' sake. "You'll feel better."

Something incomprehensible.

Brooks looked at her watch. No time for this. Her mother and Palmer would be out of the movie within minutes. She grabbed one of the beach blankets that was drying on a chair, pulled May up again, and walked her around to the back. There she spread out the blanket and set May on it. May immediately curled into a fetal position and passed out.

Traffic again on the ride back to the theater. Brooks beat on the steering wheel in agony. She got there with just two minutes to spare, only to find that someone had taken the parking space.

"No," she said, feeling everything drop out from under her. "No . . ."

Lacking an option, she parked a few spaces over and hoped that no one would notice. Then she jumped out of the driver's seat and sat on the back bumper as if she'd been waiting there for ten minutes. Her mother appeared to notice nothing amiss when she came out, but the look on Palmer's face clearly showed that she knew something was up.

"So, I got back down there," Brooks said with a laugh, "and May decided she was tired. So she went home."

"She walked home?" her mom said, concerned.

"Yeah. I think it was all the sun. She said she wanted to go back and take a cold shower."

Even Brooks was staggered by the speed of her own lie. Palmer eyed the parking space.

"We should get back, then," her mom said.

As they rode back to the camp, Brooks felt herself hitting the wall. She was exhausted in every way. All of the confusion and adrenaline had worn her out. And her mind kept replaying the moment she couldn't find May on the beach. She saw herself looking out at the water, not knowing if her sister had wandered drunkenly into the surf. It wouldn't go away.

May obviously wasn't around and waiting when they got back, so Brooks had to continue the act by jumping up and going to the bathhouse to check on her. She walked over, wandered around for a second, stared at the wet toilet paper on the ground, and returned with a false report of May's well-being.

"Well," said her mom, yawning, "I'm heading in. I'm beat."

Both Palmer and Brooks received a kiss on the forehead. After she went inside, Palmer scowled at Brooks suspiciously. Brooks could feel her skin breaking out in goose bumps.

"What?" Brooks asked, trying not to look nervous.

"What are you doing?"

"I'm sitting here."

"Want to go to the batting cage?" Palmer asked.

"Not really."

"I can't go by myself."

"Palm, why don't you watch TV or something?"

Palmer fell silent for a moment, picking at a rip in the plastic tablecloth.

"I may just sleep out here," Brooks said, faking a long yawn. "Everybody keeps saying you can see shooting stars."

The idea that Brooks would spend a night at the beach staring at the sky was extremely implausible, but she acted on it, grabbing one of the beach towels and spreading it out on the ground. Palmer couldn't seem to make anything of her motives and soon gave up and went inside. Brooks had to wait almost two hours for Palmer to go to bed before she could move her charge. This stirring caused May to be ill once again, after which she wanted to walk around the park to work off some of the dizziness. By three in the morning, Brooks was finally able to tuck her in and fall into her own bunk in exhaustion.

"So May's drunk?" said a voice from the shelf-bed above her. "That's a switch."

Brooks rolled toward the wall and put her pillow over her head.

14

"Happy Fourth of July!"

At ten in the morning May's mother threw open the flimsy piece of plastic that served as their bedroom door. Blistering sunlight poured in. May's head was revolving slowly. Pain was everywhere.

"Palmer and I are headed to the beach," her mom said, pulling her large plastic beach bag over her shoulder. "Want to put on your suit and come?"

"No . . ."

"Okay. See you later, sleepyhead."

May pulled her sleeping bag over her head for protection.

"How are you feeling?" Brooks said, standing in the sunlight, looking disgustingly tall and healthy, her blond hair loose. May felt like a small, gnarled sewer creature, something that recoiled from the light.

"Drink this," Brooks said. She held a Gatorade out to May. May struggled with the cap, so Brooks opened it for her and passed it back. May's thirst was overwhelming, and she drank the whole bottle in about a minute. Brooks took it from her, disappeared for a moment, then returned.

"Take these," she said, holding out two pills and a glass of water.

"What are they?"

"Medicine."

Okay. May could deal with medicine. Didn't matter what kind, really. She took the pills. She decided to experiment with standing up. Maybe she would feel better that way. She pulled herself out of the bed and into the living area. She didn't remember coming to bed. She had glimpses . . . walking, being outside on the ground. She was covered in bug bites.

"What happened last . . . ?" But as soon as she started the question, it started coming back in flashes and spurts. Brooks and her bottle. The arcade. The sand. The phone.

"Oh my God," she said.

"What?"

May put her hand over her mouth. Brooks dove into the cabinet and quickly produced a large plastic popcorn bowl. She shoved this under May's chin, but May brushed it away. Her problem wasn't physical.

"I need to go back to bed," May said, heading into the bedroom and slamming the door. It bounced back open.

"What?" Brooks asked again.

"You should really leave me alone," May said. "You should go as far away from me as you can."

May spent the majority of the day sleeping in fitful bursts. All of her movements were tailored to find the exact position in which her stomach would stop heaving and the flashes of pain would stop running through it. She kept sliding around on her slippery sleeping bag, which covered her tiny bed. Her pillow always seemed to be in the wrong place. One minute she'd be hot and sticky, her sunburn throbbing, and in the next second a shuddering chill would ripple through her.

When she hadn't emerged by three in the afternoon, her mother returned to examine her. Fortunately for May, her symptoms mimicked the sickness that resulted from excessive sunburn. She was smeared in aloe vera, forced to drink bottles of water and take a few aspirins, and told to stay out of the sun as much as possible for the remainder of the trip. May was fine with all of this except for the aloe, which made her shiver even more.

It took until evening for May to find the strength to get up and eat a little dry cereal for dinner. She was sick of being in the tiny bedroom, so she agreed to come along and watch the fireworks. Gingerly she pulled on a pair of running pants and a sweatshirt and slunk along behind her mother and sisters to the boardwalk. They got four Orange Juliuses and found a prime piece of railing to stand along, not far from where May and Brooks's escapade had started the night before. Just the smell of the beer was enough to almost cause May to relapse.

"Isn't this nice?" their mom said, throwing her arms over May and Palmer's shoulders.

Palmer shot May an angry look, which May didn't even feel like analyzing.

The fireworks began popping over the water, and the crowd started the obligatory oohing and aahing. May's brain was elsewhere. The illness had filled her mind with morbid thoughts, and now everything she'd been experiencing for the last few days took on a different cast. She was thinking about the word *love.* That much she could recall from the nightmarish montage of barfing, crawling, walking, and rolling around on the ground. She had used the full "I love you" construction. Not even "love ya!" or "I totally love you!"—either of which might have meant she wasn't serious. With every boom in the sky, she heard the word.

The air grew a bit cooler, and she leaned into her mother's fleece pullover. Her mother gave her ponytail a gentle tug.

There was another thing that was even harder to grasp, and she wasn't sure why this hadn't dawned on her before: They had cheated on Nell. Or Pete had, but she had definitely been a part of it. She was definitely in the middle of things now—she was the *other woman*. The more she thought about it, the weirder and more wrong it got.

For May, this was a very disturbing transition from a pleasant fantasy to a harsh reality, like a rude awakening in a horror movie—one of Pete's favorite devices, which he had explained to her several times. It went like this: Some indestructible serial killer slays half the high school. Then in the end, right after the massacre, the only surviving character wakes up on a sunny morning. All the blood is off the walls. The severed head is no longer sitting on top of her dresser. She looks around with an expression of infinite gratitude and says, "It was all a dream. . . ." At that moment the killer pops out of the nightstand wearing her deceased boyfriend's football jersey and wielding an ax. Everything goes black, but you know she is *so* dead. . . .

That was what it was like for May. Just without the ax.

"What do you think, guys?" her mom enthused. "Pretty good spot, huh?"

May numbly watched another explosion on the horizon.

"It's going to be a shame to have to go back tomorrow," her mom went on. "It's been great being here, all of us. But back to reality, I guess . . ."

15

May had been home all of an hour, and she'd spent most of it sprawled on her bed with her legs flipped over her head, yoga style. This was her thinking position. She assumed it in times of crisis to encourage blood flow to her brain. All it was doing for her now was making her stare at her calves close up. She needed to shave.

The phone rang, jarring her meditative flow.

"May!" Palmer screamed up the stairs. "It's Camper!"

She wasn't ready for this conversation yet.

"Hey," he said as May got on the phone. She could hear the smile in his voice. "I was wondering if I could drop by. Are you busy, or . . . ?"

"We're . . ." May glanced around her room for something she could be doing but came up with nothing. "I'm burned. Really burned. I'm covered in aloe. I'm sticking to my sheets. It's gross."

"You always look good."

Every alarm in May's head went off.

"No, I mean I'm in pain. I feel a little sick. You know what it's like when I get burned."

"Right," Pete said. "Want me to bring you something? Ice cream?"

"I was going to try to go to sleep."

"Oh," he said. The disappointment in his voice was clear.

"But it's only because I have the test in the morning. I have to try to be able to move and not be too swollen."

"Need a ride there?"

"My mom is taking me. I think she feels obligated since she didn't teach me."

"Afterward?"

"Oh," May said. "Yeah. Sure. Come by."

She cringed at her obvious lack of romantic suavity.

"I've really missed you," he said eagerly. "We should talk. You know. Maybe tomorrow. Or now, if you felt like it. But if you're tired . . ."

"We should," she replied, trying to sound equally as excited. "But we should do it in person."

"Sure," he agreed quickly.

The line went quiet.

"You're tired, huh?" he asked.

"Yeah. I guess I should sleep."

"So I'll see you tomorrow?" he said. "Around noon?"

"Great. See you tomorrow! Bye!"

May hung up quickly. She was pretty sure that there had been a real possibility that he was going to hang up with an "I love you," and that would have caused her to take a running leap out of her window.

May slid off her bed and pulled out the flat drawer along the top of her desk. She reached into the space underneath, retrieved an envelope, and shook out the contents. Seven Polaroids fell out. The famous Peter Camp photos. They'd had great plans for the pictures at the time that they were taken. They were going to post them online. But in the confusion that followed, they'd been put away and forgotten.

May arranged them on the desktop and turned on the light. They really were very blurry. Still, she could see enough. She could see that he had been much skinnier last year; he'd developed muscles recently. It appeared that he had very few freckles on his back. The "good butt shot" was not only an excellent photo, but it revealed a really good butt as well. The much contended issue of size was still impossible to resolve, however, even when she squinted and held the photos up to her desk lamp.

She put the photos back into the envelope quickly. She sometimes had the strange fantasy that her father could see her whenever she was doing something embarrassing, as if the dead watched the living like they were the cast of a reality show. And as on a reality show, no one would want to see the boring, virtuous parts. The bits when she was studying or when she got to work five minutes early, May was sure these were edited out. But the sight of May hunched over a photo of a naked Peter Camp—that would be included.

"I need sleep," she said to herself, crawling under the quilt. "I'll know what to do tomorrow."

Palmer sat on her bed, staring at the bronze canister. It was the first thing she'd wanted to see when she got home. She felt weird being away from it now. She didn't like leaving her dad alone in the house while they went to the beach. Using the corner of her pillowcase, she wiped away the smudges her fingers had made.

Though she was glad she'd found it, having the canister presented some problems. One, she didn't necessarily want to be its keeper. That seemed like a scary, eternal responsibility. The second was that now that she'd found it, she'd lost her desire to go through the house at night. That had been her only occupation, and now it seemed to be gone.

It had been all right at the beach, sleeping in close quarters with everyone, having Brooks and May right there with her. But now that she was home, Palmer was afraid. She was going to have to go back to the horrible feeling of waking up in the middle of the night unable to breathe. And she would have nothing to do but sit and wait until she finally managed to drift back to sleep—and that sometimes took hours.

This was not the time to be sleepless. She was already behind the other players at the camp because she'd missed the first days. The thought of games rarely made her nervous, but tomorrow she'd be playing with strangers. They'd probably be girls a lot older than she was, most of them the best players from their schools. And there might be scouts in the crowd.

She leaned back on her bed and hung her head upside down over the side. She counted her trophies. There were twenty-one, all lined up on the special shelf her dad had put up above her dresser. When her head filled with blood, she pulled herself upright and looked at the canister again. She needed to do something with it, or she was going to go crazy.

It suddenly dawned on her—May. She would tell May what she had done, and May would have a good answer. Even if she had gotten wasted over the weekend, May was still the responsible one.

Palmer slipped off her bed and went down to May's door. She knocked once, then let herself in. May was sitting in bed, reading a book.

"Could you wait for me to say, 'Come in,' for once?" May asked, looking up in annoyance.

Palmer shifted from foot to foot. How did she explain this?

"What did Pete want?" she asked. The second the words were out of her mouth, Palmer realized her mistake. She had blown it.

"You have to stop it, Palm," May said, sitting up on her elbows. "Stop watching everything Pete and I do."

"I'm not—"

"I'm really tired," May said, putting down her book and reaching over to turn out the light. "I have this stupid test in the morning. Would you please let me sleep?"

Palmer felt like she was going to cry. She wanted to tell May what she had sitting against the Orioles pillow on her bed. She wanted to tell her about her nights of prowling, and the horrible pain in her chest, and the terrible fear.

"Please, Palm." May groaned. "Go."

There was just something about her that annoyed people, that made them ask her to leave. Not knowing what else to do, Palmer turned and went back to her room.

16

Since she'd been practicing in Pete's car, May decided to take the Firebird for her exam. It was a little more similar in feel and in size than the minivan. Now that she was here, though, she wondered if it was way too old or too weird for the exam. Maybe you needed a car that didn't look like it had been stolen from the Smithsonian.

Her new examiner, a stern-looking man with a crew cut and raw red circles under his eyes, seemed much more interested in the car than in his examinee. He walked around it, inspecting it minutely.

"Firebird 400," he said, throwing open the door and taking the permit he was meekly offered. "Sixty-seven, right? Someone in the family a car buff?"

"My dad."

"He do the restore?"

"The what?"

"Okay." He glanced at the permit. "*May-zee. Maize-eee.* Mayzie? Give me your hazards while we're here."

As May demonstrated all the requested functions, she felt more like a model demonstrating a car in a showroom than someone taking the driver's exam. Her examiner even wanted to see the latch that released the convertible top.

"All right," he said, satisfied that she knew the controls. "Let's get moving."

One thing became immediately clear as May started moving the car forward—Pete had prepared her well for this. The lessons had helped, but what really boosted her confidence was the fact that she'd had so many nerve-racking experiences in the car with him. Nothing the examiner could do really rattled her. Even when she struck an orange cone on the serpentine and caused it to wobble or when she was clearly going too slowly on her thirty feet in reverse, her nerves remained steady right to the end of the course. She was actually shocked at how easy it was.

"Congratulations," the man said, checking off some boxes on his form. "Pull over in front of the building."

"I passed?"

"Yes," he said, handing her back her card and a form. "Take this inside. And tell your dad he's got a nice car here."

"Sure." May nodded, pulling into the directed spot. "I'll tell him."

It took only a few minutes to have the permit verified. When she came back out, the examiner was gone and her mother was sitting in the passenger's seat, grinning broadly. May got into the driver's seat.

"I saw you go in," her mother said. "I thought that seemed like good news."

She leaned over to give May a hug. She smelled vaguely of hospital, even though she'd showered since she'd been there last.

"You have no idea how relieved I am," she said.

"Relieved?" May asked, giving her mother a sideways glance. That wasn't quite the reaction she'd been expecting—not immediately after she passed the test, anyway.

May started the car and carefully backed out of the space. It took her almost a full minute to do this, as she stopped for every car that came down their row. She overshot her turn leaving the parking lot and almost ended up on the shoulder on the opposite side of the road. Okay, maybe the state of Pennsylvania had made a mistake—but too late now. She wasn't giving them the license back.

"Palmer has a game this afternoon," her mom said. "I'm leaving for work at six, so if you could take her, that would be great."

"Sure."

"And if you could run to the store . . ."

"Can't I be normal and celebrate for a second?" May asked. She could hear the irritation in her voice.

Her mom flashed her a quick look.

"I mean, could you wait maybe five minutes before laying the jobs on me?"

"I'm just—"

"Brooks didn't get a list of chores when she got her license," May found herself saying. "She went to a game. She had a cell phone."

"What are you saying?" her mother asked.

"I'm saying Brooks actually did stuff, had fun. I got my license because I had to. It's always been about Brooks. You let her do whatever she wants."

"Don't exaggerate." Her mother pried a few stray M&M's from the well near the shift.

"So why is Brooks practically in rehab now?" May spat. "She was like that for months, and you didn't say a word."

"If I had known . . ."

Maybe it was because she was in the driver's seat now, but May felt a sudden urge to say exactly what she thought.

"How could you *not* know, Mom? How could you not know that your own daughter was out about every other night, wasted out of her mind? Didn't you guess something was up when she quit the team? Or what about the fact that she was hung over and half dead the rest of the time? What about her grades? What are *they* like?"

Her mother put on her sunglasses and stared out the window.

"Dad liked her best," May said. "You like her best. Why can't you just say it?"

In her frustration May almost ran a red light. She skidded to a stop several feet past the white line. The nose of the Firebird stuck out into traffic. She couldn't back up because cars had come up right behind her. People wove around her to get by, some honking in annoyance as they passed.

"You're too far up," her mother snapped.

"Like I didn't notice that."

Neither of them spoke again for the rest of the ride. Once they were in the garage, her mother left the car, slamming the door behind her.

Palmer was immediately on May's heels the second she walked into the house.

"What did you do?" Palmer asked, her voice low.

"We had a fight," May replied, rubbing her temples. She pushed past Palmer and went into the kitchen, but Palmer followed her.

"Mom's *upset*."

"I know." May threw open the fridge and cursed at the empty water pitcher. "Can you leave me alone for a second, Palm?"

"What did you do?"

Palm was clenching her jaw and glowering down at May.

"I didn't do anything," May spat. "I passed my test, okay? That's what I did."

May heard a car pull up in front of the house. Pete. She hurried to the front door to check. The Cutlass was in front of the house, and Palmer was still at her back, yapping like a dog.

"You did something to her!"

"Not now, Palm! Go away!"

Palmer stomped upstairs.

May examined herself in the mirror. Her eyes were slightly red. She had her sunburn, which was almost fading into a tan and looked sort of nice against her dark blue tank top. She reached up and pulled out the twist tie that held her hair back in a knot and gave her head a good shake. Her hair was kind of bumpy and strange looking from being pulled up when it was still wet, but May decided to tell herself it was attractively wavy. She had no problems at all lying to herself in desperate situations.

She peered through the glass at the top of the door and saw Pete marching across the front lawn. He was casually but carefully dressed in long green khaki shorts and a black short-sleeve button-down shirt. His clothes even looked ironed. His hair seemed to be carefully dried and even kind of . . . arranged. His arm was tucked behind his back.

She opened the door. As he got within a few paces, he broke out into a huge grin. May clenched her hands into fists to keep them steady.

"You *are* burned," he said.

"Oh." May looked down at herself and remembered her excuse from the night before. "Yeah. I scorch."

He swung his arm around and presented her with three Gerber daisies. May pushed open the door and stepped outside to take them. They were vividly colored—red, orange, and yellow.

"I got these . . . ," Pete said. "I knew you were going to pass."

"What's this?" May said, even though they were obviously flowers.

"There's only three of them," he said, almost apologetically.

"They're great. Thanks."

"Are you all right?" he asked. May turned away and headed for the garage.

"I'm fine," she said quickly, wanting to get away in case her mother came downstairs. "Let's go . . . out here. We can sit in the car."

They sat down in the front seat of the Firebird, leaving the doors hanging open.

"So, I passed," she said. "Finally. Amazing."

Neither of them could think of anything more to say about the test. May looked down at the cream-colored vinyl seat. Traces of fabric softener fragrance wafted off Pete's shirt.

"So, your call," he began. "The other night. Did you mean what you said?"

May stroked the flower petals and found herself unable to speak. Her entire attention was on the fact that Pete's hand had fallen on her far shoulder, and this time he wasn't going to tap on it and make her turn the wrong way. He had gotten closer to her. His face was just inches away from hers. There was no question what was supposed to happen next.

Pete kept talking, his words coming more quickly.

"Because for a long time I've really . . . I like you a lot. Obviously."

All of Pete's attributes, which had seemed so appealing just a short while before, took on a threatening quality. His hair was too curly. His nose, too small and well formed. He had gotten too tall. His lips seemed especially ridiculous. They could be the most perfectly formed lips on the planet and still look like some very disturbing instruments when viewed up close for over a minute.

He slid closer to her. The hand that had been on her shoulder was now cradling the back of her head.

"Pete . . ."

Oh God, his head was even at an angle. He was ready. It was like a crowded elevator full of emotions had just risen to May's head and gotten stuck there. They were all banging around, making her feel like she was going to explode.

"Just wait." She put her hands up against his chest and pushed herself back. "Just stop, okay?"

Pete stopped moving entirely.

"What?"

"I don't want to do this, okay? It's weird."

"What's weird?"

"This!" she yelled. "Us!"

He seemed confused.

"You called and said you loved me."

"I was drunk. Brooks got me drunk. I didn't know what I was doing."

"You weren't drunk before you left."

She couldn't deny that one. She couldn't think, period.

"What about Jenna?" she asked, wondering where her words were coming from. Pete almost jumped to his side of the seat.

"What about her?"

"It just seems kind of weird to me, now that I think about it," May said. "Why you broke up with her."

Pete's eyes seemed to get bloodshot instantly. His brow lowered, and the freckleless spot between his eyes turned a bright crimson. Bizarrely, May's impulse was to make him mad. *Be vicious.* That was the only message she was getting.

"What about Nell?" she asked. "You just cheated on her, then you dumped her."

"Nell was . . . I explained this to you. What are you saying?"

"I just wanted to learn how to drive," May went on, "and you . . ."

Were nice. Helped me. Made me laugh.

". . . completely took it the wrong way. And you didn't even care what you did to her. Is that what you do? You just stay with someone as long as you feel like it? I mean, are you just going to screw me and dump me?"

May never used the word *screw*, not in that sense. The word left a hard taste in her mouth.

"Screw you and dump you?" he repeated incredulously. His voice had gone a bit hoarse.

In the silence that followed, May could hear the Stark boys gleefully using each other as lawn dart targets. Their breathless screaming drifted up over their house, through the open garage door, and passed into the Firebird.

It was hard to do, but once you made Pete angry, he stayed angry. There were times when they'd fought as kids that he'd cut May dead for days until they had made up. But those times were nothing compared to the anger she saw in him now. Now she saw a much bigger, scarier emotion. He wasn't the little boy who used to ride over to her house on his bike anymore—he was a fully grown guy.

He turned to face forward. His chest was rising and falling quickly. May leaned back and looked out her side of the car. She couldn't understand why she was so very calm when this horrible thing was exploding all around her. She actually felt a strange sense of relaxation.

When Pete left a minute later, she decided not to turn to watch him go, even though something inside her was yelling at her to follow him. Quickly. To get out of the car and catch him and stop this insanity.

That was impossible.

She sat, staring at the tool shelf. She heard Pete's car pull away.

Brooks came down into the garage and set a bucket of freshly washed dishes on one of the shelves.

"Nice one," she said, and headed back inside.

May was sitting against her bed, staring at the phone on the floor. She'd been in the process of reaching for it for an hour, wanting to call Pete but having no idea what to say—or what her voice might say, since she was apparently possessed by demons who did all her talking for her.

Brooks pushed open her door without knocking.

"It's time for Palmer's game," she said.

May shoved her star-spangled flip-flops on her feet. As she walked down the hall, Brooks followed her.

"You're coming?" May asked.

"Moral support."

"Since when have you given that out?"

Palmer was already sitting in the back of the car, silently examining her glove. Brooks hopped into the passenger's seat.

"You have a lot of problems, you know that?" Brooks said casually as May backed out of the garage. "Seriously. I think you need a psychologist."

"Not now," May said flatly.

"Really. I think you do."

"Well, when your rehab guy has some free time, maybe he can see me."

"Both of you," Palmer said from the back. "Shut up."

"What you did to Pete was cold."

"Okay," May said, backing out onto the road a bit more aggressively than necessary. "I don't think you're far enough along the twelve steps to start criticizing me. Wait until you get your sixty-day chip or something."

Palmer slammed her fist into her glove a few times.

"At least I'm not a user," Brooks continued.

"I guess you haven't used me or used Mom. I mean, we really love paying for all of your screwups. It gives us a reason to live."

"You're both retards," Palmer mumbled, but neither May nor Brooks could quite catch what she'd said.

"He's been great to you," Brooks said. "He'd do anything for you. And you treated him like crap."

"Look," May said, "I'm sorry that I didn't meet someone classy, like Dave Vatiman. . . ."

Another jab. Maybe it was the driver's seat, May reasoned. Maybe it did something to her—made her evil. But Brooks didn't seem to notice the remark.

"That's my point. You could at least be *nice* to him."

"You have no idea what you're talking about," May broke in. "He's Pete. He's an idiot. He'll get over it."

Even as May said it, she winced a bit. Why did she say these things?

Because she was crazy. Because she was a zombie.

They rode the rest of the way in silence. May brought the car to an abrupt stop in front of the clubhouse. Palmer was the first out. She pulled her things out of the backseat briskly.

"See you after," May said.

"Yeah," Brooks said over her shoulder. "Good game."

Palmer didn't answer them. She walked off to the clubhouse. May and Brooks got out of the car.

"You know what?" Brooks said, looking her sister up and down. "You deserve it. You deserve to be weird and miserable."

"Thanks," May said, walking off toward the bleachers.

Seventh inning. Three to two in favor of this team of strangers Palmer found herself pitching for. She was perspiring. This was a game she could have played better. Three obviously incompetent batters had gotten past her—girls she could have struck out with her eyes closed on any other day.

She just needed to get through this. To get home and go back to bed.

Playing always took her mind off things, but today her head was still buzzing. She was exhausted—she hadn't slept much. May had argued with her mother and left her crying. May had argued with Pete about something, and Pete had gone away. May had gotten drunk at the beach. She was used to Brooks doing these things, but now even May was falling to pieces on her. But this wasn't the time or place to think about that.

Palmer squared herself off and faced the batter, putting both of her feet on the pitcher's plate. She gripped the ball with both hands.

Then it hit all at once, without warning. The nighttime panic was here, now. The strange heartbeat, the tunnel vision. Her arms didn't work. She couldn't throw. She couldn't move. She curled her knuckles up along the stitches of the ball. It was the only recognizable sensation.

The girl at bat straightened up impatiently. Palmer tried to calm herself, but she knew that she was rapidly approaching the ten-second mark, which was the maximum amount of time she was allowed between taking her position on the pitcher's plate and beginning her pitch. The batter crowded the plate, sensing her nervousness.

Palmer had to do something.

In one smooth gesture she stepped forward, wound her arm, and released the ball. She closed her eyes. It was a solid pitch. She could see it moving in her mind—how it arced, how it slowed. The batter, confused, would move in even farther. But then it would curve and go right back toward the plate, picking up speed. And if the girl didn't move away . . .

Palmer closed her eyes right before the ball hit the girl's helmet with a sickening thud.

*   *   *

Brooks had risen to her feet a moment before the impact; her instincts had told her that something was wrong with the pitch. Palmer had waited much too long. She watched the batter stagger and fall, and her team and coaches came running. There was confusion in the bleachers and on the field. Cell phones were pulled out. A few people leapt down and ran to the fallen girl. Palmer turned and ran off.

"What's going on?" May said.

Brooks was already climbing down the bleachers in pursuit. May scrambled for her purse and trailed behind.

Palmer disappeared around the clubhouse, toward the parking lot, so Brooks increased her pace. Even though she was a little out of shape, Brooks was still an excellent runner. Palmer was fast, but she could keep up with her. She followed her through the parking lot and watched her duck behind the Firebird. When Brooks jogged up a few seconds later, she found Palm sitting on the ground, curled up into a ball.

"Go away," Palmer said in a low voice.

"What happened out there?"

"I said *go away*."

"Are you all right?"

There was heavy breathing coming from behind them. May had just caught up.

"Palm, you should really go back there," Brooks said. "Go back and explain."

Palmer screamed. Not an angry scream but a painful, high-pitched, unbroken wail. Brooks remembered screaming like that when she was a little child, so hard that she felt her throat might bleed. It carried across the parking lot. It drew the attention of everyone in the entire area. If her desired effect was to scare Brooks off, it worked. But May stepped forward and sat down on the ground in front of Palmer. Palmer scrunched her face together in what was probably an attempt at a threatening expression, but May didn't move.

"What's going on, Palm?" she said.

"It keeps happening," Palm said through clenched teeth.

"What does?"

"The thing. Where I can't breathe."

"Can't breathe?"

"It happened out there. Things get dark."

May reached out and rubbed Palm's knee.

"Do you want to go home?" she asked quietly.

The knee rubbing seemed to subdue Palmer. Her face relaxed, and she gave a heavy nod, like little kids do when they're upset or tired. May looked up at Brooks, who was surveying the activity in the distance with a dark expression.

"I don't know if we should," Brooks said. "They're going to want to know what happened."

May was already getting out her keys.

"I don't care," she replied. "Let's get her out of here."

Palmer locked herself in her room the minute she arrived home. It was stuffy and overly sunny. At least the scary, closed-in feeling was going away fairly quickly this time, probably because it was daytime and people were around.

She didn't want to think about the pitch. She couldn't think about the pitch. Not yet. Her brain was already too loud and crowded with stuff. Until she solved the problem of the urn, nothing was going to be right again. It sat there on her bed, gleaming in the sunlight that came through the blinds. She dropped down on the bed and stared at it.

"What do you want?" she asked it, hoping that by asking the question aloud, she would get some kind of magical inspiration. But the urn just slipped a bit to the right. Palmer straightened it, then lay back and stared at the ceiling.

Her life was over. She was so out of the camp. And if they kicked her out of softball, Palmer would die.

No. She could fix it. She could explain to them.

The attacks were coming in the day now. Now she really was a crazy person.

She would fix that too.

The urn . . . She just had to figure out what to do with the urn.

She just had to *calm down*.

She closed her eyes and tried to imagine the happiest place she could. Camden Yards. Definitely. Cheese dog in one hand. First inning. They hadn't taken their trip to Camden Yards this year. She had missed it.

Yesssssss . . .

The idea came as a sudden rush. Every detail was there, as if her brain had already written the plan and she had stumbled upon it. First she had to see if it was possible. She had a season schedule card pinned to her corkboard. She checked. The timing was perfect.

She looked at the urn. This was going to be hard, but she had to do it.

*   *   *

When Palmer crept downstairs a half hour later, Brooks and May were sitting at the kitchen table, holding conference over an assortment of dry crumbs, self-stick notes, and random pens. Brooks was methodically sticking and unsticking a Post-it to her forehead. May was chewing on a mechanical pencil with her back teeth, like a dog trying to tear the knobby end from a rawhide bone.

Palmer stood right outside the doorway and listened.

"It was an accident," May was saying. "Accidents happen. And those helmets are really strong. Aren't they? I mean, they look strong, and they have that flap over the ear."

"The girl's probably all right," Brooks said, putting one of the Post-it notes over her eye. "That's not it."

"Then what is it?"

"It wasn't an accident."

"What are you talking about?"

"She was head-hunting," Brooks said simply.

"She was what?"

"She aimed for the girl's head to knock her away from the plate. It's a really illegal move, but it happens."

"You're saying Palmer hit her on *purpose*?" May asked.

"I don't know. I saw her face. Something was wrong. Maybe the sun got in her eyes or something. . . ." Brooks pulled off her Post-it eye patch and started nervously folding it into the shape of a small hat.

"This is pretty bad, isn't it?" May said.

"It could be."

Palmer couldn't listen anymore. It was time to act. She strode into the kitchen, causing her sisters to lurch in alarm. Without giving them a chance to say anything, she gingerly removed the urn from the bag and set it on the table between them.

"I found it in Mom's closet," she said. "It was in a box. A shoe box."

May and Brooks said nothing. It was clear that they immediately knew what the thing was, and it seemed to affect them in the same way that it did Palmer. They flinched away from it, yet they had to look at it. Palmer took advantage of their silence to keep talking.

"I just figured it out," she said. "We didn't go to Camden Yards this year. So we have to take him. There's a home game tonight. It starts in an hour. We have to leave soon."

This concept didn't seem to click in May and Brooks's minds as quickly as it had in hers, because they looked up at her as if she'd just sprouted wings and a beak. Then they exchanged a long, puzzled look.

"You want to go to Camden Yards?" Brooks asked. "Now?"

"Right."

"And take that?" Brooks pointed to the urn but didn't look at it.

"Uh-huh."

"And do what?"

"Take him to the pitcher's mound," Palmer said. "It'll be easy. We just—"

"Are you *nuts*? You just nailed some girl in the head with a ball, Palm. And now you want us to drive to Camden Yards to go to the pitcher's mound? What the hell is the matter with you?"

Palmer had been expecting an objection from May, but not from Brooks. And she didn't like being called nuts, either.

"Where do you think he'd like to be?" Palmer snapped. "In the closet or there?"

"I don't know," Brooks said, "but he probably wouldn't want *us* to be in jail."

"We won't go to jail. They're not going to arrest three girls."

"Wanna bet?"

"There are buses to Baltimore from the city," Palmer snapped. "I know how to get to the bus station. I know which train to take. If you guys don't come with me, I'll go on my own."

She would, too, even though the bus station bit was a lie. She knew it was somewhere downtown, and people got downtown by train. She could walk to the train station and ask someone there. It wouldn't be hard.

Brooks exhaled loudly and picked at a scar in the wood. Palmer gingerly lifted the canister back up and put it back into her bag. May still hadn't spoken. She was watching Palmer as she worked. Palmer reached into the front pocket of her bag and shoved a pile of cash into May's hand. May looked at the cash in surprise, then counted it.

"Where the hell did you get that from?" Brooks asked, gazing down at the money in amazement.

"I saved it."

Brooks, who never saved, just stared in awe.

"Eighty-five bucks," May said, holding up a crisp, unused twenty.

"We have money. You can drive." Palmer nodded to May on

that one. "We have the Firebird. It'll take two or two and a half hours to get there. Same to get back. We'll probably be down there for two hours, depending on how the game goes. Mom's asleep now, so she won't notice that we've even been back from my game. She'll be at work until seven in the morning."

Nothing else was said for the next few minutes.

"So, we're talking about eight or nine hours?" May finally asked.

"You're not really thinking about doing this." Brooks shook her head at May. "*You're* going to drive all the way to Baltimore? You?"

"I'm thinking about it," May said thoughtfully. "Yeah."

"Oh my God." Brooks put her head down on the table.

"What about this pitcher's mound thing?" May asked.

"Easy. Trust me. I've got it all figured out."

"If it's so important, why don't we just wait?" Brooks asked desperately, pulling her head up. "We'll do it later."

"No, we won't," May said, rising. "That's the point. We have to do it today."

"Why?"

"Because we won't do it on some other day, when we've had time to think about it," May answered. "I won't, anyway. And she means it. She'll do it by herself. So it's better to just go."

Palmer didn't mind being talked about as if she wasn't there this time. She could see that May *got it*. She was saying exactly what Palmer was thinking. There was an energy in the room that she hadn't experienced in a long time. Something good was happening.

May started going through her purse, making sure she had

everything she thought she needed. Brooks sat staring at the wall.

"Besides," May mumbled, "today's already completely screwed up. Why stop now?"

"Come on," Palmer said, leaning down and looking Brooks in the eye. "You know you have to. Think about it."

"How's Mom going to feel when she finds out the ashes are all gone?"

"She had them in a shoe box," May said. "It doesn't sound like she had too much of a plan for them anyway."

May seemed as determined as Palmer now, and one good thing about May was that she was hard to argue with. She was always the voice of reason, and if she was going, then the plan had to be a solid one. Plus with her red hair knotted back, her neat tank top and khaki shorts, her purse resting in the crook of her elbow, and her keys dangling off her finger—May looked mature. Brooks would have to buckle. She wouldn't be able to live with herself if she was too scared to do something May was willing to do.

"Onetime offer," Palmer said. "Come now or miss out."

Palmer could almost hear Brooks's brain whizzing. Her eyes flashed back and forth, as if an argument were going on inside her head. Finally Brooks looked down at the little paper hat she had made, looked at her sisters, then slowly rose from her seat.

"We better be back in time," she said.

"Trust me," Palmer replied.

One hundred miles is a long trip when you're going at a good pace—it was an agonizing trip at fifty miles per hour, especially for Brooks, who only slowed down to that speed to go through school zones and drive-through windows. It had been even longer since she'd been in a car with no air conditioning and no decent stereo, and the open windows meant that she was bathed in that heady fuel perfume that bellowed out of the Firebird's tailpipe.

She struggled with the map in her lap, refolding it until she had a manageable-size rectangle. They were passing through Wilmington, Delaware. She located the city along I-95 and worked out the distances. At the rate May was going, they had at least another two hours of highway driving ahead of them.

"May," Brooks ventured, "can you try to go just a little faster?"

"I could." May nodded. "But I'm not going to."

"Look, if you drive a little faster, we could get there and back by the time Mom gets off. She'll never know."

"We're going to need gas soon," May replied. "You pump it."

"Why aren't you listening to me?"

"Because," May said, ignoring the other drivers who were so tired of following her that they'd begun to weave around her, "I am trying not to panic. You do not want to see me panic. If I were you, I'd do everything I could to keep me from panicking."

"Can we at least put the top down?"

"No."

"Why not?"

"It makes my hair fly into my eyes. Then I can't see. Then we crash."

"I like the top down," Palmer chimed in from the back.

"That's nice," May said. "When you drive, you can feel free to take the top down. But I have to drive, so it stays up."

"God, you sound like Mom." Brooks groaned.

"I could probably drive," Palmer mumbled. "Better than you, anyway."

Brooks felt them lose some speed. May dropped down to forty-five miles an hour.

"You have to do at least fifty, May," she said. "You can get in trouble for going too slow, too."

"New rule!" May called out. "Everyone shuts up until we get through Delaware, or I slow down to forty."

Palmer banged the back of her head against the seat back a few times but said nothing.

"I think . . . ," Brooks began.

May decelerated again. Brooks shook the map at her.

"I think," she began again, "that we should stop for gas just below Wilmington."

May gradually took the car back up to fifty miles an hour. It rumbled contentedly as she stepped on the gas.

The sun was just going down as the Golden Firebird slipped into the tunnel that led under Baltimore Harbor. Palmer went on the lookout for signs, which May carefully followed to the huge complex of old redbrick warehouses and the banner-lined road in front of them. May turned into the first parking lot she saw, which was, of course, practically miles away. She had to let Brooks slide over and actually put the car into the tiny space that was available.

Camden Yards had always reminded May of Disneyland. It was very clean, with lots of flowers and trees, and the old brick buildings that surrounded it had large, distressed signs painted on them, carefully faded, with sort of an Old West feel. Even the stadium was made of red brick. She'd never approached it before with any kind of criminal intent. Its cheery wholesomeness made her feel guilty.

The game had already started. The music was flowing up and into the night air. Palmer gazed up into the glow of the high-intensity lights that illuminated the field and grinned.

"We only need the nine-dollar tickets," Palmer explained as she ran through the front plaza to the ticket booth. "Then we can just go down to the good seats. No one will stop us."

Tickets in hand, they stepped onto the concourse that ran the circumference of the stadium, a wide ring of concrete lined with concessions and souvenirs. Hot dogs and sodas and ice cream were all a crucial part of the game experience normally, but not tonight. Tonight it appeared to be all about running. Palmer cut ahead and slipped through one of the passages that led down to the seats along the field. May and Brooks had to hurry to catch up with her. There were no seats available, so Palmer squatted on the last step. From there, they were almost perfectly level with the field. It definitely seemed like a place where they shouldn't be waiting around.

"If anyone says anything to you," Palmer counseled her sisters, "say we're waiting for our parents. Say that we got separated, and this is the only place they know to look for us."

Brooks nodded at the wisdom of this.

"Bottom of the eighth," Palmer noted. "That's good."

May silently agreed with this sentiment. She was nervous to

the point of nausea. Brooks was trying to look determined, but May could tell she wasn't doing much better.

"They're going to win," Palmer said, pointing at the scoreboard.

She was right. The ninth inning moved fast, and the crowd exploded when the Orioles won. The music pumped, the screens flashed, popcorn flew in the air—and the three Gold sisters were considerably jostled as the stands started emptying out. They grabbed three vacated seats.

"We have to do it soon," Palmer said, raising her sunbleached brows and looking over the field. She turned back to look down at May's flip-flops.

"Those are going to be a problem," she said.

"My feet?"

"Your shoes. Take them off."

May hadn't thought about the footwear issue. But she wasn't about to run barefoot across the field, so she left them on.

"All right," Palmer said, dipping her hand into her bag, "let's get ready."

She fiddled around inside the bag for a moment. May could see that she must have been going into the canister. A moment later she produced three small plastic zipper-locked sandwich bags, each full of a grayish substance that looked like coarse sand. Each bag held an amount about the size of May's fist. As Palmer passed the bags out, a man bumped into May and she nearly dropped hers.

None of this was real to May. Not the music pumping overhead, or the heavy breeze, or the residual smell of popcorn and beer.

"We go all over at once," Palmer said, eyeing the short divider that separated the stands and the field. It was only about three feet high. "Even you can jump this, May."

May looked up sourly.

"Have your bags ready," Palmer continued, "but be careful when you run with them. Run straight out to the pitcher's mound and open them up. Don't stop, no matter what happens. Then head straight for the wall over there, to the left of the Orioles' dugout. Go up the nearest steps and out into the concourse. If we get separated, we'll meet by the car. Ready?"

"What?" May asked, looking around in a panic and grabbing at her things. "No. No, I'm not."

"Then get ready. You should have put your purse in the trunk or something."

"Why didn't you tell me all of this earlier?"

Brooks straightened up and flexed her knees a few times.

"On my mark," Palmer said quietly. "One . . ."

"What if I fall?" May whispered. "I fall, like, at home. Just walking around."

"Two . . ."

"Don't fall," Brooks advised.

"Thanks a lot."

"Three!"

In various stages of readiness, the Gold sisters went over the wall.

It was a funny thing to be on an actual baseball field. It seemed much smaller than May had imagined it would be. And even though she'd seen the pitcher's mound before, in her mind it had been just a small pile of dirt. In reality the mound was crop-circle huge and rose up almost a foot at the center. Brooks and Palmer had gotten there within moments and were stopped, bags ready. As she approached them, Brooks grabbed her arm and the three pulled close together, leaning their heads in, creating a small sanctuary.

"Now!" Palmer said.

It only took a moment and it must have been invisible to anyone outside of their huddle, this trickle of dirt over a larger pile of dirt. A chalky cloud came up around their ankles. The pitcher's mound itself was kind of reddish, so the ashes stood out as three distinct piles. Palmer started mixing them in with her foot. Brooks and May automatically followed suit.

It was a strange feeling for May, grinding at the dirt. Not only was she literally burying her dad at a baseball stadium, she was doing it with a four-dollar pair of novelty flip-flops. She threw herself into the task, shaking out the very last bits in her bag and toeing them hard into the ground. She was so intent that she tried to brush Brooks off when she grabbed her arm and started pulling her. In that moment she understood what was happening. She felt his presence surround her. Her father. Then she realized that Brooks was trying to move her away from the three security guards who were quickly approaching them, speaking into walkie-talkies pinned to their shoulders.

"Oh, shit . . . ," was all May managed to say before she got the message to her legs that they should start doing their very best to propel her off the field.

Brooks and Palmer sprinted across the diamond at Camden Yards as if it was something they did every other day or so—even strides, backs straight, heads high, side by side. They turned to look for May occasionally and shouted back encouragement.

"Go, May!"

"May, *run*!"

"I . . . am . . . running!"

Thwack, thwack, thwack, thwack.

"No, RUN!"

"Oh . . . my . . . God!"

Thwack, thwack, thwack, thwack.

May's feet were striking the ground so hard that her head shuddered. The toggles of the flip-flops ripped into the skin between her toes. This was why Palmer had told her to take them off. There was probably no historical precedent for *anyone* running from the cops in flip-flops. She was in the vanguard of a whole new breed of idiot criminal.

Thwack, thwack, thwack, thwack.

The guards were catching up to her. Yelling for her to stop. As she struggled to force more air down her raw, windburned throat, she saw her impending arrest in an oxygen-deprived flash—the handcuffing, the fingerprints, the mug shot, the one phone call, the bitter and cold plastic foam cup of coffee, the good cop and the bad cop circling her ("Come on, what were you doing on the baseball field? We've been waiting long enough." "Aw, leave the kid alone, Joe. She'll tell us when she's ready . . . won't you, May?").

She thought about just stopping. Giving in to the creeping inertia that was weighing on her limbs. Giving in to the strain of holding on to her flip-flops with clenched toes. Giving herself up so that Brooks and Palmer could get away. She could take the rap. It would be the perfect movie ending—the others running away, only to turn back. . . . "Where's May?" And there May would be, standing in a pool of searchlight, surrounded by a throng of police, with a beatific smile on her face. They would know that she had sacrificed herself for them. A loving look would pass between them as May was dragged away to the sound of wailing sirens. . . .

But then she remembered—*she had the car key.*

This jolted May. Car. *Get to the car. Don't trip out of the flip-flops and die. Keep going.* She put her head forward and pushed harder. Her calves were burning, and the cutting sensation between her toes was almost unbearable. Left of the dugout . . . left of the dugout . . . Palmer and Brooks were at least leading her there; she realized too late that she hadn't been paying attention to which of the dugouts was the Orioles'. Then Palm and Brooks suddenly veered sharply to the opposite side— guards had appeared at their planned point of exit. May followed, not quite as sharply but with a wide turn to keep the flip-flops from flying off sideways.

A light, scattered clapping and cheering came from the remaining crowd left in the stands. May was almost tempted to swivel her head around to see if she had made a second appearance on the Jumbotron, but she couldn't take the time. Her focus was steady on her sisters, who had by now made it to the wall, where a few people were cheerfully helping them over. They glanced back at her, then disappeared into the crowd. Now May was alone, and some other guards were closing in on the point where they had just exited, trying to meet May.

So she zigzagged in another direction, this time cutting

across the alternating light and dark strips of grass to the wide dirt section between second and third base.

This had to be something out of a dream. It had to be.

May called up whatever reserves of power she had left in her body. She called up strength from the ground. She put it in her thighs. She put it in her calves. She was the greatest living example of what people mean when they say that someone "runs like a girl," but at least she was going faster now. She was getting off this field.

Thwackthwackthwackthwack . . .

The rail was in sight. The rail was closer. The rail was about ten more steps away, six more steps, three more steps. . . . She could almost touch the rail. . . . Her throat was so scorched with air that it no longer mattered how much it hurt. One more step . . .

A man lent her a hand to help her over and started laughing and asking her what she was doing, but she couldn't speak. She started right up the cement staircase, bobbing, weaving, and pushing her way through the crowd. She passed through the huge archway and found herself back in the main indoor concourse. It was all concrete and echoes in here, and the thwacking seemed painfully loud.

"Why . . . are . . . these . . . places . . . all . . . named . . . the . . . same . . . ?" she said, wheeling past the identical carts and shops. She ran past the pennant banners, the Russell Street exit . . . no longer even sure if anyone was after her. Maybe she should slow down, start walking? That way she would blend in.

No. Keep running.

Finally she saw the exit and tore off through it and kept

right on going, across the plaza, into the complex of parking lots, across a street. She looked for whatever signs or landmarks she could remember but found none. It was all just parking lot.

Then she saw Palm bouncing up and down in the distance, waving her in.

She didn't even care that Palm and Brooks doubled over with frantic laughter as they watched her run her strange, head-down, flat-footed run in their direction.

"The key!" Palmer was screaming. "The key!"

"I . . . know!"

Thwack, thwack . . .

"Get the key!"

"I . . . *know!*"

May's hand was already scouring the bottom of her bag, try-ing to hook a finger onto the all-important key. She found everything else. Wallet. Altoids. Millions and millions of Presto Espresso napkins, which went flying out and left a trail.

Bingo. Key.

"I got it!" she screamed, skidding up to the car. One of the shoes flew underneath, but she didn't try to retrieve it. (So they'd have Cinderella evidence as well. If they wanted to scour the East Coast trying to find the coffee-drinking girl with only one daz-zling and patriotic flip-flop, that was their business.) The adrena-line was causing her entire body to shake, so it was hard for her to coordinate her movements and get the key into the lock.

"May!"

"Shut up!"

She managed to control her hands just enough to unlock the driver's side door. She jumped in and unlocked the other

side. Ignition. Where was the ignition? The key banged fruit-
lessly into the dashboard. Palm let out a high-pitched squeal
that did little to calm May's nerves. Brooks reached over,
grabbed her hand, and directed it firmly toward the ignition.
The key slid into the slot, and the car roared to life.

"Drive!" Palm yelled.

Shift? Shift. Come on, May. Grab the shift. Her confidence
growing, May threw the car into reverse and backed the
Golden Firebird out of its parking space. *Shift again, May.
Move it to* D. *Hit the gas. Go.*

The Golden Firebird pulled off into the balmy Baltimore
night, leaving behind a star-spangled flip-flop, a fistful of
crumpled napkins, and the contents of the bronze urn.

Hysterical laughter filled the car. None of them could stop.
It wasn't necessarily a funny kind of laughter—it was a crazy,
relieved kind of laughter. Palmer was flat on her stomach in the
backseat. Brooks was doubled over, her head resting on the
dashboard. May was hugging the wheel, barely able to breathe
or see through her watery eyes. They were stuck in creeping
traffic anyway, in a long line of cars trying to get back on I-95.

"I can't," May said between heaves. "I can't drive."

"Take the shoulder," Brooks said.

Normally May would never have taken a piece of advice like
this, but all rules of her life were temporarily suspended. She
steered the massive Firebird onto the shoulder of the road, then
drove along slowly until she came to a small local road. She
turned down this and kept going until she found a gas station
with a convenience store attached.

Brooks filled the tank while May and Palmer went into the

store. May, ignoring the sign on the store entrance, kicked off her remaining flip-flop, put it in the trash, and walked in barefoot. They roamed the aisles, laughing and picking up a strange assortment of items: chips, Swedish fish, chocolate bars, minidoughnuts. When they dumped their selections on the counter, the clerk looked at them suspiciously.

"All of this food is for her," Palmer said straight-faced, pointing her thumb at May.

"I get hungry," May said.

"You're missing your shoes there," the man said, looking down at May's feet.

"Oh, right," May replied, as if just noticing this herself. "I ate them."

Once outside, they sat on the ground next to the Firebird and passed the bag around. They ate in silence for a moment, basking in sugar, fat, and impending doom.

"Do you think they know how to toe print?" May asked, looking down at the two raw and slightly bloody spots where the flip-flop toggles had cut into her skin.

"No." Brooks shook her head. "Probably not."

"Good." May stretched out her toes, and the stinging sensation from the broken skin shot up both her legs. She kept doing it anyway, trying to create as wide a space between the toes as she could. The pain almost fascinated her.

"They could check your shoes for DNA," Palmer said, shoving an entire peanut butter cup into her mouth.

"I'll tell them you made me do it."

Palmer shrugged and chewed.

"We should take the top down," Brooks said.

"Fine," May consented, still absorbed in her toe stretching. "Go ahead."

Brooks climbed into the front seat and flipped the switches on either side where the convertible top met the windshield. Palmer got up to help Brooks lower the top into the well. It was slightly stiff, but it came down without too much hassle.

"There," Brooks said as the interior of the Firebird was once again exposed to the open air. "That's more like it."

"So," May said, fishing around in one of the bags and pulling out a potato chip, "do we ever tell Mom we did this?"

Palmer was opening her mouth to reply, but Brooks beat her to it.

"No," she said.

"Don't you think she's going to notice?" May asked.

"Not if we just put the urn back," Brooks replied.

"Isn't it going to be a little light?"

"You think she takes it down and weighs it?"

"Do you know that she doesn't?"

"So we fill it with flour or something."

"She'll be able to tell the difference."

"You think she opens it up and looks at it?" Brooks said.

"Stop," Palmer said, coming over to stand in front of them. "You're ruining it. We did it, so just . . . stop."

May and Brooks fell silent. It wasn't an angry silence, either. For one of the only times in her life, May felt like she and her sisters were truly together, on the same page. But this time they had accomplished something enormous.

"You're right," she said. "We did it."

*　　　*　　　*

Brooks was sunk down completely in the backseat of the Firebird, submerged in a universe of vinyl, protected from the wind and bathing in the warm breezes. This was something that she had missed for a long time. Time moved differently here. Perspective changed. Even though she couldn't see where the car was going, she could watch herself moving quickly toward the moon. Billboards looked thin and straight, like redwoods. They seemed to be keeping time with a plane that flew overhead, probably in the direction of Philadelphia International.

Palmer was glorying in the front seat, hanging her arm over the side of the car. She took her ticket from her pocket and did as her father always used to do—she shoved it under the raised lock on the glove compartment. She examined the sight with satisfaction for a few minutes; then she watched May drive. May had gotten more relaxed. The road was fairly empty, and the route was straight and well lit. They were actually doing sixty.

"So, what did you do to Pete?" she asked.

"I don't want to talk about it," May said, tucking a stray piece of hair behind her ear.

"Why not?"

"Because."

"Those are the things that always come back and bite you in the ass," Palmer counseled.

May threw her a puzzled look.

"What things?"

"The things you try to avoid. You can never really avoid them."

Palmer was scary sometimes. May often suspected that she might have her own talk show someday.

"So what happened?" Palmer pushed again.

"We had a fight. Sort of."

"He tried to kiss her and she ripped into him."

"Thanks, Brooks," May said into the rearview mirror.

De nada.

"Why?" Palmer asked.

"I don't know," May answered honestly.

"But he likes you. And you like him."

"I don't—"

"Yes, you do. Why do you keep saying that you don't?"

"Good question," came a voice from the back. "Especially since you made out with him all night before we left for the shore."

"What did you say to him?" Palmer asked.

"It doesn't matter," May said.

They drove the next five miles in silence.

"I screwed it up," May finally said. "I screwed it up really badly."

"So what are you going to do?"

"I don't know," May said, tentatively pushing harder on the accelerator. "I guess I'll figure something out."

Right before midnight the Firebird stopped just short of the driveway. The minivan was parked in front of the house. All three Gold sisters gazed at it in horror.

"Why is that here?" Brooks whispered, leaning forward.

"I don't know," May said, eyes wide. "Maybe she switched shifts."

"We can tell her we just ran out to the store," Palmer said. "We've got stuff."

"For six hours?" Brooks said.

"Okay," May said, "it's not so bad. Well, it might be for you, Brooks. . . ."

May heard a *thunk* as Brooks fell back hard against her seat in despair.

"We just need to have one consistent story. Where could we have been for that amount of time?"

"The mall?" Palmer suggested.

"The mall closes at ten."

"Okay," Palmer said, "we went to the mall, then to a movie."

After agreeing on the details, May pulled the Firebird into the garage. Their arrival was painfully loud, with the garage door squealing as it was opened and the coughing and growling of the Firebird engine echoing through the room. Immediately the door to the kitchen flew open. Their mother stood on the threshold. Her chest was actually heaving, like a volcano in those final, huff-and-puff seconds before an eruption.

"Oh," Palmer said. "Hi."

"Where have you been?"

The question echoed through the calm night air. It shook the garage. It vibrated between the houses. It caused a neighbor's dog to start barking. A car alarm also started going off somewhere in the distance, but that was probably unconnected.

"The mall?" May offered. "And then to a movie?"

"I got a call from the league. You hurt someone today, Palmer? Then you left?"

"That was an accident," Brooks said. "Bad pitch."

Normally Palmer would have jumped at Brooks's throat for

a remark like that, but she just sat now, staring dumbly at the dashboard.

"You have your license for half a day, May, and you do this? You take Brooks out? You keep Palmer out until midnight when she's hurt someone?"

May could tell that the fight from earlier hadn't been forgotten. She sighed and looked up at the steel garage door tracks in the ceiling.

"Just get inside," her mother said, disgusted. "All of you. And go right to bed. I don't even want to discuss this tonight. I'm—"

She stopped suddenly, her eyes frozen on a spot along the dashboard. May knew in that instant what she had seen, but it was too late to do anything about it.

Her mother reached into the car and plucked Palmer's ticket from under the glove compartment lock.

17

May was lying in bed, unwilling or unable to get out, even though it was after noon and a sweet breeze was coming in through her screened window. It seemed to be trying to reach her through the sheet she had over her head, to tell her that a perfect summer day was waiting outside. But May wasn't interested. She liked it where she was, under this soft, cool canopy dotted with the undersides of little orange flowers. If she could have, she would have stayed there all day. The adrenaline of last night had worn off, and there was too much ugly stuff outside that she had to face now. But she had to get ready for work, so she reluctantly rolled out of bed and went downstairs.

May's first surprise of the day was that her mother wasn't drinking coffee at the kitchen table when she got down there— but Mrs. Camp was. She rubbed her eyes. Yes. Definitely Mrs. Camp. Her long, pale orange hair, now streaked with a few gray wisps. Her freckled skin.

"Oh, hi, May," Mrs. Camp said, pretending not to notice that May was standing in the doorway wearing only a T-shirt and her underwear. "Your mom asked me to . . . stay."

"To stay?" May repeated, pulling down hard on the hem of the shirt and trying not to move too much.

"To keep you guys company today," Mrs. Camp said, smiling apologetically.

"Keep us company?"

"I brought some cinnamon rolls," Mrs. Camp said, pushing a large white bakery box in May's direction. "And I hit a huge sale on paper towels, so I brought some of those over."

May glanced over and saw a massive fifteen-pack of paper towels sitting on the floor by the stove.

"I'm just going to . . . put on some other things," May said. "Be right back."

May ran up the stairs and to her room, shutting the door tightly behind her. First, they had, in essence, a babysitter. This meant they were under house arrest. Second, their guard was Pete's mom, which definitely put a little salt in the wound. It was entirely possible that Mrs. Camp knew what May had done yesterday—and there was so much to know: she'd fought with her mother, spat on Mrs. Camp's son's declarations of love, driven to Baltimore . . . and that was just the public domain stuff. Wait till everyone found out about the criminal trespassing and the going into a convenience store with no shoes on.

But then again, she'd brought cinnamon rolls. Who brought cinnamon rolls for heartless juvenile delinquents, anyway?

After putting on a pair of pajama bottoms and pulling back her hair, May ventured back downstairs. Mrs. Camp was busy doing the crossword now, but she looked up on May's approach.

"Am I the first one up?" May asked, looking around. "It's almost twelve-thirty."

"Actually, yes." Mrs. Camp smiled. "You all must be tired."

Cowards, May thought. And they didn't even have half of May's problems.

"So," Mrs. Camp said, detaching a cinnamon roll from the

gooey mass for May, "I heard you passed your driver's exam."

"Kind of." She smiled, automatically looking over to the key rack on the wall. The key to the Golden Firebird was no longer hanging there. Mrs. Camp followed May's gaze.

"Your mom told me to tell you to take your bike to work," she said. "It's such a nice day out. It'll be a nice ride."

Okay. She knew that they were in trouble, but she gave no sign of knowing about what May had done to her son. Mrs. Camp chatted about a trip to North Carolina they were planning on taking, about her yoga class. . . . May stuffed down a cinnamon bun. An hour went by, and Palm and Brooks still hadn't shown their faces.

"I should get showered," May said. "I have to be at work soon."

"Go ahead," Mrs. Camp said, pulling a romance novel from her bag. "I've got lots to read. You can tell Palmer and Brooks to come down anytime they like."

"I'll tell them," May said. "I don't know what's wrong with them."

"Pete was sick this morning too." Mrs. Camp nodded.

May stiffened.

"Really?"

"He came in yesterday afternoon, after he stopped by here," she went on. "He just didn't look well. He went up to his room. I didn't see him this morning either. Maybe something's going around."

"Maybe." May backed out of the room. "I'll see if they're up. . . ."

*   *   *

When May cautiously pushed open the door to Presto Espresso that afternoon, she was immediately bathed in an icy gale from the air-conditioning vent above the door. Everything seemed off. The milk stand had been rearranged, and there were at least ten customers sitting at various tables. Nell was behind the counter, humming to herself and filling oversized coffee filters.

"Okay," May said to herself, and shivered. "This is creepy."

Nell glanced up from her filters and coolly examined May's sunburned figure.

"Who are all of these people?" May asked, walking behind the counter and punching in on the cash register.

"Some church group," Nell said. "Can you go and refill all the coffee bins?"

Refilling the coffee bins was a heavy, tedious job that involved pulling out twenty-pound bags of coffee beans from the back room and topping off an entire wall's worth of plastic bins. It required using the ladder, lifting, and repacking—and it was something that May and Nell never, ever did. There was a crazy guy named Craig who worked about once a week who seemed to live to do this job.

It took May an hour to finish. When she was done, Nell asked her to dust the wall of expensive, oversized mugs that they never sold, empty and clean the pastry case, and open a new shipment of supplies and stock the metal shelves in the storage room. These were the jobs they always did on a very occasional basis and never all at once.

So she knows, May thought as she cut open a cardboard box full of cans of sweetened condensed milk. *And this is how she's going to get back at me.*

At first that felt fine to May. She thought it would make her miserable day go by a little faster. Unfortunately, she also had time to think about Pete, and she replayed their final conversation in her head nonstop as she stocked shelves in the gray, windowless storage room with the fluorescent lights.

When May came out of the storeroom, it was almost seven-thirty. Nell went off on her half-hour break to go to the little health food shop up the road to get her dinner. May leaned against the counter and tried to relax. She could see the vivid sunset, an explosive orange and red and purple filling the sky.

It was altogether too much like the flowers Pete had brought her yesterday.

Pete—he was in her head. Every part of her brain that held a piece of information about him was firing simultaneously. She could smell his skin and his shirt. She could feel the weight of his arm over her shoulders. She could hear him laughing at one of his own jokes. . . .

She couldn't lose it—not here, with Nell. She had to keep a brave face.

Nell came back in a few minutes later with a tin container of adzuki beans, seaweed, and brown rice and set herself up at one of the tables with her food and her cell phone. May listened to her chomping away and cheerfully talking to one of her friends for the next twenty minutes about some amazing deal she'd found on a flight to Budapest. May made up little jobs for herself to keep her focus off Nell. She cleaned between the keys on the cash register with a coffee stirrer wrapped in a napkin. She scraped the buildup off the milk-foaming attachment on the cappuccino machine.

When Nell had finished her call and food, she stacked everything up and quietly came behind the counter and glanced over at May.

"Ann found out about what you did with your schedule," she said as she threw away her dish.

May's head jerked in Nell's direction at the sound of Presto's owner's name.

"She said you can finish your shift today," Nell went on breezily.

Finish your shift today. . . . May ran the words through her mind, trying to pull meaning from them.

"Are you saying I'm fired?" she managed to ask.

"Pretty much."

"How did she find out?"

"I told her," Nell said plainly.

"Why did you tell her?" May asked. "You've swapped shifts dozens of times."

"Pete told me what you did," Nell said. "He told me what happened."

"So you got me *fired*?"

"Right."

May felt slightly faint. She suddenly had a flash of how she wanted it all to end. She would dramatically take off her apron and hat, throw them on the counter, and walk to the door. At the last second she would turn and say, "I think what happened was that he realized how annoying you are, like how you never stop talking about yourself. I think that may have had a lot to do with it." Then she would open the door and step out. Before she was all the way gone, she would add over her shoulder, "But I'm just guessing."

The fact was, though, it didn't really matter anymore that Nell was irritating or even that she had just deliberately caused May to lose her job. May had disrupted something personal in Nell's life. Nell could have really liked Pete, and May had ruined that for her. The score seemed even.

But May did take off her apron and hat.

"I'd like to go now," she said.

"Fine." Nell shrugged. "You have to punch out and sign a form for your uniform."

May entered her employee code for the last time, then verified that she was returning one apron, one name pin, and one hat in good (as opposed to excellent) condition. Then she picked up her bag and headed for the door. At the last moment the guilt really started to kick in. She stopped and turned back to Nell, who had taken out a backpacker's guide to Eastern Europe and started to read.

"I'm sorry," May said. "I didn't mean for it to happen."

"Whatever, Ape."

"I just wanted you to know that it wasn't intentional."

"Fine."

There was nothing more May could say, so she opened the door.

"See you later, Ape," Nell said, turning back to her book.

"Later," May replied as she left Presto Espresso for the last time.

May coasted along her street. Even though the sun had just gone down, it was easily ninety-five degrees. Despite the heat, she wasn't ready to go home yet. She skidded to a halt at the mailbox at the end of her street to cool down and watched two little kids getting dragged along by a very eager Dalmatian.

The lightning bugs were already out in full force, looking like strings of insane, moving Christmas lights. May clasped one of the bugs in her hands, like she used to do when she was little and she and Brooks used to compete to see how many they could catch in a night. The bug wandered around her palm, not particularly concerned for its own welfare. When she opened her hand and let the bug go, it didn't seem to want to leave her. She had to blow on it to get it moving. Finally it took off from her palm and lingered around her head, flashing its little yellow taillight.

She turned her bike and rode around the corner and up the slight hill to Pete's house. The Camps' rancher sat in the middle of a fairly wild yard, with lots of trees. She stopped by the edge of the driveway, near the thick wall of shrubs that marked the edge of the property.

She could do something, or she could spend the next days, weeks, or months of her grounding picking lint out of the carpet and wondering.

Her hair was probably wild, and she was definitely sticky and rumpled. She knew she probably had perspiration marks under her arms, so she took care to keep them pinned to her sides.

She knocked at the Camps' door. There was a frantic barking from deep inside the house. A thumping as someone came down the steps. And then Pete was in front of her. His skin looked very tan against the white T-shirt he was wearing. He seemed tired.

"Can I talk to you for a second?" she asked.

"What are you doing here?"

"Look," she said, "this is your chance. If you want an explanation, you have to get it now. Or if you want to yell at me. Whatever."

It took him a minute to think this one over. He opened the door and came outside.

"So talk," he said.

"Do you guys still have the glider?" May asked.

"Yeah. Out back."

"Can we go sit on it?"

Pete looked at her in disbelief, then leaned his head back to stare at the sky.

"For privacy," she said. "So we don't have to stand in the middle of the lawn."

They made their way through the rakes, shovels, bikes, and spare pieces of wood that filled the narrow passageway that separated the garage from the house. The Camp yard was overgrown, with a slightly unstable picnic bench off to one side and a brick barbecue against the back fence. The honeysuckle bushes that they used to feast on as kids were still flourishing. The people next door were cooking dinner, and the air was hot and smelled of hamburger.

"God," May said, taking a deep breath, "we haven't taken out the grill in forever."

Pete knocked some spiderwebs and leaves from the glider with his shoe, then pointed at it. May sat down. Pete sat on top of the picnic bench a few feet away and fixed her with a steady glare.

She had no idea where to begin, but she had to say something.

"I don't know why I said all those things, but I'm sorry," she said. "I was insane."

Pete said nothing to this general apology. His expression remained frozen. A cloud of gnats descended on May's head. She waved them away, but not before getting a few up her nose. She had to snort them out. Even though she tried to do this in a very low-key way, it still wasn't exactly attractive.

She decided to try again.

"Look, I know how I've been. I was just afraid all of a sudden, and I started saying whatever I could. I know that makes me seem really weird and unstable. . . ."

She could have bitten off her tongue. Now it sounded like she was talking about Jenna again.

"Let's just forget it, okay?" Pete said. He got up, took a broom from the walkway, and started cleaning some leaves and dirt from a corner of the patio. "It was a bad idea."

"What do you mean? What was a bad idea? Us? Dating?"

"Right. So it's over. Let's just forget it happened."

"I don't think it was a bad idea," May said quickly. "I think it was a really good idea."

Pete didn't answer. He swept.

"If it makes you feel any better," she added, trying to get a response, "Nell just got me fired."

"Yeah, that makes me feel great."

"I don't know. I thought it might."

"Why would I be happy about that?" he asked, never once taking his eyes from his work. "Do you think it's my fault that she got you fired? Do you think *I* told her to do it as part of my plan to screw you over?"

From the way he'd said the word *screw*, May could tell that her words had definitely not been forgotten.

"No," she said.

"So what's your point?"

That corner of the patio had probably never been so clean.

May put her head down and told herself not to cry. This was not the time for that. This was the time to become a genius and say something amazing. Unfortunately, nothing was coming to mind.

"I don't know, Camper," she said. "I didn't really have a plan. I wanted to explain, but I guess I don't have an explanation."

"I guess you don't. Like I said, it was a bad idea. Can we drop it now?"

There was a swell of emotion building up in May. It was huge. It seemed to spread over every thought in her mind.

"Brooks didn't have these problems," she said, mostly to herself. "Why is that not surprising?"

Pete stopped sweeping for a minute and leaned into the broom, looking down at the supremely clean bricks.

"I mean, he liked Brooks the most," May went on. "Brooks was perfect. Palmer too. It was like they had a little club. Maybe if I played sports, it would all have been okay."

Nothing like another little attack of Tourette's to spice up a conversation, May thought. She really didn't seem to be in control of her own speaking voice anymore. Pete looked like he was about to say something (maybe call for help), but the patio door opened and his mom came out. He moved on to another corner of the patio.

"May?" Mrs. Camp said, clearly surprised to see her and even more confused by the weird silence that lingered between her son and May.

"I was just on my way home from work," May said. "I was giving Pete a message."

"Oh. Right. Does your mom—"

"No, I know. It's fine. I'm going home now."

"Okay."

Mrs. Camp looked between the two of them, then went back inside. Pete stood there with his broom, not moving.

"I'm kind of in trouble," May said. "It's a long story. I should probably go."

He didn't say anything.

May got up and walked back through the covered passage toward the front lawn. She tripped over the Weedwacker in her haste. It didn't matter. There was no reason why she should try to be graceful. She just wanted to get out of there as quickly as possible.

Out of the corner of her eye she saw Pete coming through the walkway. He came halfway down the driveway and stopped a few feet away from her.

"I'm sorry you got fired," he said.

"It's not so bad," May replied, grabbing her bike. "I won't have to smell that cabbage stuff Nell eats anymore."

Pete leaned against the Cutlass.

"Hey, Pete!" his mom called from the front doorway. "Can you start up the grill?"

"Um . . . yeah," he said. "Just a second."

His mom lingered by the door for a moment before disappearing back into the house. May could see her walking past the living room window. She was watching.

"You'd better go start the grill," she said.

"I know."

For the first time in the conversation, May saw a look on Pete's face that seemed somewhat familiar. He was staring off down the street, squinting just a little, wrinkling the top of his nose.

"Why'd you say all of that?" he asked.

"All of what?"

"That he didn't like you as much."

"Because it's true."

"No, it's not," Pete said. "Your dad never shut up about you."

"Trust me, okay?"

"How do you think I know all your grades and all your scores and stuff?"

"You do?" That was news to her.

"Yeah. He talked about Brooks and Palm sometimes, but it was usually about you."

"He never talked to me, though. Not like he did to them."

"Come on," Pete said. "You always used to get those little jokes he'd put in your lunch in grade school. Or we'd come over to watch a game and he'd be quizzing you and we'd have to wait."

"That's not the same," May said. She had no idea why she was having this conversation with Pete at all. Stuff was just coming out of her mouth faster than she could keep up with it.

"What's your problem?" he said angrily. "You get mad at people a lot. You think they're doing things to you. You're pissed at Brooks, at your dad, then you got pissed at me."

"I already said I was sorry. . . ."

She was crying, she noticed. There were tears running down her face. She wondered how long that had been going on before she became aware of it. Pete was just watching her now.

"Sorry," she said, sniffing and wiping her eyes with the back of her hand. "I'm stupid. I'm going to go."

She was about to swing her leg over the guy bar when another thought came into her mind. It flew out of her mouth in the next second, unchecked.

"Sometimes I feel like I've been waiting for someone to tell me when I can be normal again," she said. "I keep thinking I'll get a letter or something. Or a call. When does it happen?"

Pete looked like he wanted to walk toward her, but then he fell back against the car. The staring contest between them went on for almost a minute, and finally Pete exhaled loudly.

"It's okay," he said.

May could have been wrong, but it seemed—it *seemed*—like he was forgiving her.

She couldn't keep still any longer.

She ran up to him, stretched up onto the tips of her toes, and kissed him. It didn't matter to her that she looked gross, or that he might still be mad, or that his mom was clearly gawking out the living room window. At first he seemed startled. He stood up quickly. After a second or two, though, he wrapped his arms around her. May didn't know if it was a romantic embrace or just an attempt to keep her from losing her balance and falling backward onto the blacktop—and it didn't matter. Pete was holding her, and he was kissing her. She was getting his entire face wet in the process.

When they separated, the freckleless spot between Pete's eyes was bright red. Before anything else could be said or done, May grabbed her bike and hopped on. She waited until she was six houses down to turn and see if he was still standing in the driveway watching her.

He was.

She stopped for just a moment, and they caught each other's eyes. Then he slowly started walking backward toward the house. May couldn't see that well, considering that her eyes were still a little blurry and he was far away, but it looked like he was smiling.

May arrived home to find Brooks, Palmer, and their mom in the living room, freezing from the overfunctioning window air conditioner that shot out small pieces of ice along with cold breezes. Her mother was quietly crocheting a pale yellow baby blanket. Obviously a gift for someone. Crochet was a new thing for her mom. She had picked up the habit from some of her friends at the hospital. May thought it seemed like a weird activity for someone who used to go to clubs in outfits made of black trash bags, but it did seem to relax her.

"You're home early," her mom said.

"It was dead at work," May replied, trying to look as casual as possible.

"What's wrong with you?" Palmer said, looking May up and down. May was sweating profusely. Her shoes were covered in grass, her face was flushed, her eyes were red, and she was breathing a little too quickly—not things typically associated with a night spent at Presto.

"It's hot out."

May sank down on the floor. She immediately felt her energy leaving her, like the final, dying flickers of a battery indicator light sending those last-gasp warnings before blinking off. She had spent all of her emotions, and now she was going to slump on the floor and think about nothing. If she tried to analyze the Pete thing now, she'd go insane. As for her job, she'd think about it tomorrow. She'd definitely have the time.

Brooks flicked through the channels, trying to find something remotely interesting. Palmer didn't seem to care. She sat on the floor with her legs stretched out, looking content with everything—CNN, golf, a documentary on the evolution of the battleship, a Spanish soap opera. . . .

"Maybe we should get a movie," Brooks said.

"We have plenty of stations," her mom answered. "Find something to watch."

Brooks sighed and clicked away.

So this was how it was going to be for the next few weeks, May thought. They would all be like Palmer now—dumbly staring at the television, never speaking. She focused on a commercial for some kind of wonder spatula. Usually infomercials entertained her. She liked the way they would always show people who were apparently so incompetent that they couldn't flip a burger without putting out an eye or roll their garden hose without an ambulance crew on standby. That was why they needed product XYZ—they had very serious problems.

They were just getting to the part where they offered to send two wonder spatulas for the price of one if May called right now when Palmer suddenly spoke.

"We took Dad's ashes," she said. "Last night. We took them

to the field, to the pitcher's mound. That's what we were doing at Camden Yards."

From the way she said it, you would have thought that Palmer was just mentioning what she'd eaten for lunch. It was a very stealth move. May swung her head around and saw the old maniac gleam in Palmer's eyes, even though they were still steadily focused on the television. May looked the other way to find Brooks backing up in her seat, looking like she wished the recliner would swallow her up.

The only thing that could be heard in the next minute was the Starks' infrared bug zapper along the back fence.

May slowly turned to see how her mother was taking this news. Her hands were frozen midway through a stitch, and she was looking right at May. Not at Palmer, not at Brooks. Just at May. And her expression said it all very clearly: *Tell me what the hell Palmer is talking about.*

"We . . ."

That was as much as May could come up with. Palmer had just said it all. There was nothing to deny, nothing to add.

"We did it all together," Palmer said, picking up from there. The light was still in her eye, but she was balling up her fists and releasing them over and over. She was afraid. "He's gone. We did it. All of him is there, right in the middle of the field."

At the moment May expected the blowup or the violent outburst of Dutch, her mother simply stood up and left the room.

One in the morning and hot. Hot, hot, hot. A million percent humidity. A universe of hot soup. The clickity fan did nothing but push heat from side to side. On nights like this one, the

Gold sisters frequently camped out in the living room to bask in the air conditioning. But no one was down there tonight. They'd all scattered. Everyone was sweltering alone, in safety.

May had lived about three lifetimes in the last two days, so she wasn't too sure where she stood on Palmer's surprise announcement. On the one hand, she was glad not to have the secret hanging over her head. On the other, she was completely worn out. Brooks had freaked, completely. She'd screamed at Palmer. Palmer had just sat there and taken it. May had just wearily trudged up to her room in the middle of their fight.

For the last five hours she'd moved seashells around on her desk, stared at the wall, reorganized her bookshelf, and examined the cuts between her toes. She had nothing to get up in the morning for. Nothing to get ready for. Nothing to look forward to. She could stay in her room for the rest of the summer and count the ponies on the wall.

What she wanted to do was run out right now, in her boxer shorts and old T-shirt, and go to Pete's and sit on the glider. But she figured that she could only turn up at his house once a day looking scruffy and desperate.

This heat was going to kill her.

She needed something to drink. If she was quiet, she could go down to the kitchen without attracting any attention. Peeking out into the hall, she saw that all the doors were shut. There was no light coming from downstairs. She was safe. She crept along on her toes down the stairs and through the hall to the kitchen.

May was surprised to see her mother sitting at the table, looking strangely young in her bleach-stained scrub shirt and her ruffled, spiky hair. She had both of her feet on the chair, and her knees were drawn up to her chest. May almost tried to back up and disappear, but her mother had seen her. She nodded toward an empty chair.

"Sit down," she said.

May sat down. She was so stupid. She should have known better than to leave her room. Now she was going to go through this all over again.

"How did you get them?" her mom asked. She sounded exhausted, not angry, which was somewhat of a relief.

"Palmer found them."

"Was it Palmer's idea to take them to Camden Yards?"

"She was upset," May said, nodding. "She said she was going whether we went with her or not. So I drove there."

"So she wouldn't go on her own?"

"Yeah . . ."

Zap. Another bolt of purple light from the bug whacker shot through the room. Another bug moved on to bug heaven. May stared at the microwave clock for a moment until her focus gave and the numbers went fuzzy.

"Who took them to the field?" her mom asked.

"All of us."

"Didn't someone try to stop you?"

"They tried," May said. "We ran. We got away."

She couldn't really blame her mother for looking so surprised. It was still a little hard for May to believe that she'd successfully run away from a group of grown men. Her mom tucked her head between her knees and scrunched her lips together. She looked a little like Palmer when she did this.

"Sometimes I don't know what to do," she finally said. "I'm not like your dad. He always knew."

"Knew?"

"He knew how to talk to Brooks and Palmer. I don't. I always felt like I had more in common with you. I was just like you when I was sixteen."

"Right." May snorted. "Because I always wear fishnets."

"I was quiet," her mom said. "Shy. The hair, the makeup—that was me just pretending I wasn't. It was easy to fake it that way."

"You were faking it?"

"Sort of," her mom said, smiling slowly. "I liked some of it. But a lot of it was just trying to fit in. Your dad didn't have to try that hard. He never seemed to be afraid of anything. He was totally comfortable with himself and with everyone else. I liked that. I wished I could be like that. And he knew who I really was, even under all that makeup and stuff. He liked me."

There was something in her voice that May had never heard before. Her mom wasn't talking like a mom—she was talking like someone with a huge crush. It was the same kind of voice that May heard in her own head when she thought about Pete.

"What you said yesterday," her mom went on. "You were wrong. Your dad didn't like Brooks or Palmer best. They're a lot like him, so he understood them. But he could never believe that he helped make you. He thought you were amazing. When you got into Girls', he couldn't stop talking about it. He'd tell anybody he met about his May. You were always his May."

"Why didn't he tell me that?" May said quickly. "He always told Palm and Brooks how great they were."

Her mother leaned back and thought about this.

"I think," she said, "that he didn't know how. He tried. He was almost in awe of you, May. You're smart. You're mature. It was almost as if he thought he couldn't keep up with you."

Having just heard something similar from Pete, May couldn't help but feel ashamed. She couldn't even remember why she'd thought her father hadn't liked her. Now she remembered it all clearly—the way he'd managed to find the money for her school, the fact that she alone had been allowed to have the kitchen table for homework, and even how he'd called her "the professor." It all made sense now.

There was a noise by the door. May didn't have to turn around to know that Palmer was lurking somewhere in the darkness of the hall. She must have heard them talking. Evidently, her mom knew she was there as well.

"You can come in," she said.

To May's surprise, Palmer wasn't alone. She had brought Brooks with her. Brooks shot her a look as if to ask, *What's the damage?* May could only shrug.

"There's something I want to know," her mom said to the three of them. "Why didn't you ask me to come with you?"

The bug zapper claimed another victim in the ensuing silence.

"Wouldn't you have stopped us?" May asked.

"Of course I would have stopped you."

"That's why," May replied, puzzled.

Her mom nodded, as if this confirmed something she had been thinking.

"I never knew what to do with the ashes," she said. "I never believed they were really him. So I just put them away. You did a dumb thing. Something could have happened to you."

All the control she'd been keeping herself under dissolved all at once as she said that, as if the thought of anything happening to them was more than she could even bear to contemplate.

"You're good girls," she said, her eyes filling with tears. "You know that? You're in a lot of trouble, but God—you're really amazing girls."

The four Gold women slept in the living room together that night, with the air conditioner blasting. May's mother took the sofa, with Palmer splayed out all over the floor by her side. They were the first to fall asleep.

Brooks took the recliner. May claimed a patch of floor by the television and made herself a little nest of blankets and pillows to defend herself against the icy gale that was coming straight at her. She wriggled down into the plaid flannel depths of an old waterproof sleeping bag that she had opened up and wound around herself. The recliner groaned softly as Brooks shifted.

"It's either kill-you hot or kill-you cold," May whispered. "It's never just right."

"It's better than sleeping upstairs," Brooks whispered back.

May heard a tiny chip of ice rattle around before flying loose from one of the AC vents.

"What are you doing tomorrow?" Brooks asked.

"I don't know," May said, staring up at a moving shadow on the ceiling that was a car passing by. "My schedule's pretty wide open."

"Mine too."

Lots more shifting around coming from Brooks's direction. The footrest banged back into starting position.

"You want the chair?" Brooks asked.

"I'm good."

"I can't sleep here. Can I share those blankets?"

"Sure."

She made some room in her warm pocket to accommodate Brooks, who managed to completely destroy the careful arrangement May had set up. But Brooks also acted as a human shield against the blast, so temperature-wise things were more or less the same.

"Hey Brooks?" she whispered.

"What?"

"Do I seem different to you?"

"What?"

"More unpredictable? Not as boring?"

"What?" Brooks said again. But this time it was a softer "what?" A "what?" that meant yes to anyone who spoke Brooks.

"Thanks," May said.

"Go to sleep." Brooks gave a tug on the blanket.

May took the suggestion and closed her eyes. She knew she would wake up on the living room floor, still grounded and unemployed, with Brooks's hair in her face and no covers at all. But these things didn't seem as bad as they would have even a few hours before.

Within a few minutes, Brooks was snoring in her ear loudly enough to cover the thick, icy coughs of the air conditioner. This didn't bother her either. In fact, it was lulling, reassuring. Her eyes grew heavy. She was right at the point where the real world gets taken over by dreamy haze when she felt a bump as Palmer rolled over and joined them.

ACKNOWLEDGMENTS

Many thanks are due to Leslie Morgenstein, Ben Schrank, Josh Bank, and Claudia Gabel at 17th Street Productions, and Abigail McAden at HarperCollins. They are the reason this book made it to the shelf.

Jason Keeley, Karen Quarles, John Vorwald, Joey Sorge, Matt Zimmerman, "the real" Linda Fan, and Chris Blandino provided inspiration and information. The Fasslers provided the starting point. Joseph Rhodes committed an act of kindness simply out of the desire to help a writer.

I would be lost without the assistance of my friend and long-time partner in crime, Kate Schafer. And it was Jack Phillips who—among millions of other things—explained to me how to remove corrosive buildup from the nodes of a car battery.